Treaty Violation

Treaty Violation

Anthony C. Patton

EMPIRICUS
BOOKS

Cambridge, England

First published in Great Britain 2017
by Empiricus Books
The Studio
High Green
Great Shelford
Cambridge CB22 5EG

www.januspublishing.co.uk

ISBN 978-1-85756-863-9

Cover Design: Lev Brodsky

Printed and bound in Great Britain

Prologue

December 31, 2009

Dear Leslie Burns,

Ten years after the fateful events in Panama that changed my life in so many ways, I am pleased to finally submit to you a copy of my manuscript for *Treaty Violation*. I see this story as my own *Iliad* and *Odyssey*. As we discussed during the writing conference last summer, I believe my story is a good fit for Atreus Publishing, and I look forward to working with you on this project. If I have not said it enough times before, I am greatly indebted to you for your guidance and mentorship, from your inspirational classes in the creative writing program to your personal attention outside of class.

I have had a lot of time to think about the question you asked me so many times: What is the story *about?* Suspense, intrigue, betrayal, and the joy and sorrow of love aside, I finally concluded that this story is really about my personal vision of the American Dream—how I as a foreigner viewed it, how I became entranced by it, and how I ultimately learned to live it and embrace it. I have not forgotten what you taught us regarding how the best modern novels about the American Dream are often ultimately about the failure of the American Dream, but perhaps my perspective as an outsider makes me uniquely qualified to comment on the American Dream with less cynicism, without resorting to naïve platitudes or abstract ideals. Each year, millions of hopeful foreigners still line up for visas or risk death for their chance at the American Dream. I believe that only someone born and raised inside the American system could cast such a critical eye. As you know, my pursuit of the truth as a journalist for *El Tiempo* in Panama landed me in jail and nearly ruined my career, but that same pursuit of the truth in America has been celebrated and liberating in so many ways.

Although this story is based on true events, I have taken a few liberties to construct the narrative toward a satisfying conclusion, as should be expected with any story. Reality truly is stranger than fiction. I will not spoil the surprises, but some of the people who survived the events have read the story and liked it, to include my husband Nicholas, whereas the people who did not survive cannot speak for themselves and now inhabit the underworld. Unfortunately, my health condition has not improved. The doctors say I could live a few months or a few years, which is why I have been working so hard to finish this novel, as my last will and testament to the truth. Although I polished the other characters and made them as empathetic as possible, I offer no such solace to myself.

Finally, you will note that the manuscript is not quite complete. I am still putting the final touches on the last few chapters and will send them to you as soon as possible. The truth is I have been dwelling on how to finish the story during the past months, especially after reaching this point in the book. I cannot rule out the possibility that it will take another month to finish the book, but I also know how busy you are and wanted to give you the opportunity to start the manuscript now. For all I know, you will not like it and will not ask to see the rest! If this were to be the case, I would understand that it was a professional decision, not a personal decision. I look forward to hearing from you soon and wish you the best of luck in all of your endeavors.

Sincerely,

Lina Lowe-Castillo

Chapter One

Panama City, Panama, December 1999

Lina Castillo drove down Balboa Avenue along the Pacific coast of Panama City under the gentle glow of the moon and the neon lights of the businesses and restaurants. Her modest Nissan Sentra was a practical choice for a young journalist starting out in the business without the advantage of family pedigree to provide a modicum of affluence during the early phase of her career. A radio newscast provided updates on the ongoing investigation: "Authorities have officially ruled the death of Helena Hernandez a suicide, but police sources tell us that foul play is suspected. Ms. Hernandez fell to her death from the penthouse of Cesar Gomez, who is suspected of being involved in criminal activity, but sources have confirmed his alibi that he was not present at his penthouse at the time of her death. The family has asked for privacy and has not provided any details about the autopsy results."

Lina tapped a preset button on the radio to find some soothing salsa music and turned up the air conditioner another notch as she veered right off Balboa Avenue to Italy Avenue in the Punta Paitilla neighborhood. Upon entering the residential area of densely packed condominium towers, she got held up by a procession of vehicles slowly passing by the site of Helena's death in front of a ritzy condominium tower. Outside, scores of people with candles wept and prayed for the woman who in so many ways symbolized beauty and class in Panama, for rich and for poor. From her participation in the Miss Universe contest to her minor role in a Hollywood film, where she seduced audiences around the world with a stereotypical accent she never used in Panama, Helena was the woman who launched a thousand ships. The biggest question in Panama was which lucky man would win her heart, and that question appeared to have been answered, until her tragic death. Many admirers tossed violets on the mourning site, Helena's signature flower. As Lina passed by, she caught a glimpse of the inner sanctum, where a poster-sized photograph of Helena looked down on the mourners with her eternal smile.

After Lina was in the clear, she rounded the corner, made a quick turn, parked on the street a safe distance from the condominium tower, and walked the rest of the way to push the button at the entrance.

"It's me," she said.

The door clicked.

Lina knocked on the door and waited. After a short delay, Tyler Broadman, with an uncharacteristic scruffy beard and bloodshot eyes, opened the door wearing an untucked polo shirt and jeans. About six foot two with blond hair, he managed a smile as he looked at her like the first time they met so many months ago. He embraced her with one arm, kissed her on the cheek, and gestured for her to enter.

"How about a drink?" he said, and she nodded.

She got comfortable in the swank apartment she once knew so well and admired the view of the city and the Pacific Ocean as he dropped the ice cubes in the glasses and opened a can of soda to mix with the rum—Cuba Libre, her favorite; he remembered. When she saw his reflection, she turned and leaned against the window.

"Here you go," he said and gestured to the couch. They sat.

"How are things at work?" she asked.

He shrugged and shook his head with exhaustion. "I'll get to that soon enough, but as you can imagine, I'm still struggling a bit with the death of Helena. Most people don't know we were planning to get married and move back to the States."

She sipped her drink and set it down. "Actually, it was probably the worst-kept secret in Panama. The social pages were irate that you were planning to take her away. Some of her admirers proposed declaring war on America to keep her here."

He managed a smile and shook his head, then leaned forward and rested his face in his hands. "Can I trust you with some very important information?" When he looked up, she nodded. "Do you remember when you told me you heard that Helena was going to Cesar's penthouse to get some cocaine?"

She grabbed her drink with a nod and sipped it.

"So get this, I went there to confront her," he said and paused as she set her drink down. "Needless to say, I didn't kill her. I mean, can you imagine? She was tanning by the pool, sleeping, in fact, probably stoned for all I could tell."

"Oh my God," she said and touched his arm. "What did she say?"

He took a healthy swig of his drink and squeezed her hand. "The usual nonsense about this being the last time she would use cocaine and how she had sex with Cesar only once a long time ago. She apologized and begged me to forgive her, but I told her I needed time to think about it. I was honestly thinking about calling off the engagement."

She kissed his hand and allowed him to think about it.

"So what the hell happened?" he asked rhetorically and stood. "I've worked this out a million ways in my mind, and I just can't figure it out. Not long after I left, she mysteriously falls to her death. It doesn't make sense." He sat next to her and leaned back with a groan.

"We never know what makes people do something like this," she said. "Perhaps she was depressed from her cocaine addiction. Perhaps she thought things were over with you."

He appeared deep in thought. "The other odd thing is that the security tape from the lobby is missing for the whole week, which I know from someone at the embassy who is working with the Panamanian National Police on the investigation. This means that someone out there probably knows I entered and left the building not long before Helena died. I can hardly sleep just thinking about it."

She held his stare. "That would make sense that the lobby has a security camera. You're sure it's not the police that has the tape?"

He shrugged. "Could be, but why wouldn't they talk to me about it?" He grabbed a large envelope from the coffee table and waved it. "And on top of all of that, as if this wasn't enough, there's some crazy shit going on at work. I've been thinking about getting out for good, so I plan to use this if the CIA objects."

Lina watched as Tyler walked to the bedroom and set the folder inside the nightstand drawer. He ran his fingers through his hair as he returned to the living room.

"I suppose that's top secret stuff you can't discuss with me?" she asked playfully, glancing at the nightstand.

He managed a smile. "Something like that. After so many years of this shit, I'm getting to the point where I'm ready to quit, move to the States, and do something else. Maybe I'll write a book or start a business."

She walked over and hugged him. To her pleasant surprise, he wrapped his arms around her and kissed her on the forehead as they returned to the couch.

"I sometimes think the biggest mistake I ever made was giving you up," he said. "We never had these problems."

"Take me with you," she said.

He looked at her with skepticism. "After what I did to you, I'm surprised you're even talking to me now."

"I'm a pretty good catch," she said with a friendly wink, "but I'm willing to consider your relationship with Helena a case of temporary insanity. I guess what I'm saying is that I can understand why you would pick her over me, no matter how much it hurt. After all, I would have dumped you for George Clooney."

He laughed and looked out the window as she rested her head on his chest. "You probably imagine America with white picket fences."

Lina looked at him, surprised. "You've known me long enough to know I don't have any childish fantasies about life in America. I want to work as an investigative journalist without fear of reprisal from the government, businesses, or wealthy families. I want to work in a country where the pursuit of truth is valued."

He smiled. "That makes two of us, if only such a place existed. I hear what you're saying, but all the big media outlets in America are beholden to political parties and special interest groups. Don't get me wrong, you would be fantastic, but profits overshadow the truth. I would recommend writing a book if you want to pursue the truth."

She leaned closer and cautiously kissed him on the lips. He kissed her back as a smile filled her face. "I also like the idea of spending my life with a man who won't feel compelled by his culture to enjoy mistresses or prostitutes."

He stared deeply into her eyes. "I really made a mistake letting you go."

"It's not too late," she said.

They gazed into each other's eyes as their lips met. She moaned and ran her fingers though his hair as she slid onto his chest and kissed his neck. He slid up her skirt and caressed her as she lifted her head, breathless, and started removing his shirt.

Tyler's cell phone rang on the coffee table.

"I have to get that," he said, to her dismay, and slid from underneath her. "Sorry," he added and looked at her with a wink as she sexily removed her blouse and skirt and waited for him with nothing but a bra and a thong. He grabbed the cell phone, resisting a smile. "Hello?" He listened intently and looked at his watch. "Really? I wonder what he wants. OK, consider it done. Talk to you tomorrow."

He hung up the cell phone. "I'm really sorry, but I have to do something for work that can't wait. If you promise to wait for me looking just like that, with two glasses of red wine in the bedroom, I'll hurry back as fast as I can."

She beckoned him with a finger and kissed him. "I'll be waiting."

"We have to clarify a few things about white picket fences," he said.

"Don't ruin the moment," she said.

He kissed her, grabbed his cell phone, and waved as he walked to the door.

Alone, Lina strolled through the apartment in her bra and thong sipping her drink, admiring the paintings on the walls and standing before the window with a panoramic view for the whole world to see. She entered the bedroom, slid herself under the Egyptian cotton sheets with a wistful deep breath, then grabbed a white Turkish bathrobe from the bathroom and strutted confidently to the kitchen with a bounce in her step to open a bottle of red wine.

With two glasses of wine, she returned to the bedroom, let the robe fall to the floor, slid under the sheets, and turned on the television.

After some channel surfing, she settled on a *telenovela*, watched with a few laughs, and slowly drifted off to sleep.

Lina woke with a gasp when she heard the sound of car doors slamming outside. She jumped out of bed, put on the robe, and rushed over to the window in the living room to see two police cars below with flashing lights. The apartment buzzer sounded.

She gasped, grabbed her clothes from the couch, and ran to the door, but then stopped and paused, returned to the bedroom, and grabbed the large envelope in the nightstand drawer. In the hall, she reached for the elevator button but could hear the elevator running as a gentle vibration shook the floor. She ran to the stairwell and pulled the door shut as two policemen exited the elevator and knocked on Tyler's door. She held her chest to control her breath and continued down the stairs.

She emerged from the stairwell wearing her clothes and walked purposefully to her car parked just down the road, careful not to look at the policemen. As she drove away, she passed by the mourning site again and slowed to watch a young woman toss a handful of violets in front of the picture of Helena.

Chapter Two

Nicholas Lowe headed north on the George Washington Parkway in his black BMW 5 Series as the sun was rising over the Potomac River. The ground was blanketed with snow as far as the eye could see as he donned his sunglasses, with the prominent Georgetown University architecture looking down on him. He turned the heater down a few degrees, triggered a single swipe of the windshield wiper to clear some snow, and turned up the radio as the silent scenery outside zoomed past him: "Stocks futures are down slightly today as the Federal Reserve considers changes to short-term interest rates. This has been NPR news."

He reached the top of the hill, made the exit onto Dolly Madison Boulevard, or Highway 123, and then made the right turn into CIA Headquarters. His tires crunched the snow as he slowed to present his identification to the security officer and then hit the gas and made his way to his reserved parking space. He set his cell phone in the glove box, stopped the car, and wrapped a scarf around his neck. Outside, he buttoned his wool overcoat, checked his watch, and started the trek for the entrance, where he presented his identification to another security officer and removed his sunglasses as he made his way to the cafeteria. His wooden-heeled dress shoes clicked the polished floor each step of the way. The pleasant, elderly woman with a hair net behind the counter looked at him with a smile.

"Black coffee, please," he said.

As she poured the coffee, he glanced at his watch and waved to a few colleagues walking down the hall.

"Here you go," she said and accepted his payment and generous tip.

He raised the coffee respectfully and strode to the elevator, which took him up a few floors to the Office of Russian and European Analysis, where he entered a corner office with a view, removed his overcoat and scarf, and sat down to log on to his computer. A folded piece of paper was inserted into the keyboard. He opened it to read: "Please report to the Office of Asian Pacific, Latin America, and Africa (APLAA) Analysis, to assist with a Peru–Ecuador task force. Sincerely, Louise." He crumpled the piece of paper and tossed it into the garbage with a groan.

On the other side of the building, Nicholas entered the front office for APLAA and approached the secretary. A smiled filled his face when he saw Ms. Peterson with her red dress with white polka dots and salon-styled hair. He admired the dozen red roses in a crystal vase and raised an inquisitive eyebrow as she finished a phone call, after which she presented a cordial smile and folded her hands.

"Good morning, Ms. Peterson," he said. "I had the pleasure of receiving the invitation for your dinner party tonight."

"My husband's only request is that you don't make passes at me again, Mr. Lowe," she said with golden-age class. Her spirit was forever young, even among the Beltway Bureaucrats. She looked at the roses and blushed. "Please call me Louise, I insist."

He admired her distinguished air and smelled the fragrant roses. "You Italian lover must be in town," he said playfully and teasingly reached for the card. "In all seriousness, why did you summon me here today? I've been trying to stay away from Latin America for the past ten years. Is there any way I can call in sick?" Latin America was one part of the world he wanted to forget, but the tide was strong.

"The team is waiting for you, Mr. Lowe," she said.

He gestured to a small conference room containing four people. She nodded.

"Would it be possible to get a black coffee, like the old days?" he asked.

"Right away, Mr. Lowe," she said.

"How did I ever get along without you," he said. "Oh, and please call me Nicholas, Ms. Peterson, I insist."

With a nostalgic smile, she watched him walk away. "Welcome back, Nicholas."

Tom Langford, the Chief of APLAA, and three lovely ladies, each with a coffe, stopped talking and looked at Nicholas when he entered the conference room. Tom wore a gray suit with black polished shoes, the professional analyst look—but not stiff, as his Hispanic roots could attest. As a case officer who was certified to operate overseas, Nicholas could still get away with khaki slacks and a navy blue blazer, tie optional.

The three lovely ladies, probably recent M.A. graduates, all wore silk blouses with skirts and nylons. The shift in the CIA hiring to include so many attractive women had resulted in a notable uptick in the spy-versus-spy marriage game, which made the spy community even more insular that it already was, and which had a limited impact on the unusually high divorce rate. The Latina exuded femininity; the northeast Ivy League type next to her probably attenuated her IQ to appease insecure men; and the Asian woman next to her had all the trappings of someone who had benefited from the rigors of a Dragon Mother. The alchemy of their perfume induced an oriental rhythm in his heart. Things were looking up.

Nicholas and Tom moved closer for a firm embrace with slaps on the back.

"How the hell are you, Tom?" Nicholas asked.

"Hanging in there," Tom replied and turned to the ladies. "For those of you who don't know, Nicholas and I go way back. He's a regional expert, which is why I personally selected him for this task force."

"So I have you to blame for this," Nicholas said in a joking manner as he shook hands with the three ladies and sat, but he was serious. Tom was a nice enough guy, but he should have given him the opportunity to say no before having him reassigned.

Louise knocked on the door and entered to hand Nicholas a mug of black coffee.

"Thank you, darling," he said.

"Will there be anything else, Mr. Lowe?" she asked.

"Please hold all my calls," he added matter-of-factly and then looked at her with a smile and a subtle wink.

Louise nodded deferentially with a smile and excused herself.

Tom shook his head with a Twilight Zone look on his face and started the meeting. "I wanted to begin by saying welcome to the team and to thank you for accepting the call to assist with this task force. Some of you are new to analysis, but I plan to leverage your fresh minds for some out-of-the-box thinking."

"What's the latest?" Nicholas asked.

"The Peru–Ecuador border dispute is hot again," Tom began. "We were tasked by the Director to provide daily assessments and to work with State Department, which is trying to mediate the dispute."

Nicholas checked his watch. "I'm so glad to hear that State Department is on it. That should keep this task force running at least through next fiscal year." Tom and the four ladies didn't seem sure how to react—sarcasm? "This Peru–Ecuador thing has been dragging on far too long and has generated far too much attention."

"If that's really your assessment," Tom said with a tone of disappointment, "we look forward to hearing your rationale. I, for one, think the situation more complex than it used to be and merits our attention."

"I'm sure you're right," Nicholas said and turned to the three ladies. "You know, back in the day, we would have locked the two presidents in a room and slapped some sense into them, or used less traditional methods to get the outcome we wanted."

The three ladies looked at Nicholas with a combination of shock and intrigue—*that's why I signed up for the CIA! Can we really do that?*

Tom forced a smile. "Why don't we humor ourselves for now and see whether we can find a lasting solution that takes into consideration the broader historical context and the current political situation."

The lovely Latina looked at Nicholas and raised her hand innocently with a submissive arch of the eyebrow. "So, are you an analyst or an operations officer?" Her floral scarf was tied loosely around her neck, her toned calves resting on her high heels.

The animated Ivy League leaned forward. "They didn't teach us about locking presidents in rooms. Do we really do that?"

Tom rolled his eyes and cleared his throat. "I'm sure Nicholas would love to regale you with war stories some other time. Besides, when was the last time you were in the field, Nicholas—about ten years ago?"

"About that," Nicholas said, "as far as you know. If you're tired of hearing the stories, the rest of us can chat about the good old days during happy hour." He turned to the ladies, who seemed to like the idea. "Something tells me this task force is going to drag on for at least a few months, so we might as well get to know each other in a less formal setting."

Tom took a deep breath and checked his watch. "Well then, I promised to keep this short. Now that you've all got acquainted, why don't we break for the day and report back the same time tomorrow with your initial assessments." As the three ladies stood, he added, "And, Nicholas, if you could stay back a minute."

The Latina passed by and handed Nicholas a business card. "I can arrange a happy hour if you tell me what day of the week is good for you."

"Surprise me," Nicholas said. "I have no previous commitments."

Ivy League slid her business card across the table and waved. The Asian woman started to walk away, then paused, returned, handed Nicholas a business card and scurried out of the conference room, where the three ladies huddled briefly before going their separate ways. Nicholas fanned the three business cards in his hand, feigning surprise.

Tom shook his head and seemed to resist a smirk. "That's just perfect, Nicholas. Still up to your old ways. I'm trying to build a team here."

Nicholas raised an incredulous eyebrow. "Your idea of building a team is selecting the three hottest analysts in the Agency, in three different flavors? We both know no policymakers are really interested in this Peru–Ecuador thing, so we might as well have some fun."

Tom smiled and shook his head. "I suppose it wouldn't be unfair to characterize my selection process as biased, but we have to keep this professional and do a good job. Besides, I'm happily married with three kids, as will you be one day, I hope." He drummed his fingers. "More important, do you really want to be on this team?"

Nicholas took a deep breath and sipped his coffee to think about it. "To be honest, the short answer is no, but I'll do whatever needs to be done. I'm starting to lose interest in the Caspian Sea oil projects."

"Nicholas," Tom said, "from one friend to another, I know what happened ten years ago wasn't easy to deal with, but I and many others are getting the impression that you're just spinning your tires here until retirement, which is no way to live. You're a good analyst, but your heart clearly isn't in it. Have you given any thought to going back to operations?"

As Nicholas thought about it, Louise interrupted with another knock on the door. "Excuse me, Mr. Lowe, but K would like to see you. He's waiting for you at the ranch."

Nicholas' heart raced. The name K stirred a reservoir of dormant emotions—anger, resentment...exhilaration. K, his mentor and now the CIA's Deputy Director for Operations (DDO), was requesting his presence. *What does he want?* He resisted a temptation to answer that question and then reached deep within to sculpt a mask of indifference.

"Thank you, Louise," Nicholas said. "Tell them I'll be right over."

Tom leaned back and nodded approvingly.

Chapter Three

Nicholas headed west on Interstate 66, beyond the strip malls and densely packed single-family housing developments that were built around the blue ribbon public schools of Fairfax County. Whereas federal jobs like the CIA had once been the purview of the adventurous sons of elite families, with a notorious history of derring-do and toppled governments in response to the communist menace, many of these jobs were now seen as stepping stones for middle-class America to establish a foundation for future generations of university education and wealth building, while at the same time injecting a new level of caution and morality into the business that could withstand Congressional scrutiny.

After exiting onto a county highway, he passed through a small town with a three-digit population, a run-down gas station with a convenience store, and a small strip mall with a vacant store. A few miles down the road, he glanced at the map on the passenger seat and the odometer as he approached a stone and timber gate. He turned, stopped at the gate, lowered his window, and pushed the button.

"Nickie, is that you?" a raspy voice asked cheerfully.

He took a stroll down memory lane and smiled as he remembered the secretary who struggled the most with the federal government's no smoking policy. "Yes, Janette. The rumor around the office is that you're off the market."

"Stop it, Nickie!" Janette laughed. The buzzer sounded and the steel gate opened.

The driveway wove through some snow-covered fallow fields before entering a grove of oak and elm trees that shielded the single-floor rambler. When Nicholas parked in front of the house, Janette was waiting for him. As they embraced, her sapphire eyes beamed through the deep wrinkles on her face.

"He's expecting you in the study," she said and squeezed his hands. "The Directorate of Operations just isn't the same without you."

"The good old days look much better from this perspective," he said.

"At least we have our memories," she said with a wink and a gesture.

He entered the house, hung his coat and scarf in the closet, and warmed his hands by the fire before making his way to the study. He knocked on the door and peeked his head inside to see K sitting at his desk reading the *Wall Street Journal.*

"You asked to see me?" Nicholas asked, entered, and eased the oak door shut until the brass latch clicked. Books from Aristotle to Zen lined the left wall. A world map hung on the right wall behind a large floor globe flanked by two burgundy leather chairs. A Persian rug lay before K's desk.

K looked up with a smile and walked over. He wore a tailored navy blue suit with a starched white shirt and a crimson tie. His graying hair was cropped around the ears, and the lower rim of his glasses rested in the wrinkles under his eyes. His posture, his composure, and the confident tilt of his head radiated a regal air. He was a complete man of an aristocratic cast who feared insignificance more than death. They met with a firm embrace.

"Thanks for coming out on such short notice," K said.

Nicholas gestured to the newspaper. "Anything interesting?"

"The NASDAQ continues its climb," K said. "The list of new millionaires is growing by the day and we're balancing the budget with capital gains taxes, but it's a casino, not disciplined investing, which never ends well." He gestured to the two leather chairs. "I heard you were reassigned to the Peru–Ecuador task force."

Nicholas paused to digest the comment as they sat, which meant K was probably weaving a plan that would not be clear for several moves. The aroma of single malt Scotch and cigars inside the globe blended luxuriously with the smell of the leather chairs. "I'm not excited about working on another task force, but I am a big fan of the CIA's new hiring policy. Have you seen some of the women walking the halls?"

"I consider part of my plan to help you find you a wife and settle down," K said with a subtle smirk. "I suggest you take advantage of it."

After a pause, Nicholas continued, curious: "I really appreciate your taking time out of your busy schedule to see me."

K nodded and looked pensively at the wintry scenery outside. "Unfortunately, I have some bad news to share." He lowered his head. "Tyler is dead."

Nicholas shifted in his chair, his heart pounding, staring in disbelief. "What do you mean? I just spoke with him the other day."

K folded his hands. "One of his agents triggered an emergency meeting. When Tyler arrived, he was shot dead."

"By the agent?" Nicholas asked.

"We're not sure," K said. "Later the same evening, the agent was also found dead, which suggests one of two things. First, the agent killed Tyler and was himself killed coincidentally later the same evening, which seems unlikely; or second, the killer coerced the agent to take him to the meeting, killed Tyler, and then killed the agent."

"How did the killer know the agent worked for us?" Nicholas asked.

"The agent was a low-level drug trafficker with powerful contacts in the Colombian cartels," K said. "He might have told someone about his relationship with us. It's not clear." They sat in silence. "I can't tell you how sorry I am. Tyler was one of the best. On top of this, the death of his fiancée Helena Hernandez is a mystery as well."

"He told me," Nicholas said, and stood to gaze upon the scenery. "I can't believe they killed him. Do the cartels think we won't respond? Have they lost their minds?"

"Tyler was running a sensitive operation that was having great success against the drug cartels," K said. "We work in dangerous situations. Think about how many people would probably have wanted to kill you in El Salvador, if they had known who you were."

Nicholas lost some friends in Central America during the 1980s guerrilla wars, but no one recently, and certainly not since the peace dividend following the collapse of the Soviet Union. "What's the plan? How do we strike back?"

"Until we figure out what happened, we have to continue with the operation," K said and gestured for Nicholas to sit. "Our Chief in Panama, Dylan, called me today and suggested that you replace Tyler. I told him I agree."

"Dylan...Dirk?" Nicholas asked and raised his hands defensively. "The same Dylan Dirk who ruined my career ten years ago?"

"You can't blame him for that," K said. "He was forced to give sworn testimony at a Congressional hearing. The Agency was under great pressure after the atrocities. No one asked that you stop working in operations to become an analyst. The only demand was that we remove you from El Salvador and terminate our work with the agent."

And just like that, ten years of frustration suddenly boiled Nicholas' blood. While working in El Salvador during the late 1980s to help the Salvadoran government and the Armed Forces defeat the Farabundo Marti National Liberation Front (FMLN) communist guerillas, who were receiving support from Cuba, the Soviet Union, Vietnam, and other communists around the world, Nicholas was tasked to recruit a retired Salvadoran Army sniper trained by the CIA who was no longer fit for service due to medical issues but who could be used to assassinate high-level leaders of the FMLN. The primary plan was to use him to assassinate viable communist presidential candidates leading up to the next election, but in the meantime, he was used to kill FMLN military commanders. The CIA knew the FMLN had penetrated the Salvadoran Army with spies and was concerned the FMLN would begin assassinating Americans if they discovered the CIA assassination program.

The plan worked, but not in the way the CIA had intended. The FMLN was never able to link the actions of the assassin to the CIA, but the CIA, and therefore Nicholas, lost control of the assassin as he went on a killing spree that included women and children, always leaving his calling card to claim credit—the ace of spades, the two of spades, the three of spades, and so on, which is why he was known as the spades assassin. Fortunately, he never reached the face cards. Good tradecraft had shielded the CIA from public exposure of the atrocities, and the White House was in no position to offer a public apology, but the Congressional oversight committees were more conspiratorial, with some committee members even suggesting that the assassin was never under the CIA's control and that the Salvadoran Army had used the assassin to launch their own atrocities, with the CIA taking the fall if the operation ever leaked. When Dylan testified that Nicholas had headed up the operation, removing Nicholas from El Salvador and cutting CIA ties with the assassin were seen as reasonable solutions to an otherwise complicated situation.

"You really believe my career wasn't ruined?" Nicholas said.

"You were offered the opportunity to work in other countries," K said. "We had people who had cleared the way with Congress and I gave you my word that I would personally see to it that your career got back on track, but you wouldn't listen."

"You know it was more than just the job," Nicholas said.

K was one of the most prominent members of the Order, an old boys' club that provided much of the young blood for the CIA during the early years. In an age when the elites were still expected to serve on the front lines, such as World War II, the Order walked the delicate line of maintaining the privileges of the elites while demanding that their sons risk life and limb in the name of national security, the same way Greek warriors had sought glory on the shores of Troy. After the great wars and the advent of global prosperity, with the United States of America becoming the industrial capital of the world, many of these families eschewed public service and focused their efforts on accumulating wealth. Not to mention, with the tradition of primogeniture, many of the elites were offering up the sons that were not in line to inherit the family businesses, which resulted in a notable drop in quality. In response, K, the most prophetic of the old aristocrats, saw the need to recruit a new elite of men and women whose success in life could be attributed primarily to personal effort and who were motivated to serve for reasons that could not be captured in a spreadsheet or the family's last name.

Nicholas was a rising star of this new elite when K first introduced him to senior members of the Order for vetting, who all fingered him for greatness. Nicholas faced the ire of many wealthy snobs who were tired of their fathers comparing them to Nicholas, and was the talk of the town with the eligible daughters who were courted in ways that were reminiscent of old families merging their balance sheets. Despite several discreet offers to "get to know each other," only one woman caught his eye: Julia. She wasn't from the elite of the elite, but she did promise a life of financial stability and access to an elite club, none of which mattered to Nicholas. Many members of the Order were humbled by Nicholas' display of romantic love during the engagement, with no apparent concern for forming a merger with the elite of the elite who were only too willing to welcome him. With the fall-out in El Salvador, however, the Order made a strategic decision to distance itself from Nicholas. Even more painful, Julia suddenly got cold feet and returned the ring.

K nodded knowingly. "I tried my best to secure your membership to the Order, but too many members wanted to delay it. Besides, you never seemed like the kind of person who was interested in stodgy old social clubs. The Order is a dying breed."

"It was never really about joining the club," Nicholas said. "What bothered me was losing Julia and being judged for something that wasn't my fault."

Janette knocked on the door and poked her head in. "Excuse me, sir, but you have an important phone call."

K stood. "I'll be right there. Please take Nicholas to the stables." K turned to Nicholas. "We have more to discuss."

Chapter Four

Nicholas rubbed his hands and exhaled a cloud of steam as he walked to the horse stables behind the house. He admired the hilly, rural terrain, with no other houses as far as the eye could see. The ranch had a brook down the hill with a water pump, rows of fruit trees and a large garden, solar panels on the roof of the house, and a barn with chickens. A chilly wind swirled as his shoes crunched the snow underneath. Inside the stables, he walked down the concrete aisle to admire the dozen horses in stalls on either side. A shovel and a wide broom hung on the wall, but the aisle and stalls were cleaned and polished to perfection, although he had helped K clean them in the past.

K had a knack for keeping the family wealth grounded in the aesthetic beauty of the land from one generation to the next, in a way that would allow him to live off the grid if the situation were ever to arise, something he conceptualized long before preppers began forecasting the apocalypse. K inspired admiration, not resentment, even from people who rejected everything his class represented. He was known to play cards with the local farmers and contributed to bake sales at a simple church down the road, even though few people knew where he worked. Nicholas' introduction to the Order was at this same ranch during a crisp fall day that included a fire in the back yard, a hay ride for the kids, and a horse race for the ambitious young men as the young ladies watched. Despite having less training, Nicholas outran the others, mostly because he didn't know what to fear. The final leaps of the fence and the brook left the older generation nodding approvingly as their sons made excuses about why they didn't make the same calculated risk. This victory caught the attention of Julia, who gave him riding tips during a private excursion later the same evening.

The stable door opened and closed. Nicholas turned to see K, who stopped at one of the horses, stroked its head, and whispered something. When K arrived at the end with Nicholas, he rubbed his hands and gestured to an office with handcrafted furniture, a bar, and a window with a view of the ranch. They set their cell phones in an insulated storage box outside the office and entered. K closed and locked the door, turned on the heater, and walked behind the bar to pour two glasses of Scotch. They sat, toasted, and sipped their drinks.

"If I had known a few days ago that we were going to meet today," K said, "we could have had the horses prepped for a ride."

"That would have been nice," Nicholas said. "So many years have gone by, but everything looks the same."

"Yes, well, a lot of hard work goes into creating the appearance of stability," K said and gestured to the stalls. "One of the horses is owned by President Mendoza from Panama. He offered me his prize horse while discussing a strategic plan for his country a few months ago, here in this same room. I told him I couldn't accept any gifts, so he agreed to keep the horse here until next summer after his shot at re-election. If the situation were to call for it, he could sell the horse and retire comfortably—less conspicuous than gold or Swiss bank accounts."

K had deftly linked Nicholas' fond memories of Julia at the ranch and a potential operation in Panama in a way that seemed thoughtful, not manipulative. At this point, it would be bad form to not let the discussion play out, but Nicholas had to lead the way to show the kind of initiative K expected. "I've been out of Latin America for some time, but the last I recall, the Constitution of Panama doesn't allow for re-election."

K nodded and sipped his drink and gestured to the room. "I had this room specially designed for these conversations. I don't know the technical details, but they assure me it's a smart room with real-time monitoring to detect bugs." K gestured to an electronic box with a green light on the bar. "They tell me that if a Soviet were washing that window outside, we would be safe discussing our communist spying program inside." After a pause, he continued: "The tragic death of Tyler has been a shock for all of us, but we have important and sensitive operations in Panama that have to continue."

"I'd love to help," Nicholas said, "but I've been assigned to this Peru–Ecuador task force, which I'm assured is a matter of national security." At this point, it occurred to him that K might have gotten him assigned to the task force in the first place.

K smiled. "I'm sure I can pull a few strings to change that. As background, we're not comfortable with how things are shaping up in Panama just as we're getting ready to close all of our military bases and turn over the Canal by December 31st. For that reason, we're working with President Mendoza to help him get re-elected. In return, he'll allow us to maintain some of our military bases post-1999."

Nicholas nodded slowly and sipped his drink, impressed with how K could make the most loaded statements sound so natural and bureaucratic. First, maintaining U.S. military bases in Panama post-1999 was a violation of the Carter–Torrijos treaties of 1977, which were ratified by the U.S. Senate. Giving away one of the engineering marvels of the modern world probably didn't sit well with K. Second, manipulating a foreign political process or election fell under the rubric of covert action, which required a presidential finding and Congressional notification. Underlying all of this was the fact that the United States in 1903 had worked with rebellious Panamanians to secure their independence from Colombia, which was not a legal process by any stretch of the imagination.

"I'm surprised to hear our president is making such an aggressive move in Panama," Nicholas said, making his next move.

K smiled and nodded. "Given the sensitive nature of this operation, we would prefer to keep this one off the books. Some of the other federal agencies definitely wouldn't support the plan, so we can't risk a leak. The plan, which is known as operation Delphi Justice, is quite simple: President Mendoza has a good plan to win the referendum, which will allow him to run for president again, and we're funding it."

Nicholas resisted a smile in response to what K didn't say, such as not mentioning whether the U.S. president knew about the operation. "I understand our wanting to keep this off the book, but how do we hide the funding?"

K stood, opened the door to make sure no was outside, checked the electronic box with a green light on the bar, and sat. "Now we get to the sensitive part. We've found a creative way to raise money that doesn't involve any of the Iran–Contra problems that got us into trouble during the 1980s. Are you familiar with a Colombian drug trafficker named Cesar Gomez?"

Nicholas jogged his memory. "He was a FARC guerrilla leader in Colombia back in the day. Didn't Helena Hernandez fall from his penthouse?"

K nodded. "Cesar has been moving cocaine shipments with his old guerrilla comrades on the north coast of Colombia. He was our top Linear target for years and we were close to getting him." The CIA, DEA, and other federal law enforcement and intelligence agencies nominated Linear targets to focus the efforts of the United States government on eliminating drug kingpins rather than petty dealers—cutting off the head, so to speak. "Knowing that we were onto him, Cesar approached us and offered to give up his remaining inventory of cocaine in exchange for his freedom."

Nicholas cocked his head, confused. "I don't understand. How do you propose we monetize his cocaine?"

"Cesar knows some new buyers who want to dip their toes in the business," K said. "By the time anyone figures out that Cesar is losing his shipments, he'll disappear. The way it works is that we step in as the middle man, arrange to deliver the cocaine, and arrange for the cocaine to be seized after we have collected the money from the buyers, what we call a controlled shipment. That way, we collect the money and seize the drugs in one step. Cesar gets his usual cut from each shipment and then he goes free when we're done."

Nicholas was still skeptical. "Can we trust him?"

K shrugged cautiously. "Dylan and Tyler spoke with Cesar in person. He's getting old and is ready to move on. Not to mention, if he says anything, his fingerprints are all over the shipments, so he'll go to prison."

"Honor among thieves," Nicholas said.

"Something like that," K said. "The first two shipments were successful, and the proceeds went to supporting President Mendoza's referendum campaign. Cesar has enough cocaine for three more shipments, which should produce enough money to push us over the top and allow us to keep some U.S. military bases in Panama post-1999, which is a critical national security objective. I can't think of anyone more qualified than you to take the job."

Nicholas resisted a smile and a quick acceptance. K had a way of motivating people that couldn't be denied; however, age, maturity, and discipline had allowed Nicholas to think through these issues more dispassionately. "The absence of a presidential finding and creative funding are two things the CIA doesn't do well. Not to mention, we're discussing this at your ranch, not at your office. Would I be out of line to suggest the Order is behind this?"

K shook his head. "You wouldn't be out of line. The members of the Order, myself included, certainly want to keep U.S. military bases in Panama post-1999. Most of the members these days are primarily concerned with making money, but they've agreed to finance the operation with their own money."

"I'm interested in taking the assignment," Nicholas said, "but I don't want to be the scapegoat again if things go south. Can you assure me there are no other details you're not telling me? Is this really nothing more than raising money for President Mendoza?"

K took a deep breath and looked at Nicholas, perhaps disappointed he had to ask such a question. "I promise you there's nothing else going on here. We're raising money for President Mendoza. Like I said, the days of the Order making foreign policy are behind us."

"In that case," Nicholas said and paused to think about it, "I'm sure no one would object to offering me membership to the Order if I complete the operation."

K finished his drink with a wry smile to suggest he was pleased with how Nicholas had manipulated the discussion. "Why would you want to join these old dinosaurs who dwell on the past and obsess about protecting their wealth?"

"To hedge my bets and to make sure they're serious," Nicholas said. "Things might not seem this way from your perspective, but membership still has benefits, even with the recent push to hire people like me based on merit. Trust me, the world is filled with intelligent and hard-working people who never make it."

K nodded, excused himself, and stepped outside. Nicholas walked to the bar to freshen his drink and admired the scenery outside. He felt surprisingly relaxed but didn't want to lose sight of the fact that someone had killed Tyler, and that this person would pay for his crime. This alone was a sufficient justification to take the assignment in Panama and would be the focus of his efforts, but with the direct or indirect involvement of the Order, he had to take steps to ensure he wasn't the victim of another Congressional inquiry.

K entered and closed the door. "I made a call. Assuming you have a successful operation, the members of the Order would be pleased to welcome you to their ranks."

Nicholas and K shook hands.

Chapter Five

Panamanian Minister of Foreign Affairs Victor Hernandez, late sixties and balding, but tall, dark, and handsome in his black suit and crisp white shirt, entered the hotel bathroom, splashed cold water on his face, and gazed in the mirror. He exuded the refinement of a gentleman, but inside the pain was unbearable. Outside, applause thundered in the conference room. He removed a photograph of his daughter Helena Hernandez from his suit-coat pocket and raised it to his nose to smell the violet-scented perfume as the tears returned.

"I miss you and love you so much, honey," he said. "I promise I won't stop until Cesar Gomez is brought to justice." The pain of Helena's death was something he would have to learn to live with.

The arrival of another man in the bathroom summoned him back to reality. He tucked the photograph of Helena into his suit pocket, dried his eyes with a paper towel, and acknowledged the man, who lowered his head in a gesture of respect. In the hall of the hotel, amid a group of people drinking and smoking, a stunning young mulatto woman, Sheena, wearing a skintight red dress and with delicious chocolate skin, was sitting alone at the bar sipping champagne. Victor approached the bar and made fleeting eye contact with her. She discreetly passed him a plastic hotel room key, with a scintillating touch of her skin; he surreptitiously slipped it into his coat pocket with a subtle smile and then grabbed a book of matches from the bar before walking the other way.

Inside the conference room, Victor sat next to his wife, Ivonne, who looked at him inquisitively, sensing something wrong. She looked regal in her black dress, diamond-encrusted jewels, and salon hair, like the other wives sitting with their prominent husbands. Victor forced a smile and squeezed her hand to assure her everything would be fine.

"Panamanian sovereignty at last!" President Mendoza thundered and pounded his fist on the podium. The audience burst into a round of applause. The stout president wore a navy blue suit, French blue shirt, and a patterned yellow tie. He stood with aplomb under the bright lights, and removed a handkerchief to wipe the sweat off his rounded, pinkish face.

Victor groaned to himself—*the damned phrase again.* Unfortunately, social "progress" in Panama, which meant allowing even more unqualified people to vote, had upset the regime and forced him and his president to pander to common sentiments with phrases like "Panamanian sovereignty," as if the masses had any clue what the word meant. Democracy wasn't bad in principle, such as the original suffrage restrictions in the Constitution of the United States of America, but democracy worked only when the citizens allowed to vote were informed, intelligent, and forward thinking enough to make wise decisions, which any civilized man knew wasn't the case in Panama, or most countries, for that matter.

"With the Canal, Panama's greatest natural resource," President Mendoza continued, "we manifested our destiny. Today, we stand before the next millennium awaiting our third and final freedom." He sipped his water and acknowledged the crowd's applause.

Victor hated the clichés "natural resource" and "third freedom," but the audiences loved them, which is why they included them in the speech—to motivate the base. For natural resource, the president was referring to the Panama Canal, which was anything but a natural resource; it was an engineering marvel made possible by the United States. Without it, Panama would be a mosquito-infested backwater country, as sad as that was to admit. For third freedom, the president was referring to independence from Spain in 1821, from Colombia in 1903 (with a U.S.-sponsored *coup d'état*), and finally, though only symbolically and with a heavy dose of irony, from the United States on December 31,

1999, when Panama would assume control of the Canal and all the U.S. military bases. The paternalistic imperial actor that had made Panama possible was being asked to leave.

Victor checked his watch and rose as the applause erupted into a standing ovation. The departure of American troops certainly wouldn't help Panama's future, no matter how good it felt to imagine or how obsessed people were with feeling emancipated. He would naturally prefer to live without rowdy American GIs strutting around the streets and sweeping up the lower-class girls in bars, if only to reduce the number of disgruntled young Panamanian men without access to women, but the gringos provided money and stability, two things desperately lacking in Panama. All nations depend on law and order and wise leadership from the men who are bred to lead and are naturally suited to lead. If he had things his way—and the president assured him he would—the American military would remain in Panama post-1999, despite what the naïve populists preached about sovereignty.

"We've proven ourselves capable," President Mendoza said as the applause faded and the people returned to their seats. "We'll maintain the pride of the Canal. It will continue to serve the world as a center for international shipping. I might add that it would be an honor to lead Panama into the twenty-first century."

The crowd hooted and hollered; a few boos fizzled.

"Success in the next century," President Mendoza continued, "will hinge on our relationship with the United States, our partners in economic development and regional security." More boos bellowed—not a good sign—but he raised a confident fist. "This, my distinguished guests, is our promise, from the people of the Republic of Panama to you and the rest of the world. Thank you."

Victor and Ivonne stood to applaud as President Mendoza gathered his notes from the podium and waved to the cheering crowd before being escorted out of the room by his security detail. As they made their way out of the conference room, they stopped in the hall with a group of friends as a waiter passed out glasses of champagne. Victor moved mechanically from one person to the next to discuss politics; he checked his watch and sipped his champagne as he watched Sheena waiting in the periphery. Finally, she gave him a wink, turned, and walked down the hall to the elevators, with Victor watching her every step of the way.

"Honey," Ivonne said and tapped him on the shoulder, "can we go? I'm tired, and this is the third event this week."

Victor kissed her on the forehead. "I have to work late tonight. I have some money issues to discuss with the president." He gestured to a man wearing a suit by the door, who rushed over. "The driver will take you home."

"Honey, how can you work at a time like this?" she asked.

Victor leaned forward to whisper. "If we lose this election, we'll lose many of our business interests," he said, "which will force us to sell some of our properties. You know this is tearing me apart, but what choice do we have?" The driver arrived. "Can you drop my lovely wife at home and come back to pick me up in about two hours."

"Yes, sir," the driver said.

"Don't stay out too late," Ivonne said and leaned forward to kiss him on the cheek.

"I won't," he said and waved as she walked away.

Victor looked up blissfully as Sheena straddled him on the hotel suite king bed, the headboard rhythmically pounding on the wall. Victor caressed her ass and breasts, but was overwhelmed and closed his eyes as he reached orgasm with a delightful moan.

"Oh, dear God," he said, gasping, as Sheena snuggled up next to him. "You're like a magic spell that makes me young again." He caught his breath. "You make my body do things that never happen with my wife, even with pills."

"You're not old," she said, "and this is really good for both of us. You work so hard, with so much stress, and you gave me a good job to help me pay for college."

He caressed her cheek. "I hired you because you're the best."

"You're so sweet," she said and smiled. "I don't see anything wrong with a powerful man like you hiring a beautiful woman like me."

"As long as I'm paying your salary and your college," he said while stroking her cheek gently, suddenly serious, "I won't have you sleeping with any other men."

"I understand the arrangement," she said, walked to the bathroom, and sat with the door open to pee. "How are you and your wife holding up with the loss of Helena?" The toilet flushed, and she appeared again.

"I'm still numb," he said and gestured for her to join him under the sheets. "It's really true what they say: there's nothing more painful than losing a child. I hope that bastard Cesar Gomez is brought to justice."

"Hope?" she said.

Victor smirked suavely. "I can't give you all the details, but we're working on a plan to bring him to justice."

"I wouldn't bet on hope," she said. "You know he'll bribe everyone in the legal system and will probably never serve time in prison. The Panamanian justice system is a complete joke. You should just kill him."

"I can't just kill him," Victor said and sat up.

"Why not," she said. "You're a minister with a lot of power. I'm sure you know people who could do it for you and keep your hands clean."

Victor thought about it—*why not?* "I should kill that son of a bitch and make him pay for what he did to Helena."

"I know some of the girls who go to his penthouse," Sheena continued. "They all say he's a real bastard, like his information guy, Manuel."

"Manuel Espinosa—the big time rice farmer?" Victor thought about it—*My God, he's a prominent party member!* "What do you mean by information guy?"

"He gets information to help Cesar move drugs," she said. "Everyone knows it. He also stores cocaine in his rice warehouse."

Victor paused to think about it. She was right. Cesar would never serve time in a Panamanian prison, and any attempt to extradite him to the United States would probably turn into a circus as the corruption links in the Panamanian government were revealed. *The exercise of power was such a rush!* He smiled, pulled her close, and began caressing her body and kissing her neck. "Are you ready for round number two?"

Sheena reached under the sheets and grabbed hold, surprised. "Wow, Minister, two times in the same night. Someone's taking his vitamins."

Chapter Six

Nicholas emerged from Tocumen International Airport in Panama City, Panama, inhaled the sweltering air, and donned his sunglasses after stepping into the piercing sunlight, which shone down as a phalanx of black clouds retreated on the horizon. A taxi drove by and splashed a puddle. He scanned the palm trees and the chaos of passengers and vehicles and concluded that not much had changed in Central America during the past ten years.

About fifty meters down, Dylan Dirk tossed a cigarette to the ground, crushed it with his tasseled loafer, and waved. Nicholas gestured for the Kuna Indian luggage man to follow. The tropical sun had tanned Dylan's skin; his salt-and-pepper hair and mustache were neatly trimmed; and the gray pin-striped suit magnified his Napoleonic frame. They had not spoken in ten years, since the Congressional hearing, but Dylan offered a top-of-the-day firm handshake followed by a one-armed hug and slaps on the back.

"Welcome to Panama," Dylan said. "You look good."

Nicholas gestured to him, eager to inquire about Tyler's death, but glanced at the driver and managed a professional smile. "You too."

Dylan gestured for a driver to load Nicholas' luggage into the SUV in front of them and gestured for Nicholas to sit shotgun in a maroon Mercedes Benz. Nicholas sat in the cool and crisp air and turned down the salsa music on the radio a few notches as Dylan got in.

"It's hotter than balls out there," Dylan said and checked his watch. "The driver will get you checked in at the hotel and drop off your luggage. We need to stop by the office first."

Nicholas gestured for a first down. "Let's do it."

As Dylan drove aggressively through the traffic and made small talk—gossip at the embassy, corruption in the Panamanian government, some hot women who showed up at the Marine House happy hour—Nicholas viewed the school-of-fish flow of Panamanian traffic and felt oddly at home, as if he had picked up where he left off ten years ago. He was back in the field working operations again. He tried to follow Dylan's humorous tales, but he couldn't help but feel skeptical about Dylan selecting him for this assignment. Granted, Dylan was testifying under oath when he threw Nicholas under the bus, but there must have been another way to protect someone doing the mission in the field.

A strange combination of memory and intuition kicked in for Nicholas as they entered downtown Panama City and wove through the one-way streets and narrow alley shortcuts opening up to major roads. While zipping down Balboa Avenue along the Pacific Ocean coast, they passed the prominent black iron fence surrounding the U.S. Embassy compound with the stars and stripes flapping proudly in the wind. Street vendors pushed wobbly carts around the honking cars as passengers stepped off colorful buses—*diablos rojos*. Blue *Si* and red *No* signs were plastered on the walls and telephone poles—*Si* favoring the referendum for the president, *No* opposed. A lone policeman stood below a broken traffic light doing an inefficient job of keeping the vehicles moving. A red Toyota Corolla taxi swerved at the last second from oncoming traffic and cut them off, prompting Dylan to swear and honk, then smile and nudge Nicholas as a midnight blue Mitsubishi Montero pulled up next to them. Nicholas turned to see a gorgeous Latina with flowing black hair and Gucci sunglasses driving with blasting Panamanian reggae. The place was *loco* but so full of life—*Que Panama!*

After a left turn, they entered a posh sector of town with exclusive homes and a small commercial building. Dylan stopped at the front gate, honked twice, and waved at the security guard who slid open the steel door.

* * *

Nicholas and Dylan waited for the security guard to open the door to the building, thanked him, and walked up the stairs to the office. They took a load off in Dylan's office with marble floors, leather furniture, a panoramic window with a view of the Pacific Ocean, and a nice blend of Panamanian-themed paintings, sculptures, and maps.

"Any news on Tyler's death," Nicholas said, getting down to business. Discussing it in the car would have been a bad idea, for security reasons, but he couldn't wait another minute. "There's a lot of confusion in headquarters about exactly what happened."

Dylan nodded solemnly. "The Panamanian National Police are all over it, but we have to withhold a lot of information from them for obvious reasons. I was working late when one of Tyler's agents signaled for an urgent meeting, so I called Tyler to let him know. A few hours later, I got a call from the police saying they had found him."

Nicholas nodded pensively. "So Tyler goes to the meeting the same night. Do we think the agent killed him? If so, why?"

Dylan shrugged. "Here's the thing: Tyler was killed near the meeting site, which suggests the agent killed him, but the agent was found dead later the same evening. The agent was a low-level drug trafficker who had moved one of our controlled cocaine shipments for operation Delphi Justice, so we can't rule out the possibility that he was compromised by his cartel and forced to kill Tyler."

"How do we know the agent was killed?" Nicholas asked.

"While discussing the investigation of Tyler's murder with the police," Dylan said, "they mentioned they were investigating another homicide, our agent, who they knew was involved in drug trafficking. Of course, I had to act like I never heard of the guy."

Nicholas drummed his fingers. "It's certainly plausible, but I really find it hard to believe one of these cartels would kill a CIA officer. They have to know we would figure it out and take the fight back to them."

Dylan pointed at him with a serious nod. "That's exactly why I selected you for this assignment. I knew you would be passionate about completing the mission and helping us find the person behind Tyler's murder. You have to be careful, but any clues you can find about his death would be helpful—probably a lot more helpful than the Panamanian National Police."

"And we're sure Cesar Gomez isn't behind this?" Nicholas asked.

Dylan nodded slowly. "He would stand to lose a lot by killing Tyler, so I doubt it, but you never know, so don't let your guard down with him. He's capable of anything."

As with everything Dylan said, Nicholas didn't know whether to believe him or trust him; perhaps the bias from ten years ago was still clouding his judgment, but there was one way to find out. Dylan never seemed the type to welcome outsiders to his exclusive club, the Order. "I'm not sure whether you heard, but K convinced the Order to approve my membership after completing this operation."

Dylan shot him with a finger pistol. "Of course I know. I lobbied the other members of the Order to approve it." He leaned forward. "Look, I know you probably blame me for what happened in El Salvador—the assassin, the atrocities, the Congressional committee—but you know I couldn't lie under oath. Besides, we all tried to help you get back in the game and back on track with your membership to the Order but you retreated to headquarters to work as an analyst during the past ten years."

"Well," Nicholas said, struggling to take Dylan at face value and allow his actions to speak louder than words, "here we are."

"Here we are," Dylan said with a clap, checking his watch. "Now, operation Delphi Justice and Panama. I have to go to a meeting at the embassy soon, but nothing has changed here. State Department still has utopian fantasies for human nature and the military still wants to rule the world with an iron fist. What was it that guy said? If things are going to stay the same, things are going to have to change."

"Some Italian guy," Nicholas said.

"That's right," Dylan said. "Now, big picture, no one cares about Panama per se, but the Panamanians don't understand why our president doesn't have them on speed-dial. They're too small to concern us as a trading partner and political instability would have minimal consequences for the region."

"So why the top secret plan to keep military bases?" Nicholas asked.

"We're running some successful counternarcotic operations," Dylan said, "and we want to have resources in place to respond to an emergency at the Canal. More important, they use the U.S. dollar here and have a massive offshore banking system that is a magnet for money launderers, all of which is easier to monitor with a large footprint in the country. Needless to say, the president and many senior policymakers are counting on you; all of this hinges on making sure that President Mendoza gets re-elected." He checked his watch. "I've got to run, but read Tyler's files and schedule a meeting with Cesar Gomez as soon as possible."

After a firm handshake, Dylan showed Nicholas to an office with a box of files and then headed out. Nicholas looked at the files and observed a moment of silence before sitting and opening the box. He was committed to studying every nuance of every word. What had Tyler done, thought, observed? Who were his agents? What were their motivations for providing secrets to the CIA? Had he found people willing to reveals secrets for ideological reasons, or just for good old-fashioned money? What clues could he find about his death?

Tyler's insights were brilliant. More important, they were uniquely *his*. Nicholas could hardly hold back a smile when he read passages like, "Our assistance with the medical treatment for his wife, under the guise of a special research program, seems to be a good fig leaf for him to sustain the relationship, but he certainly knows, at some level, what is really happening and that continued medical assistance will be contingent on providing classified documents from his work," or when he described one contact as, "corpulent, yet elusive." Of particular interest, Tyler had recruited Minister of Foreign Affairs Victor Hernandez, the father of his ex-fiancée, Helena Hernandez, and played a key role in convincing Cesar Gomez to work with the CIA in exchange for not facing legal prosecution. The information Minister Hernandez provided, about the plans and intentions of the Panamanian government vis-à-vis the Panama Canal and the possibility of maintaining U.S. military bases in Panama post-1999, was critical for setting the stage for operation Delphi Justice—two major successes.

As Nicholas tried to piece together what might have happened the night Tyler was killed, it occurred to him that it seemed like only yesterday that the two of them were eager young case officers starting their new careers. Their first stop was The Farm, the secret training base where they learned the arcane tradecraft of espionage and the martial skills that would keep them alive in the field. The monastic seclusion hardened their bodies and minds and exposed their weaknesses, which they chiseled away day and night until they reached the smooth, rounded core of their true self. They were part of a team, a fortress of stones piled high defending their nation; and the one thing that unified them more than anything else was the feeling that destiny was leading them, that they were key players with a divine mission. Their next stop was the real world of espionage and covert operations.

Central America during the 1980s was like the Wild West. Military dictators and insurgent guerrillas were regular items on the menu—not to mention civil wars, drug trafficking, and weapons trafficking. The U.S. was in the thick of every Machiavellian plot. While some American citizens protested the covert operations, the majority selectively ignored the dirty work being done by their government in defense of their freedoms. Many names were forgotten—the Contras and the Sandinistas in Nicaragua, the FMLN in El Salvador—but they were forever etched in the lexicon of U.S. covert operations.

Nicholas and Tyler were there, sometimes together, sometimes not. Ultimately, Tyler was a casualty of the Iran–Contra affair. Unfortunately, the generals and senior bureaucrats had grabbed all the chairs before the music stopped, which was a setback for Tyler's career, about the same time Nicholas quit the Directorate of Operations after the fiasco in El Salvador with the spades assassin and the atrocities. Both were reassigned to Washington—Nicholas by choice and as a punishment, Tyler as a guest in purgatory.

Nicholas had admired the way Tyler took things in stride and worked diligently to prove he deserved a second chance. He'd ruffled some feathers and obliquely questioned the integrity of those prosecuting him. He didn't let the bastards grind him down. Eventually, he was reassigned to the field, one successful mission after another, until he was selected for duty in Panama, until a bullet took his life.

After a few hours of reading, Nicholas walked outside to the parking lot to stretch his legs and feel the hot sun on his face, still shaken by the loss of his best friend. The sight of Tyler's silver BMW parked in a covered space grabbed his attention. He looked around to ensure no one was watching and then approached the car and apprehensively opened the driver's door. Steamy, putrid air stung his nose and dissipated, but a chemical odor remained. The smell was a blend of detergent and whatever it had cleaned, probably Tyler's blood. He held the door open as a gentle breeze stirred the air and then sat in the driver's seat. Unmistakable blood splotches stained the passenger seat and the top, suggesting Tyler had been shot through the driver-side window when it was lowered because it wasn't broken. *Did he recognize the killer?* He felt ill as sweat trickled down his neck. He gripped the steering wheel with both hands and closed his eyes, imagining what Tyler's last thoughts might have been. A horrible image flashed in his mind of Tyler recognizing that he was about to be killed and trying to drive away.

The sound of the security guard tapping on the glass jolted him back to reality. He opened the door.

"Mr. Dylan say no sit in car," the security guard said.

Nicholas nodded, exited the vehicle, and walked to the other side of the parking lot with the cell phone Dylan had given him. He reflected for a moment and dialed a number. A man answered on the second ring.

"Hello," he said, "Cesar Gomez, please."

Chapter Seven

"Shake that ass!" Cesar Gomez yelled over the blaring merengue on his penthouse patio with its view of the Pacific Ocean and the city. He stroked his mustache and admired his two ladies' tanned bodies by the swimming pool. Adriana, a topless blonde from Eastern Europe wearing a leopard-skin thong, kicked water at him and flipped him the bird. Maria, a brunette Latina with tan skin wearing a mauve bikini, lowered her copy of *Cosmopolitan* and imitated her friend's playful gesture. His body once had been something to admire, during the glorious days of fighting the revolution in the jungles of Colombia, but what dignified man didn't gain a few pounds before middle age? He loved these feisty beauties, though. They were the perfect ornaments for his penthouse, the loves of his life! He had big plans for the three of them, including a peaceful home away from the city.

Tyler Broadman's tragic and mysterious death and the canceled cocaine shipment had turned his world upside down. He'd completed two of the agreed-upon five cocaine shipments but the Americans hadn't yet called him to explain the next steps. Dylan Dirk had said he would remove him from the Linear list after five shipments, to finally retire in style, but the Americans had no idea they were freeing him to pursue his revolution in new and exciting ways.

He finished his dose of Aguardiente, a savory Colombian anise liquor, and set the glass down. "I don't know why I put up with their shit," he joked as his assistant, Gloria, arrived with the bottle.

Gloria, a young Colombian beauty with wavy black hair, indigenous features, and a three-inch scar on her left cheek, made stern eyes with Cesar and filled his glass. "Are the hookers asking for another raise in their allowance?"

"How dare you disrespect me like that," Cesar said, holding her stare, "after everything I've done for you."

Gloria downed Cesar's shot of Aguardiente, set the bottle on the table, and walked away in a huff. The cordless phone on the table rang. She stopped, walked back, and forced a smile before answering the phone. "Hello?" She listened intently, then covered the mouthpiece and handed it to Cesar. "Sounds like an American."

Cesar breathed a sigh of relief. "Give me that!" he demanded and gestured for Gloria to stay put. "Hello?" He nodded. "Yes, Mr. Lowe, we should meet soon." *Back in business!* "Perhaps we can meet at my office. Are you familiar with Josephine's Elite?" He laughed. "You have an office there as well? In that case, see you at eleven."

Cesar hung up the phone. "Funny guy," he said and thought about the familiar name. "Gloria, would you be so kind as to check my records for any information we have on a guy named Nicholas Lowe—please."

Gloria's glare transformed into a smile. She filled Cesar's glass, sat in the chair next to him, and began reading a worn copy of *The Communist Manifesto*.

"Why are you reading that crap?" Cesar asked.

"You're the one always talking about the revolution," Gloria said defensively, still focused on the book. "I saw you reading it ten minutes ago."

Cesar scoffed. "I read it from a critical perspective, you see. That so-called manifesto actually contributed to enslavement of the working class." He sipped his Aguardiente and exhaled. "To understand the revolution, you must listen to my words and follow my lead. I am the revolution."

The buzzer from the lobby sounded.

Gloria tossed the book aside and stood. "Good luck with that."

Cesar watched her walk away and then turned his attention to the two beauties by the pool. "Ladies, we have a guest." Adriana and Maria slipped on caftans and walked over. "Who do you love?" he asked.

They kissed either cheek and escorted him to the penthouse. The touch of their hands sent a chill up his spine. Unfortunately, the scent of the coconut tanning oil coating their divine bodies diluted his ardor.

Helena Hernandez had smelled of coconut oil the day she died.

"Ladies," Cesar continued, "you remember I told you I was looking for a house? I found the perfect place—quiet, tranquil, just the three of us. What do you think?"

The ladies looked at each other and shrugged.

"Make it a Monday," Maria said. "We don't want to miss any fun here in the city." She tugged Cesar's arm. "And bring some cocaine. If we're going to be locked up in the middle of nowhere, I want to be high."

"For sure," Adriana seconded. "And don't forget—our rate is higher for vacations."

Cesar laughed to himself. His ladies were always angling for an increase in their allowance! "I don't think you understand. I was thinking we could move there, for good, just the three of us. We could start a family."

"No way," Maria scoffed. "A family? With you? No thanks."

"Yeah," Adriana agreed, "no thanks."

"I promise you you'll love it," he assured them. "We'll go for a few days. If you don't like it, we'll come back."

Most women thought the world revolved around their happiness, which was why they needed men, like Cesar, to keep them in line. They would love the house after one weekend, he was sure of it. He reached down and slapped their shapely asses.

"Go get ready so we can party tonight," he said.

"Actually," Maria said, "we're going out with some friends. Remember?"

Cesar had taken them away from the world of topless dancing and young horny men, but they sometimes had reunions with their old friends.

"We'll stop by tomorrow," Maria continued. "You promised to take us shopping."

Adriana kissed his cheek. "We saw some beautiful clothes today," she said, adding seductively, "very sexy clothes."

Cesar didn't remember making any promises to go shopping. He couldn't remember everything. Who could?

"I have a meeting tonight anyway. Big business," he said and squeezed their asses.

Adriana rubbed his shoulder. "We're a little short on cash."

Cesar laughed. Women had no fiscal discipline: give them money, and it was gone before you could say blowjob! He reached into his pocket and removed a wad of twenties. He handed half to Maria, because she seemed the more disciplined one. Adriana grabbed the other half."Ah, yeah, have a good time."

"Bye," they said in unison and strolled to the penthouse. Maria apparently told Adriana a joke because they both laughed hysterically.

Cesar entered the study and admired his vast library, mostly books with the word "revolution" in the title. He'd read all of them—well, almost— the seeds of his brilliant philosophy that would revolutionize the way revolutions changed society. Unlike most revolutionary theories that never worked or only kind of started to work after millions of people had been summarily executed, his wasn't based on the traditional ways of thinking. No, his was the result of an ingenious insight.

Since the middle of the nineteenth century, revolutionary geniuses had discovered different facets of the Truth, to include material forces and social classes. Their primary error, however, had been confusing physical evolution for the evolution of consciousness, meaning that consciousness was a reflection of the material world, not the other way. They all assumed the fundamental force of their philosophical system was the clashing social classes in space and time in response to the material conditions of their particular society. However, as Cesar had discovered, the unfolding universal consciousness was the fundamental force and the key to the Truth. That is, consciousness shaped matter as much as matter shaped consciousness, a symbiotic relationship that unfolded in a logical and rational manner in time. (When someone pointed out to Cesar that his ideas were reminiscent of Hegel, who played a critical role in shaping the thought of Marx, he scoffed and insisted his ideas were original.) Therefore, the corrupted manifestation of the materialist system—civilization—had to be destroyed so the individual could return to his roots and express himself naturally through pure consciousness. Cesar's destiny was to reveal this Truth and save humanity—from itself.

He sat in the leather chair behind his desk and gazed at the rifle hanging on the wall, the one he'd fought with in the jungles of Colombia for the glorious revolution against the oppressive oligarchy that relied on the iron first of military power to enforce its will, along with millions of dollars from the Americans. The Truth had set him free, though. He understood that the masses had no reason to feel ashamed for being poor. Cruel and systematic exploitation by corrupt groups was the cause of poverty. For centuries, the exploiters perpetuated the lie that a person's lot in life was the result of a natural hierarchy. He saw through this perverted conspiracy. Vicious groups like the Order enslaved the masses and created unjust social systems that perpetuated their grip on power and their ability to print money at will. Armed with this knowledge, Cesar joined the leftist Revolutionary Armed Forces of Colombia (FARC) in the jungles to fight this force of evil. Initially, despite the horrible violence, the war was glorious. Eventually, however, he learned a dark truth: many FARC leaders had transmogrified into the power-hungry despots he originally had set out to destroy.

The first indication of this unfortunate transition was the alliance with the drug cartels. Cesar wasn't opposed to this on principle—as long as the imperialists snorted the cocaine and the profits supported the revolution—but he opposed targeting local villagers, the people they were supposed to be liberating. Once-beautiful Colombian women had resorted to prostitution to support their disgraceful drug habit. Cesar took great pleasure in secretly killing the man who had cut Gloria's cheek with a knife and threatened to sell her as a sex slave to the cartels. Gloria had been with him since that time, first in the jungles of Colombia, and now in urban Panama City. The second indication was the attacks on innocent villages. People who didn't pay enough "taxes" to the FARC or provide enough sons as soldiers were killed or forced to live like slaves. Their dead bodies were shown to the media and made to look like the work of the right-wing paramilitaries. Cesar's career in the jungle ended when he refused to wipe out a village. He couldn't kill his own people.

Shattered and heartbroken, he started his own revolution. Keeping in mind the Anglo-Saxon fear of mind-altering substances and his

43

desire to free the consciousness of humanity from its material bondage, he began transporting cocaine to the United States and Europe in the hope of unraveling the social fabric of those oppressive cultures. Thus began his world crusade. The rifle now hung on his wall as a reminder that he was always willing to fight for a just cause. If the right situation were ever to present itself, he would no doubt grab that gun off the wall and use it, with the same precision that made him legendary in the jungles of Colombia.

A knock on the door jerked Cesar back to reality.

"Anyone home?" Manuel Espinosa asked. He wore a white linen shirt—the top three buttons undone, with enough chest hair to mow—and tan linen slacks. He sat and lit a cigarette with an attitude so typical of someone from wealth. He exhaled the smoke and posed dramatically, like someone from one of those *telenovelas* that more often than not fail to move the plot forward in any meaningful way during any given episode.

"I saw Adriana and Maria," he said with a smirk. "They looked joyful—another good pay day, I assume?"

Cesar glared at him, not pleased with his tone, and mustered a confident smile. "If they looked joyful it was because they were with me." He hated to associate with the local capitalists, but Manuel was a great source of information, although he never would have survived in the jungles of Colombia. Wealth had made Manuel lazy. He had broad shoulders and a face that women raved about, but money had chipped away his moral convictions.

Cesar offered a glass of Aguardiente.

Manuel nodded approvingly with a raised eyebrow. "Any word on your next shipment?"

Cesar nodded assuredly. "I have a meeting tonight with a client." Manuel didn't know about his special deal with the CIA.

"What's his name?" Manuel asked. "I'll check him out."

"Not necessary," Cesar said.

Manuel set his cigarette down and sipped his drink. "The word on the street is that you ordered the hit on Tyler Broadman."

Cesar leaned back. He expected that rumor to surface eventually, and the good news was Manuel had no idea he was working with the CIA or Tyler. He respected Tyler and stood to gain nothing by killing him. No one would believe it, of course, so he'd become the prime suspect. "I had nothing to do with that."

"They're saying he wanted to kill you for what you did to Helena Hernandez," Manuel said. "The CIA—"

"Fuck the CIA!" Cesar yelled and pounded his fists. How dare anyone accuse him of killing Helena! He would never do such a thing. Anyone who knew him could attest to that. He jabbed an accusing finger. "I'm untouchable, you hear? No one fucks with Cesar Gomez. And who the hell is this *they* you keep referring to?"

"I have friends," Manuel said calmly and refilled his glass. "That's what you pay me for—information, no?"

Cesar mumbled an apology.

"I'm watching out for you." Manuel crushed his cigarette in the ashtray. "You should invest some money in legitimate businesses. I have a few ideas if you're willing to listen."

"Legitimate?" Cesar scoffed. "You'd better think twice if you think Cesar Gomez is going to join this consumer culture in its prolonged state of arrested development."

Manuel lit another cigarette and took a deep puff, not fazed. "You can't live like this forever. First, you pay for your women."

Cesar restrained himself. Paying beautiful women an allowance **for sex** was normal. Husbands did it all the time, and often got no sex!

"Second, you're a loner. Why don't you settle down with a nice wife, like Gloria, and have some little Cesars?" He grimaced with amusement. "Then again, maybe not."

Cesar glared at him. He would settle down and start a family, but he would continue his revolution in new and exciting ways. He had yet to define what that meant, but he had confidence in himself and in his vision for the future.

"Cesar Gomez knows what he's doing," he said. "I'll run drugs, hookers, whatever it takes to smear the capitalists in their own slime. Do you think I left the glorious revolution in the jungles of Colombia to become a vulgar bourgeois? No offense, my friend, but you live a boring life running your little businesses."

Manuel puffed his cigarette. "I'm worried about you, that's all."

"Cesar Gomez is in control of the situation. I'll continue to live this life, doing my part to destroy the imperialists. See if you can get that word on the street!" He stood and gestured to the door. "Thank you for stopping by. I should have a shipment ready in a few days. Get me all the information you can on what air and maritime assets the Americans and Colombians will have available."

"Sure thing, boss," Manuel said with a wink and excused himself.

Cesar couldn't hold back a smile as he strolled outside to the patio. He could have won an Oscar for that performance! Manuel had no idea he was working for the CIA. Three more cocaine shipments and his life would change, forever—a numbered Swiss account and a private beach house on a Caribbean island.

His elation ended, however, when he rested his hands on the ledge and looked down at the patch of grass below, where Helena had fallen to her death. The last thing he remembered, she'd agreed to stop using cocaine—right here, on his patio, face to face with him on that fateful day. He removed the photograph of Helena from his shirt pocket, admired it, and raised it to his nose to smell the lingering violet-scented perfume.

Gloria approached from behind, tapped him on the shoulder, and handed him a stack of papers. "I got the information you asked for about Mr. Nicholas Lowe."

Cesar cleared his throat and examined the pages. "Let's see…El Salvador…yes, yes…well, well, well." He looked at Gloria and smiled. "It seems the famous Nicholas Lowe is back in the game."

Chapter Eight

Dylan Dirk arrived at the U.S. Embassy gate, presented his ID to the local security guards, and turned off the engine. The security guards checked the vehicle—pop the hood and trunk, rolling mirrors underneath, glances in each window—then opened the gate and waved him past. He rolled into his reserved parking space near the main entrance and presented his ID to the U.S. Marine at Post 1. The Marine acknowledged him and pressed the button to unlock the door.

One of the frustrating parts about working in an embassy was attending meetings, all kinds of meetings, listening to other federal agencies talk about what they are doing and providing just enough tidbits about CIA activities and successes to keep everyone intrigued yet silent. Even more frustrating was the fact that the federal government seemed to be promoting a new generation of do-gooders who developed inflated egos from giving away hard-earned U.S. tax dollars to foreign-aid programs with negligible benefits to the recipients or to U.S. national security interests. As should surprise no one with a keen grasp of human nature, people were simply less likely to strive for autonomy if the Uncle Sugar paychecks kept rolling in, regardless of results. And many of these young lefties, especially from the U.S. State Department and the U.S. Agency for International Development (USAID), had the nerve to question the CIA about the way it conducted business. Thus, it was no surprise that he spent most of his time talking to the military and law enforcement agencies (FBI, DEA, DOD, and so on, alphabet soup), the reasonable ones in the room who understood that the world was filled with evil people who wanted to harm U.S. interests and who understood that showing strength and resolve was the best way to motivate other countries to behave.

However, at the end of the day, there were many things Dylan couldn't discuss with even his military or law enforcement colleagues. In the National Security Act of 1947, as amended, the CIA was entrusted with important authorities that couldn't be delegated to other agencies and couldn't be open to consensus or groupthink. When the president of the United States concluded that nontraditional methods would be required to achieve a particular national security objective, he called on the CIA. When the president had to make an important policy decision that hinged on the most reliable information, he called on the CIA. For this reason, although Dylan had to keep the ambassador in the loop for all of his activities, he enjoyed a level of autonomy that other agencies did not enjoy and could only envy. And when it came to the activities of the Order, all the rules were out the window. There were some things even the ambassador didn't need to know, sometimes even the president, and who were only too willing to live with the positive results after the fact. At the core of American national security rested the cold, calculating logic of the Order—doing what has to be done for the survival of the Republic.

Dylan casually entered a conference room kept frigid by a noisy air conditioner and with a view of the Pacific Ocean. The conversations dissipated, and the gazes of everyone settled on him as he moved to the head of the large rectangular table, where a half dozen agency heads were seated, along with a dozen or so mostly military personnel seated around the perimeter of the room. The Department of Defense usually invoked the principle of mass for even the most routine meetings. Dylan gestured to a young man seated at a computer to start the PowerPoint presentation. He nodded and clicked the mouse, spawning a welcome slide.

"Good morning, ladies and gentlemen," Dylan said. "The purpose of this meeting is twofold. First, the ambassador requested our ideas regarding Panama post-1999, from an intelligence perspective. Second, I wanted to discuss operation Delphi Justice." He gestured to the bald, stocky Air Force officer sitting to his right, the only one in the group wearing camouflage. "Colonel, would you do us the honor of going first."

Colonel Lance Dupree gestured to the young man sitting at the computer. He looked battle hardened, as if he'd gripped the enemy's throat with his bare hands. "Despite the reduction of U.S. forces in Panama," he began, "the war on drugs continues full throttle, make no mistake about it. Although corruption and poor training often prevent the Colombians and the Panamanians from making drug seizures, we've had many successes this quarter—seven planes destroyed. Next slide.

"Panama is facing an uncertain future," he continued. "Political stability is absolutely necessary when Panama assumes control of the Canal on December 31st. One of the greatest threats to stability in Panama will be the influence of drug traffickers. Drugs destabilize nations, and the associated problems like addiction and corruption tear apart the social fabric. For this reason, we must maintain military bases in Panama post-1999—to continue fighting this war, despite what the 1977 treaties say. Hell, if I had it my way, we'd keep the Canal; but since that ain't going to happen, we should do this at a minimum."

Colonel Dupree paused and continued: "In addition to stabilizing Panama, maintaining military bases will have other advantages." He listed items such as geography, logistics, the looming threat of China (as the young man at the computer clicked from one beautiful PowerPoint slide to the next), and the capability to deploy assets in support of "other operations," which was a euphemism for covert action and Special Forces.

He finished and pounded his fist lightly—no polite comments, no thanking the audience for their time. Dylan liked his style: to the point, no bullshit. Once the leadership had made a decision, he was the kind of guy you wanted on your team.

Thomas Rendall was next. He was the State Department Political Counselor, a New England liberal with a condescending smirk. He wore Continental wire-rimmed glasses, and his gray suit couldn't disguise his frail frame. He gestured to the young man sitting at the computer and waited for his PowerPoint slide to appear.

"Those were some compelling points, Colonel Dupree," Rendall said, "but reality is less propitious. Although funding for counterdrug operations shows no signs of waning, the key to Panama's future, including the Canal's, is economic reform. Next slide, please.

"About fourteen thousand ships transit the Canal annually. Recent profits have been low. Because shipping companies have other options, Panama won't have the luxury of increasing tolls significantly. Only reduced costs and increased efficiency will make the Canal profitable during the next century.

"Being shielded from economic competition has fostered Panama's oligarchic, monopolistic culture; income disparity is at dangerous levels. Economic reform is required to promote a level playing field and to transform Panama into an entrepreneurial culture with a strong middle class. The only way to achieve this is by promoting competition and by moving toward compliance with World Trade Organization standards. As a final word, I must stress that any attempt to violate the 1977 treaties, to include keeping military bases here post-1999, would have disastrous consequences for U.S. foreign policy in Latin America and around the world. The world is watching. If we violate this treaty, we'll lose credibility, which will damage our ability to sign other treaties in the future."

He gestured to Dylan to say he was done.

"Thank you, gentlemen," Dylan said. "I selected you to present two sides of the issue because Panama's future will be determined by political and economic factors."

"He's living in a fantasy world," Colonel Dupree said with a gesture to Thomas. "This is the third world. Panama occupies a strategic location. Our only concern should be security and stability, not building an *entrepreneurial culture.*"

Thomas chuckled condescendingly. "In case you didn't hear, Colonel, the 1977 Carter–Torrijos treaties require our military to leave Panama by December 31st of this year. Does the concept of national sovereignty mean anything to you?"

"Not if it interferes with U.S. national security interests," Colonel Dupree said bluntly.

"Besides," Thomas said, unscathed, "even if political stability were the primary goal, we can't provide that. The biggest problem in Panama is income disparity. Economic reform will create a middle class and promote the stability you are looking for."

Colonel Dupree's gaze shifted around the room. "That would take decades. In the process, Panama might collapse, which would threaten the Canal. It's not worth the risk."

"Gentlemen," Dylan interjected, "as we can see, the issue is complex. Please give me a copy of your PowerPoint presentations. I'll include them in my report to the ambassador and all the key players in Washington. From what I understand, the White House and the National Security Council are watching this issue closely."

Colonel Dupree and Thomas nodded respectfully.

"Moving on to the second item," Dylan said and gestured for the next PowerPoint slide. "Operation Delphi Justice, for those of you who don't know, was a sting operation to arrest Cesar Gomez. We've had—"

"What do you mean *was*?" Colonel Dupree asked. "Why would you stand down on a plan to take down that son of a bitch? And why didn't I know about it?"

Dylan raised a finger to put the colonel on hold and to keep center stage. With the tragic deaths of Helena and Tyler and the police investigations that followed, he couldn't rule out the possibility that details of operation Delphi Justice might leak. To prevent other agencies from learning about the controlled cocaine shipments that were being run with Cesar, the narrative going forward had to be that the CIA was entrapping Cesar to take him down. Therefore, by providing a few tantalizing details about the operation, he was taking steps to ensure the truth of it never saw the light of day.

"Most of you know that Tyler Broadman was tragically murdered Saturday night," Dylan began. "What most of you don't know is that we received information indicating his death might have been related to this operation to take down Cesar, perhaps retaliation." The next piece of the puzzle would make the big lie even more believable. "The most likely suspect is Cesar Gomez, but we don't have any proof—"

"I tell you what," Colonel Dupree said, "he probably killed Helena Hernandez—I don't care about his alibi—so I wouldn't be surprised if he killed Tyler as well."

Many heads around the table nodded.

"We don't know for sure," Dylan said, playing it cool. "The bottom line is the operation is on hold until we get more information."

"Is that a good idea?" Thomas asked. "Cesar might flee with his money."

"Now he wants to get his hands dirty," Colonel Dupree said.

Thomas glared at Colonel Dupree. "Tyler was a good friend, Colonel."

Colonel Dupree leaned back and lifted his hands defensively. "Please forgive me for that. I was out of line," he said. Thomas accepted the apology.

Dylan nodded like an impartial judge watching two sides reach agreement. The move of partially exposing the operation with Cesar was risky, but the seeds of deception were planted and seemed to be taking root.

"I'm sure others of you at this table have a lot of evidence we might be able to use against Cesar Gomez," Dylan said as the heads around the table moved north to south. "Our preference is to let the dust settle and determine whether the lawyers have enough evidence to build a case. In the meantime, I would ask that you all keep this information within this room and don't take any further steps without consulting me."

More nodding heads around the table.

"You were right to keep Cesar as a Linear target," Colonel Dupree said. "I knew that son of a bitch never stopped dealing cocaine."

"Guys like that never do," Dylan said.

"In the meantime," Colonel Dupree said, "I'm going to track his shipments and convince the Colombians to shoot them out of the sky. That son of a bitch won't get another kilogram of cocaine out of Colombia, not as long as I have anything to say about it."

Thomas leaned forward. "I'll talk to some of my banking friends to see whether Cesar is moving funds out of the country."

"I appreciate that, Thomas," Dylan said, "but let's lay low until after the referendum. If Cesar gets word we're onto him, he might flee to a country without extradition, as you said. Rest assured, we'll have him behind bars soon enough."

Unfortunately, defending U.S. national security in the modern world often meant lying and manipulating the same people who work with you.

"Speaking of the referendum," Thomas said, "did any of you read the editorial today in *El Tiempo*?" No one responded, which wasn't a good sign. "It suggested President Mendoza is funding his referendum campaign with drug money."

"I wouldn't doubt it," Dylan said calmly and resisted his bulging eyes. An editorial in *El Tiempo* about the president, the referendum, and drug money could mean only one thing—the journalist Lina Castillo. "Who wrote that editorial?" he added and slid his pen into his shirt pocket, taking a deep breath to control his nerves. The big lie was about to become even bigger and even more complex.

Thomas looked at the paper and shrugged. "It's anonymous. No direct accusations, only references to offshore funds and the paper's intent to investigate the story."

"Most campaign contributions in Panama have cocaine residue on them, if you know what I mean," Dylan said with a wink, getting a few laughs. "Probably just a bitter journalist spreading a nasty rumor."

"But a potentially devastating rumor," Thomas said.

Chapter Nine

Nicholas Lowe entered the Radisson Hotel reception and spotted Dylan Dirk on the other side of the room near the buffet table. A banner welcomed the guests to the 15th Anniversary of *El Tiempo* newspaper—celebrating 15 years of exposing corruption and reporting the truth. In many ways, journalists were a lot like spies—seeking the truth—so events like these were often a great way to gin up new business.

Nicholas accepted a glass of red wine from a passing waiter and strolled along the buffet table toward Dylan. The food line offered more for the senses: a tropical fruit salad, ham and turkey cuts with dinner rolls, chicken wings and meatballs, and finger desserts. A portly chef at the end sliced a large roast under the amber glow of a heat lamp.

"Good evening," Nicholas said as if to a stranger.

"Hey, Nick, glad you could make it at the last minute," Dylan said and turned to his wife, Ellen. "Honey, look who's here—back from the dead."

"Oh my, Nicholas Lowe," Ellen said and hugged him with a firm kiss on the cheek. Her sandy blonde hair smelled of strawberries, and her black dinner dress revealed her shapely figure, no doubt the result of yoga, Pilates, and an organic diet. She was in her late forties, but still a head turner, not the kind of woman you would expect to see with someone who looked like Dylan, if it wasn't for his money and family name. "Gosh, it's been so long," she whispered with a friendly squeeze on the arm and leaned closer. "I think we were drunk the last time we saw each other."

"I don't remember a thing," Nicholas whispered back, remembering her flirtatious offer to take a walk with a bottle of champagne during an event at K's ranch prior to his assignment in El Salvador, the same day he met Julia. To this day, he couldn't rule out that Dylan knew about it and held it against him.

"Dylan tells me you're working in Panama now," she said.

Dylan joined them with a smile. "He's back in the game," he said.

"Excuse me," she said playfully, "but I need some alone time with Nicholas." She led Nicholas away from the food line and whispered in his ear: "Congratulations on your membership to the Order. There are many eligible daughters who will be thrilled to hear the news—still single, right?"

Nicholas leaned back to a safe distance with a smile, probably blushing, and noticing Dylan watching them out of the corner of his eye. "How's Julia?"

Ellen raised a seductive eyebrow. "*Julia.* I knew you still had a thing for her." She looked around and leaned closer. "Last I heard things didn't work out so well with her fiancé, and now she's back on the market. I'll put in a good word."

Nicholas waved to Ellen as she walked away. He felt oddly uncomfortable with what should have been a good-news conversation—Julia was available—but he couldn't rule out the possibility that Ellen's affections were staged and calculated. The members of the Order were elite and exclusive, and weren't known for embracing outsiders who weren't in their circle of trust. Then again, the last thing he wanted to do was ruin a good thing by being paranoid.

Nicholas joined Dylan at the food line and grabbed a plate. "Ellen is in good spirits."

Dylan grabbed a dinner roll and a slice of ham. "She's an amazing woman." He split the roll and dabbed some mustard.

Nicholas reached for the pincers, tested it like a curious lobster, and flipped open the lid of the stainless steel chafing dish. He waited for the steam to clear and retrieved four chicken wings. "Any new clues or leads on Tyler's murder?"

Dylan shook his head and scooped some Swedish meatballs onto his plate. "The police are checking blood samples. All the evidence indicates the agent killed him." He tapped the spoon on the edge of the chafing dish, closed the lid, and looked at Nicholas. "But he's dead, so we aren't getting much information from him."

"No, I suppose not," Nicholas said and focused on the fruit salad.

"Did you call Cesar?" Dylan asked.

"I'm seeing him later tonight at a strip club," Nicholas said and nodded when the chef offered a slice of roast beef.

"Cesar is such a scumbag," Dylan said. "He's screwed every prostitute in this country."

Nicholas got to work on his chicken wings.

"Stay focused," Dylan said. "No matter how you feel about Cesar, we have to run three more shipments with him to raise enough money."

"K was clear about my objective," Nicholas said calmly, suggesting he took his orders from a higher power.

Suddenly alert, Dylan pointed. "You see that young, attractive woman over there talking to Minister Hernandez?"

Nicholas turned and focused on the Latina beauty as he chewed an overcooked chicken wing. As she and Minister Hernandez enjoyed a laugh, she turned and held his gaze for what seemed like an eternity, before turning back to her conversation.

"She's a journalist with *El Tiempo*—Lina Castillo." Dylan's eyes narrowed as if deep in thought. "I suspect she might have written the anonymous editorial in *El Tiempo* today about the president allegedly taking drug money for the referendum."

"Why?" Nicholas asked, unable to take his eyes off her, then dropped the chicken wing on his plate and turned. "Is it possible she knows?"

"I have a good feel for how she writes. She likes to investigate these kinds of stories." He looked at Nicholas. "I know you'll be busy with the operation, but I want you to get to know Lina. Find out what she's up to. If you can find anything resembling proof of her allegations, take it. We can't let her mess this up."

Nicholas looked longingly at the roast beef, set his plate down, and grabbed two glasses of red wine from a passing waiter.

"She wrote a good story about the Panamanian banking industry last week," Dylan said. "Be careful with this one."

Nicholas nodded and made his way across the room, then paused as he passed by. "Excuse me," he said as Lina and Minister Hernandez turned, "aren't you Lina Castillo? You wrote that insightful piece on the Panamanian banking industry last week."

"I'm glad you liked the story," she said. "Although, most people don't compliment me on my banking reports."

Pins held up her brown hair. Her intellectual glasses detracted attention from her figure. Her white business suit balanced professional with feminine. She definitely had the sexy librarian look going on, but Nicholas couldn't discern whether she was self-made or under the patronage of a sugar daddy, perhaps Minister Hernandez.

Nicholas clumsily looked for a place to set his extra glass of wine. "Could you hold this?" Lina accepted the glass as he kissed her on the cheek. "My name is Nicholas Lowe. Wow, your story was insightful." He sought acknowledgment from Minister Hernandez.

"She's the best," Minister Hernandez said: "the only journalist I can trust to not misquote me, although she's not a member of the President Mendoza fan club." Everyone enjoyed the humor. "Is this your first visit to Panama, Mr. Lowe?"

"Not the first or the last," Nicholas said and shook his hand, intrigued to be speaking with one of Tyler's best spies. Minister Hernandez acted appropriately smug for a minister: firm handshake, polished manners, and his mind on more important matters.

"Forgive me," Lina interjected. "This is Minister Hernandez."

"I recognize you from the newspapers," Nicholas said. The appropriate thing would be to offer condolences for the loss of his daughter, but that would be revealing. "I know some people in Washington who think very highly of your work."

Minister Hernandez seemed to appreciate the comment, but he didn't flinch, probably the result of Tyler's superb training.

"Panama is great," Nicholas added. "I'm sorry. The two of you were probably in the middle of something important. I'll just—"

"No, no, I was just leaving," Minister Hernandez said, checked his watch, and extended his hand to Nicholas. "It was a pleasure, Mr. Lowe." He touched Lina's shoulder. "Take care," he added and walked purposefully to the exit.

He lifted his glass to Lina. They toasted. "Here's to Panama."

He sipped the wine and gestured to the conference room exit. They walked to the ledge overlooking the lobby. The crowd noise faded to a buzz.

"Being a journalist must be exciting," he said.

She shrugged innocently, probably concealing her pride. "I can't think of anything more satisfying than using the newspaper to pursue the truth. I interview interesting people, like Minister Hernandez, and many stories I write have an impact, but the pursuit of the truth can be dangerous for journalists in Panama."

"The pursuit of the truth has been riddled with danger since the beginning of time," he said, which she seemed to appreciate. "Have you written anything else recently that you are particularly proud of?"

She glanced upward, apparently deep in thought. "No, not really."

Nicholas shrugged it off nonchalantly. "I work at the U.S. Embassy. I understand your newspaper was critical of my government when we liberated Panama from that dastardly dictator Noriega in 1989."

She smiled. "So now it was a liberation?"

"We promote democracy," he said with hint of sarcasm, figuring it would win points with her. "I heard about Minister Hernandez's daughter, Helena."

Lina rested her hands on the ledge and looked down. "Believe it or not, she and I were good friends when we were younger." She stood erect and stepped back.

"I'm sorry," Nicholas said. "I didn't know—"

"No," she said, "it's all right. I knew her for many years. We didn't exactly come from the same social circles, but Panama is a small country."

Lina obviously had normal human emotions. The next test, however, wouldn't be easy. "I know how you feel. Her fiancé, Tyler Broadman, was one of my best friends. In fact, I was sent down here to replace him."

She paused and stared at him. "I'm so sorry. Tyler was such a dear friend."

"You and Tyler were friends?" he asked, intrigued.

"We dated," she said cautiously, "before he met Helena." Her face seemed to be pleading for recognition. "He never mentioned me?"

Nicholas jogged his memory and feigned recognition. "Now that you mention it, I think he did—yeah, Lina—but we hadn't spoken for some time."

Lina seemed relieved as she removed a picture of Helena from her purse and handed it to Nicholas. "Every year she had a photograph taken of herself."

Nicholas concealed his admiration. Helena smiled as if possessing the secret of life. His eyes focused on the pearl necklace with a golden heart-shaped locket.

As if reading his mind, Lina pointed at the picture. "Tyler gave her the necklace during their engagement party."

Nicholas flipped the picture to read, "Eternity is the Bliss of Passion," written in calligraphy. He raised it to his nose to smell the lingering violet-scented perfume. He could almost feel her smooth Mediterranean skin, her silky black hair cascading through his fingers, the tide of her blue eyes a siren call pulling him toward the rocks of self-destruction. He smelled the perfume again and handed the picture to Lina.

"Like I said, we used to be good friends," she said and forced a smile.

"If you don't mind my asking, how long did you and Tyler go out?" he asked

"About a year," she said. "It was off and on at the beginning, but we were getting serious toward the end, or so I thought. Then he met Helena," she said and sipped her wine. "They got engaged two months later."

Nicholas winced empathetically. "Two months?" For some odd reason, none of this sounded familiar.

Lina shrugged to suggest she could be reasonable about the whole thing. "I guess I just didn't expect things would turn out that way."

Lina spotted someone on the other side of the room and handed Nicholas a business card. "I have to talk to someone for a story I'm writing. If you need anything—"

"Perhaps we could have dinner some time?" Nicholas asked, getting down to business. "I'll get up to speed on your stories and we can discuss Panama."

Lina paused, surprised, but seemed to warm up to the idea as she looked at him.

"Or," he said, "if you don't have time—"

"No, I would like that very much," she said.

"Perfect," he said and leaned forward to kiss her on the cheek.

Lina walked backwards a few steps and waved before turning.

Chapter Ten

Minister of Foreign Affairs Victor Hernandez entered the Presidential Palace with a newspaper tucked under his armpit. The secretary was busy on the telephone and raised a finger to signal the wait would be short. Victor opened the edition of *El Tiempo*, flipped to the editorial, read a few words, and groaned.

"The president will see you now," she said.

Victor opened the door to see President Mendoza pacing behind his desk and smoking a cigar, admiring the moon hovering over the Pacific Ocean. He set his cigar down, sipped his whiskey, and raised a newspaper off his desk.

"Have you read this?" he asked in an accusatorial yet inquisitive way.

Victor nodded and gestured to his own newspaper. "I was as surprised as you are. I have no idea why they would publish such lies."

"Did that Castillo woman write this?" President Mendoza asked. "She quotes you a lot in her stories."

"Mr. President," Victor said, humbly, however much it pained him to address a younger man in such a respectful manner, especially someone whose family wealth could not be traced back more than one generation, "I assure you that I have told Ms. Castillo nothing about our plan with the Americans. I just spoke with her at the anniversary party for *El Tiempo*. I raised the issue delicately, but she revealed nothing. As you know, Mr. Dirk is wiring money to your offshore account to help finance the referendum campaign. Besides, this editorial makes reference to drug money, which we know to be untrue and which suggests to me that Ms. Castillo did not write this. This is clearly an attempt by the newspaper to smear you."

President Mendoza clenched his fist and finished his drink. "If I find out who is behind these lies, there will be hell to pay!"

"I understand, Mr. President," Victor said. "On the other hand, if we can prove that these accusations are false, your poll numbers should rise because the voters will recognize it as a smear campaign."

"Except that some of the information is true," President Mendoza said and took a deep breath. "If anyone finds out we're taking money from the Americans under the table, we're finished." He paused. "Antonio is on his way over to discuss this, so I wanted to talk to you first to make sure we're on the same page."

"I will follow your lead, Mr. President," Victor said.

Moments later, there was a knock on the door. First Vice President Antonio Romero, mid-fifties, balding, with a department store suit that could use some tailoring, entered the room and offered firm handshakes to both of them. President Mendoza gestured for them to sit on the leather sofa and chairs.

"The president and I were just discussing his speech the other night," Victor began. "I think it made a positive impression on the voters."

"It was a fantastic speech, Mr. President! So full of passion," Antonio said with his usual greasy smirk that suggested he had an angle. He was an obnoxious drunk and a self-professed idealist who had slithered up the ranks of his ragtag movement by pandering to common sentiments, which was why it was such a painful decision to add him to the election ticket to win the support of his minority political party.

"Aside from some of the negative comments that were made about our strategic plan with the Americans," Victor continued, "I think we're on the right path to convincing Panama to vote yes for the referendum."

"And as you know," Antonio said, "many of those negative comments came from me and my party. We need to kick those American soldiers out of here for, what did you call it, Mr. President—our third freedom. Nicely said."

Victor resisted an urge to groan and handed an article printed from the Internet to President Mendoza and Antonio, who donned his reading glasses. "I am going to work under the pragmatic assumption that we want to win this referendum. As you can see from the most recent polling, we do not have a comfortable majority in the polls. And as you can also see, the people overwhelmingly support our relationship with the United States. I happen to believe that our national defense strategy should hinge on our relationship with the Americans, but as you can see, it is also good politics."

President Mendoza examined the article and squinted to view the charts. A true pragmatist with brains and charisma, he was an effective cocktail of "third way" sound bites to satisfy the masses and conservative policies to keep the country running. With a penchant for gauging public opinion and formulating divide-and-conquer tactics, he had garnered a little under half the vote in the last election, with a little help from Antonio's party, to win a plurality. A win is a win.

"The error factor has us over 50 percent," President Mendoza said.

"Or below 50 percent, Mr. President," Victor replied.

"Speaking of the referendum," Antonio said and removed a copy of the *El Tiempo* editorial from his pocket, "I noticed a big increase in our advertising. Our numbers are going up. That's great."

Victor nodded, but he smelled something rotten behind Antonio's greasy smile.

"I favor getting re-elected as much as the next guy," Antonio continued, "but where's the money coming from?"

Victor gestured to the article. "If you're referring to that absurd editorial in *El Tiempo,* you can rest assured that those accusations are false. In fact, the president and I were just discussing ways to take legal action against the newspaper."

"We can't start attacking newspapers," Antonio said. "If they present some evidence, we'll address it, but an unfriendly response will be viewed as an admission of guilt. We're all in the same boat, right? So, working under the assumption that all the claims in the editorial are false— taking money from the Americans that is linked to drug trafficking—it still raises questions about all the latest spending."

President Mendoza leaned back and crossed his legs. "You are correct. We have seen a nice rise in donations. I don't have a list with me," he said and looked around as if one might be handy—Victor shrugged in agreement—even checking his inside breast pocket, "but we have many supporters. We're a popular party with a mandate from the people. Businessmen, civic leaders, many people believe we represent Panama's future."

"We don't disclose that information to the public," Victor added. "As the first vice president, you of course have the right to know how we raise money." He had no intention of admitting they were taking money from the Americans. "I'll talk to the party treasurer," he continued, "but getting a complete list could take some time."

Antonio laughed. "I didn't ask for a list. I only wanted to know where the extra money was coming from." He paused and clucked his tongue as he looked at President Mendoza. "Funny how the increase in advertising coincided with your proposal to allow the Americans to keep military bases in Panama post-1999."

Victor jabbed an accusing finger. "You are out of line—"

"No," President Mendoza said. "That's a fair comment. Let me ask you a question. Speaking hypothetically, would you accept money from the Americans if it was the only way to get re-elected?"

Antonio shrugged. "I'd rather not take money—"

"I didn't ask you what you'd rather do," President Mendoza said calmly. "Given the options of re-election or defeat, would you accept money from the Americans?"

"I suppose I'd take the money," Antonio said, "but I wouldn't sell out Panama."

"You wouldn't sell out Panama," Victor repeated as if deciphering the words of a moron. "I suppose you know what's good for Panama? Let me guess: all that communist nonsense you and your comrades were spouting at the university as you continue to live parasitically off the wealth of others?"

"Panama doesn't need those damned Americans soldiers," Antonio said. "Have you no pride? Have you no shame?"

Victor shook his head in disgust—he was not taking the bait. The Americans were the masters of geopolitics—like a gentleman, he could admit that without resentment—and they, like he, knew that keeping U.S. soldiers in Panama post-1999 was in both nations' interests. Leaders worked in gray areas to make the world appear black and white to the masses, where people like Antonio fomented revolutions.

Antonio folded his arms and faced the window. "You want those damned American soldiers here reminding us we can't take care of ourselves?"

Victor jabbed an accusing finger but decided not to respond. After all, he had a point: Panama's dependence on America was disgraceful, but the world was full of harsh realities.

"If I may, gentlemen," President Mendoza said.

Victor and Antonio apologized.

"Antonio has a good point," President Mendoza said. "I agree that selling out Panama for the sake of re-election would be reprehensible," he paused to gesture to Antonio, "which is why we would never take money from the Americans. But I truly believe that forming a strategic alliance with the Americans is the right choice. Do you really think we have the resources to keep our country safe?"

Victor nodded approvingly as Antonio grumbled.

"Drugs are a threat," President Mendoza continued. "The American military presence provides stability and security, which is good for the Canal and for business. We both know the drug traffickers are lining up to move in with their money after the Americans leave."

"Exactly," Victor said.

"But when will we walk on our own two feet?" Antonio asked and threw his hands up in defeat. "How long will we ask the Americans to protect us from ourselves? Panamanians must experience freedom, which also means assuming responsibility. We will probably slip and have problems, but we'll work it out in the long run."

Victor groaned and sipped his drink. The idea of complete freedom sounded nice, but Panama just wasn't ready.

"All people want to be free," Antonio continued. "And freedom in our case means the departure of American soldiers. Can you imagine what allowing them to remain would do to our national psyche? It would perpetuate our dependency mindset, which would be shameful and irresponsible. We can do better than that."

"All the polls indicate the people favor a continued U.S. military presence." Victor hated to invoke polls, but this one was convenient to his purpose. "If the citizens are so eager for the Americans to leave, why do the polls not reflect that sentiment?"

"Because they're afraid!" Antonio said. "The Americans are their hedge against government incompetence—us. So let's show them how to govern. Economic reform, not military bases, is Panama's most important issue. The other problems are merely symptoms of social injustice."

President Mendoza nodded and puffed his cigar. "I will find a way to allow the U.S. military to stay here post-1999, regardless of what the 1977 treaties or the Legislative Assembly say." He silenced Antonio with an open hand. "Economic progress, as you said, is also important. We must make Panama more competitive if we plan to succeed in the twenty-first century. We must conform to World Trade Organization standards."

"Mr. President," Victor said, shocked, "surely you don't mean total conformity? Panama first needs law and order, or an open economy will result in chaos."

Antonio laughed. "Real competition would threaten your business interests. You don't want to help Panama; you want the Americans to protect your bottom line."

Conspiratorial nonsense, Victor thought. He was not boiling oil to protect himself from a peasant revolt. Hell, he had provided thousands of jobs to those ungrateful bastards who had no idea about how to turn a cash investment in to a positive cash flow business that provided jobs. "Panama isn't ready for radical economic change," he said calmly. "Change takes time."

"I intend to take time," President Mendoza said. "I'm creating a comprehensive plan to make Panama more competitive in the twenty-first century. The changes will affect some sectors more than others," he paused with a gesture to Victor, "but forcing companies to compete fairly is the best way to create a better future for Panama."

"Well said!" Antonio said triumphantly and stood, holding the editorial. "I must be off. Thank you for your time, Mr. President. I will advise the members of my party that there is absolutely no truth to this editorial. They will all be so relieved by your assurances."

President Mendoza waited for Antonio to leave before turning to Victor. "He doesn't believe us."

Victor shook his head, wondering what could have inspired his trusted friend Lina Castillo to write such an outrageous piece of nonsense. Then again, given that Lina never got the story wrong, *what kind of trouble are we in now?*

Chapter Eleven

Nicholas Lowe departed the El Panama Hotel along Via España dressed in khakis and a white linen shirt. The night air was perfect. The U.S. military enlisted hangout on the corner, My Place—filled with reggaeton music and American GIs grinding with the local talent—was hopping. After the 1989 invasion, someone had tossed a grenade into the bar after masses of Panamanian women started dating the gringos who'd invaded their country, ushering in a saga of broken promises and single mothers.

An ethnic medley of taxi drivers with surprisingly colloquial English—"Hey, man, you want a beautiful girl?"—offered free trips to the gentlemen's clubs, and undoubtedly charged gringos twice the regular fare for respectable destinations. He assured them he didn't require their services. He wanted to enjoy the walk, to acclimate himself.

Garbage littered the street where an elderly woman was cooking shish kebobs on a tinfoil-lined hibachi. The coals weren't glowing and the marinated beef was still raw, but the gray smoke acted as a perfume for the city's stink. By three in the morning, she'd be one of the most popular women on the street as the GIs began their exit.

Past adventures flashed in his mind as he waited for the traffic to clear on Via España. He was amazed more than ten years had passed but the place had not changed much. He hadn't honed his case officer skills during that time, but he'd learned a lot about the intelligence business by watching the key players from the White House and the National Security Council use his analytical reports to construct geopolitical strategies that shaped world events, although the policy decisions were often made before reading the intelligence reports, which meant that many policymakers spent a lot of their time mining for intelligence reports to support their policy decisions. When the traffic finally cleared, he dashed across the street, strolled past the Citibank building to the right, and turned left on the next road leading up the hill to Josephine's Elite.

He stood below the purple and pink neon lights. Many foreign agents had divulged secrets in exchange for bombshells with insatiable lusts for carnal pleasures. He'd used sexual currency on many occasions to satisfy his agents' peccadilloes, or what were viewed as natural desires in most countries. Paying for dancers and hookers was often cheaper than wiring money to numbered Swiss bank accounts.

The bouncer frisked him and wished him well. Inside, two beauties rattling promises of sensual satisfaction escorted him to a chair. The white lace lingerie contrasted nicely with their cinnamon skin. He sat in a chair two rows from the stage and opened his arms as they slithered onto his lap. Their perfumes enveloped him.

"*Hola, papi,*" they whispered and kissed him on the cheek.

"Two drink minimum," a waiter said.

Nicholas looked up and focused his senses. "Scotch," he said. "Tell Cesar that Nicholas is here to see him."

"Nicholas," the beauties said in unison and kissed him again.

"A drink for the ladies?" the waiter asked.

Buying a drink for a dancer was a bad investment, considering bang for your buck, but the ladies looked thrilled, and he wasn't spending his own money. "Of course," he said. "Two glasses of champagne."

"*Gracias, papi,*" they said and kissed his neck.

Stenciled words on the acrylic napkin holder advertised "Regular" dances for $10.00 and "Special" dances for $25.00. A woman on stage with a black robe was dancing dramatically to a techno version of Carl Orff's *Carmina Burana*. The final fling of the robe was anticlimactic and didn't quite capture the bacchanalian passion of the music.

The waiter set the drinks on the table. "Start a tab," Nicholas instructed and clinked the ladies' glasses of champagne.

"Excuse me, sir," the waiter said. "He will see you now."

Nicholas savored his blended Scotch.

"The ladies will show you the way," the waiter added.

The two beauties escorted Nicholas past a dimly lit room filled with feminine shadows casting spells atop moaning men—the "Special" dance room. They opened a door at the end of the hall and announced Nicholas' arrival. A man inside voiced his approval. The urge to hesitate overwhelmed him.

A red light illuminated the small room. Cubicle speakers attached to the wall played the music from the DJ booth. Bottles of liquor, a bucket of ice, various carafes, and a circular mirror with lines of cocaine covered the table. Cesar sat with a naked woman on either side, his hands groping their bodies.

Nicholas cleared his throat. Cesar looked up and unfettered himself. He extended his hand but couldn't reach. He looked like a caricature of evil in this sleazy setting. Nicholas had spent many years taking down guys like Cesar Gomez. However much it pained him to be working with him, he would follow orders and get the job done.

"Get out!" Cesar told the women. "Cesar Gomez has business to take care of." When they protested, he screamed, "Get the hell out, you dumb bitches!"

The ladies left. Nicholas sat next to him.

Cesar snorted a line of cocaine and shook his head to quell the jitters. "Cesar loves this blend. Do you want some?" he asked and slid the mirror.

"Nicholas is trying to quit," he said without emotion.

Cesar snapped his fingers and pointed. "Funny guy." He looked Nicholas up and down with a spent redness in his eyes. "I like that, a sense of humor. Besides—" He stopped suddenly. His eyes fluttered as he moaned.

Nicholas felt something slithering at his feet. A young lady crawled out from under the table. She wiped her mouth, grabbed a hundred-dollar bill from the table, and scurried out of the room. Cesar awoke slowly from his reverie.

"Sorry about that," Cesar said. He shook his head to regain his bearings. "No," he continued and pointed at the cocaine. "I was testing you. Cesar Gomez doesn't do business with people who use the stuff.

I only test the quality." He moved the cocaine to the other side of the table and wiped the excess powder off his hands. "How about a drink?" He gestured to a bottle of Aguardiente and filled two glasses.

Nicholas analyzed his inexplicable urge to choke Cesar to death. All the evidence suggested Cesar had nothing to do with the deaths of Helena or Tyler, but his gut assessed otherwise. "How pathetic."

Cesar set down the bottle and looked up. "What's that?"

"The way people keep buying cocaine," he said, aware that Cesar knew he worked for the CIA. Normally, he would have a spy within Cesar's network to take him down from within. As much as he hated it, they were partners.

Cesar gulped his drink. "Cesar Gomez says you can rely on three things."

Nicholas arched his eyebrows, ready to be enlightened.

"First, the human desire for material goods is insatiable; people will work themselves into their graves to buy more stuff. I call that consumerism." Cesar was obviously hoping for a reaction, but Nicholas gave him a blank stare. "Second, people will sell their souls for economic security. I call that slavery. To quote your philosopher Herbert Spencer, we haven't abolished slavery; we have nationalized it."

"Spoken like a good Marxist," Nicholas said.

"Marx was an idiot!" Cesar yelled and slammed his empty glass on the table. "Why does everyone credit him with every good idea? He was a capitalist pig!" He cleared his throat and relaxed. "You have to read between the lines, of course."

"Of course," Nicholas said. "What's the third thing?"

Cesar stroked his mustache. "Oh yes, the masses, left to their own devices, will live a life of self-destruction. People need other people to tell them what to do. I developed my revolutionary theory from these truths."

"That's a cynical view of human nature," Nicholas said, noticing the irony of Cesar speaking with such conviction about corrupted human nature. A vivid vision of Cesar writhing in his grip appeased his tension. "Sounds like you believe people are driven by primal desires, not by reason. What kind of revolution is that?"

"Reason rationalizes the self-deceptions caused by layers of oppressed desires," Cesar said and grinned.

"Did Marx say that?" Nicholas asked, laughing to himself.

"I said that!" Cesar yelled as his eyes narrowed. "Oh, I see, funny guy."

Nicholas changed the tone. "Humor aside, a lot must have happened during the past ten years for you to go from being an idealistic leftist FARC guerrilla in the jungles of Colombia to being a cynical cocaine trafficker." He arched a subtle eyebrow. "We know about your past."

Cesar glared at Nicholas. "My cynicism is a reflection of the times. Your country is responsible for converting the masses around the globe into money-hungry consumers. Unlike you, I still have my ideals. I have a plan to change the world, if you'd like to hear it."

"I'd probably find your plan intriguing," Nicholas said, "but I don't think we're here to discuss political philosophy."

Cesar's intellectual vigor faded. "We're here to make a deal. My third deal, by the way. Make sure Dylan doesn't lose count. Two more shipments after this one and I'm finished."

"That's the deal," Nicholas said.

"I get paid up front. No credit." Cesar handed Nicholas a business card. "That's my bank account number." He smiled sheepishly. "I'm planning to use the money to buy a retirement home and live the good life after this is finished."

Nicholas gave Cesar no reason to believe he gave a rat's ass about his plan. "I'll wire the money after your men have loaded the plane," he said. "Can I assume a rate of three thousand dollars per kilo?" Cesar nodded. Tyler's reports had indicated the price from the first two shipments. "Five hundred kilos should do."

Cesar opened a map of Colombia and set it on the table. "Tell your pilot to file a flight plan to Santa Marta. When he approaches the tower he should descend to one thousand feet and pass this call sign." He pointed to the word BORNEO. "The tower will make an official record of the plane landing, but the pilot should continue at the lowest altitude possible to this coordinate." He pointed at a remote airstrip on the Guajira Peninsula. "My men will be there to load the plane, slap on a fake tail number, and sell extra fuel."

"Can you provide my pilot with enough fuel to fly past the island of Hispaniola?" Nicholas asked. Tyler's first two shipments had gone to the Bahamas, but there was no reason to advise Cesar.

Cesar nodded. "He'll have more than enough fuel. Don't forget, my men don't load the plane until after I collect my money."

Nicholas checked his watch and nodded. "Sure thing."

"Before you go," Cesar said and then unfolded the *El Tiempo* editorial and slapped it down on the table, "care to comment on this?"

Nicholas feigned ignorance and perused it. "Looks like someone with a political axe to grind is manipulating public opinion."

"I don't care what you guys do with the money," Cesar said, "to include helping President Mendoza get re-elected, but I would be really disappointed if you guys are sloppy enough to let this kind of information leak. I think we both agree that this is more than a coincidence." He poured two more drinks. "Keep this in mind: I have recorded our meetings, which you should probably assume, so any attempt to back out of our deal or leave me high and dry will expose our activities together. If I go down, you go down—that's the beauty of working in the criminal world."

Nicholas slapped him on the shoulder. "Honor among thieves."

"Stop by my penthouse Saturday night," Cesar said. "Tell the security guard at the front desk you're one of my bankers."

Nicholas arched an inquisitive eyebrow. "What is Colombia's track record for shooting down airplanes?"

"They track most planes on radar," Cesar said, "but they destroy only one or two a month. Not if I have anything to say about it, of course."

"Of course," Nicholas said with discreet sarcasm.

"Cesar Gomez never blows a deal," he said confidently.

Nicholas feigned veneration and sipped his Aguardiente. The anise liqueur warmed his throat and left his tongue pleasantly numb. The lingering aroma triggered memories of hard candies in crimson wrappers.

"Unless we have any other business to discuss," Nicholas said, standing, "I'll see you Saturday night." He stood to leave, ignoring Cesar's outstretched hand.

"Your plan is hopeless, by the way," Cesar said as Nicholas reached for the door. "You know, the Order, the group responsible for so much misery and oppression around the world." He chuckled. "You see, Mr. Lowe, I know a lot about you as well."

Nicholas turned.

Cesar continued: "I know about the millions of lives the Order has destroyed in its rational quest to rip humanity from the jungle, but the plan won't work. I also know about the work you did in El Salvador and how the Order made you the fall guy. Life is never nice and tidy when we hire assassins, am I right?"

Nicholas was shocked that Cesar knew about him, the Order, El Salvador, and the spades assassin. "I don't know what you're talking about."

"Yes, you do," Cesar said, laughing. "The Order will never accept someone like you, someone who knows the difference between right and wrong. I can't help but wonder what happened during the past ten years to make you still want to join them."

"I'll see you Saturday," Nicholas said. One more minute of this nonsense and he would resort to the choking option.

"Don't worry—it was a compliment," Cesar said.

Outside the room, Nicholas gathered his composure. With a deep breath, he decided that he wouldn't let Cesar get under his skin, and then walked to the exit. To his surprise, the two cinnamon beauties were waiting for him, bought and paid for, wearing jeans and tight T-shirts. They held either arm and kissed him. "*Vamos, papi.*"

Nicholas accepted a card from a waiter. He opened it to read: "Two special gifts for a virtuous man." He paused to admire the beauties, then kissed them on the cheek and waved as he left the building.

Chapter Twelve

After navigating the new inefficient system of one-way streets and shortcuts through the morning traffic, Nicholas arrived at the Panama City World Trade Center complex. The trip would have been difficult for any foreigner—Panamanians relied on memory to get from point A to point B, not on street signs or sequentially numbered roads—but because the old system was still etched in his long-term memory, he was twice confused.

The affluent strip connecting the high-rise condominium towers in Punta Paitilla and Calle 50 had changed since his last visit. Modern buildings, ritzy shopping boutiques, and fast-food franchises lined the avenue. Patatus, once a watering hole for enlisted gringos on Fridays, now struggled for business while hip joints like Rock Café and La Cantina prospered. A haven for the affluent—white-collar workers by day, spoiled teens and young professionals by night—this Petri dish of Americana was a fragile experiment amid the city's chaos and poverty.

Nicholas entered the parking lot of the Radisson Hotel, the shorter tower of the World Trade Center complex. The business day was under way. Uniformed bellhops hailed taxis for stodgy old fair-skinned businessmen. Attractive, fashionable ladies unlocked the front doors of retail stores like Chanel, Tommy Hilfiger, and Façonable. Everything was polished and pristine, but just outside the perimeter, the road was bumper-to-bumper chaos with honking traffic that had managed to turn three lanes into four.

*   *   *

The brass nameplate for the suite on the top floor said "Enterprise Associates," but there was nothing to indicate this office was any different from the others, aside from the fact that Dylan had told Nicholas this was the office handling the finances for operation Delphi Justice. The Order preferred to keep things above board with Congressional funding, both to backstop the activity and to avoid using their own money, but some operations were too sensitive for general dissemination. Nicholas knocked on the door and heard the rapid click of high heels on marble. The dead bolt twisted, and the door opened until the chain was taut. A seductive blue eye inspected him.

"Hello, my name is Nicholas Lowe," he said.

The woman opened the door and posed with a smile, then gestured for him to enter and closed the door behind him. Her wavy blonde hair rested fetchingly on the shoulders of her elegant navy blue dress. They hugged and gave kisses on the cheek.

"Jessica, how have you been?" he asked. "You look great." He looked around. "What are you doing here?"

"Now it's Jessica Porter," she said with a gesture to her glittering diamond ring. "I can't believe we haven't seen each other since the weekend at K's ranch."

Nicholas jogged his memory. "Porter...wait, Barry Porter?"

She nodded matter-of-factly. He did his best to smile in approval, but he hated to see such a beautiful woman marry a man so clearly for the money. Barry was overweight and a little goofy, but his family had a financial empire that included offshore banks, which obviously included Panama. Apparently, the family was making him pay his dues in the developing world before moving up the corporate ladder.

"I was so excited when I heard you were coming down," she said. "Does this mean they agreed to approve your membership?"

"That's what they said," he said. The members of the Order made a point of never saying "the Order."

"I'm so glad to hear that," she said. "Many of us were very upset with how they treated you after El Salvador." She leaned closer to whisper. "Dylan is such an ass." They paused for eye contact, and then she gestured to lead the way. "Shall we?"

The office was spotless, immaculate, and decorated with enough artwork, furniture, and plants to satisfy a dozen wealthy clients. Fanned out magazines and stacked newspapers covered the tables. Two fresh pots of coffee were receiving their last drops. He sensed an eerie perfection for which only the Order could be responsible. He laughed to himself when he noticed himself admiring his alluring guide. Her hips swung like a metronome with each click of her heels.

She sat at the desk and folded her hands. "I was getting bored at home, so I decided to help out at the family business. How can we help you today, Mr. Lowe?"

He appreciated the contrast of someone like Jessica playing the role of secretary or office assistant. "I would like to wire transfer one point five million dollars," he said and handed her the business card with Cesar's bank account number. "I will also need one hundred and twenty thousand in cash."

She removed a form from the top drawer, fit it into a clipboard, and began filling it in. She made some check marks and handed it to him. As he started filling it in, he noticed the *El Tiempo* editorial on her desk.

"Interesting editorial," he said.

She took a deep breath with a nervous look in her eyes. "Yes, well, Dylan just called to say two members are flying down to talk to us." She forced a smile. "You and Tyler were good friends, right?" she asked, and then frowned when he nodded. "I knew him only a few weeks," she added. "His death, Helena's death—it was all such a shock."

He didn't want to face any painful emotions, but she might have some insights or clues about his death. "How did he seem, toward the end?"

She sighed and rested her elbows on the desk. "I think something was really bothering him, even before Helena died. After that, of course, he wasn't himself."

"How so?" he asked.

"Well, a few days after Helena died he came here to arrange the third wire transfer. He hadn't shaved and his eyes were bloodshot. I asked what was wrong, but he didn't want to talk about it." She leaned forward with an upraised eyebrow. "I heard a rumor that Cesar Gomez—he's a Colombian drug dealer—might have killed Helena. Judging by his mood that day, I would say he wanted to kill Cesar."

He nodded to provide feedback. "You said something was bothering Tyler even before Helena's death. What did you mean?"

"I can only speculate," she said.

He didn't expect anything more, with the caveat that women often offered such caveats before speaking the truth.

"Helena liked to party," she said. "She used cocaine. People talk, you know."

He nodded, surprised.

"One night a few months ago she overdosed at a party. No one will discuss it, but I heard she was raped." She pronounced rape at a cautious whisper.

He gestured for her to continue.

"More recently," she whispered, "she found out she couldn't have children."

"Because she was raped?" he asked. She shrugged and nodded. "What does that have to do with Cesar?"

She looked embarrassed for having not stated the obvious. "Helena was raped at Cesar's penthouse during a party. Not by Cesar himself, mind you," she added, "but he was the one who gave her the cocaine, or so I heard."

He gritted his teeth. Cesar probably gave her cocaine in the hopes of satisfying his own perverse desires. He couldn't begin to imagine the pain Tyler must have felt. "I had no idea—"

"Jesus Christ!" a man yelled and slammed a door. He loosened his tie and stormed down the hall yelling a medley of four-letter words.

She smiled apologetically. "You'll have to excuse Nash. He's our futures trader. The market must have taken a turn for the worse."

"Actually, the markets are breaking new records every day, especially the NASDAQ," Nicholas said. "I'm guessing he must be short." He noticed her confusion. "Short means he's betting the stock market will go down."

She smiled. "That explains more than you can imagine. That's why Barry handles the money. How about I give you the official tour?"

He gestured for her to lead the way. She walked to the back of the office and gestured to the room the enraged man had left. "That's

Nash's office. He spends most of the day at the computer watching the markets and placing trades for our clients." She continued down a short hall. "That's the bathroom," she said and pointed to the closed door. The faucet was running, and Nash could be heard mumbling expletives. "I think Nash is really upset," she whispered and turned to the other side of the hall. "This is our conference room. Please," she added and gestured for him to enter.

He entered the room, walked around the conference table, and stood before the window. He observed the silent city below as cool air from an air duct showered him. Most Panamanians probably had no idea what this building looked like from the inside.

He turned to see Jessica standing next to the words "Enterprise Associates" emblazoned on the projection screen. He sat in a leather chair and drummed his fingers on the oak table. The Order definitely owned this company: it was running the finances for operation Delphi Justice and the decor was exquisite. Besides, million-dollar wire transfers and six-figure cash withdrawals weren't things U.S. government agencies did without lots of paperwork and Congressional oversight.

He focused his attention on Jessica, who was outlining the benefits of owning a Panamanian corporation: anonymity with bearer shares, no taxes on revenue generated outside of Panama, and no financial reporting requirements. Enterprise Associates, EA in the company's parlance, created corporations, trusts, and foundations for people who had reason to believe their assets were in danger of repossession, or for "tax planning" purposes. EA also offered a complete line of offshore mutual funds and a brokerage service.

This presentation was probably designed for inheritors of wealth or members of the Order who had to be initiated into the arcane craft of wealth preservation. The seasoned members of the Order who met in this conference room not only understood offshore finance, they probably made the rules and paid modest fees to Panamanian politicians to ensure they remained the law of the land.

They left the conference room and returned to the reception area. The faucet was still running when they walked past the bathroom.

"Nash must be really upset," he whispered and stopped to look inside his office. The computer was big enough to run a small corporation.

She led the way to the front door. He gave in and admired her ass every step of the way, each tick tock of the metronome. At the door, she spun around, wrapped her arms around him, and kissed him passionately, then gently bit his lip as she backed away and smiled.

He looked into her eyes—*interesting*. "So, Barry? I never saw that coming."

"You," she said and touched his lip, "had your eyes set on Julia, who is still not married, by the way." She kissed him again. "I figured you were off the market, and Barry is obscenely rich. It's all about choices, Nicholas."

Chapter Thirteen

Minister of Foreign Affairs Victor Hernandez sat on the chair facing away from the hotel suite window, legs crossed, ready for the decisive moment. "Gentlemen," he murmured, gesturing to the empty sofa, envisioning his two recruits, "before I outline my plan, let me offer you a drink." He stood and adjusted the bottle of Scotch, the bucket of ice, and the three tumblers, and then slapped the surface of the wet bar. Everything was perfect. He walked to the window and rested his hands on the ledge as he looked outside. The unsuspecting citizens of Panama had no idea he was about to make history—here, inside a hotel suite.

"Damn!" he mumbled and closed the curtains to prevent anyone outside from seeing him. He'd made no mistakes up to this point. He had Sheena pay cash for the room—no credit cards, no trace. He scheduled an informal meeting with the Peruvian ambassador in the lobby bar after lunch to establish an alibi. If this story didn't work and he found himself caught in the act, he could reluctantly admit to having an affair with Sheena, which would ruffle only a few feathers in a place like Panama. After the meeting, he took the elevator to the twelfth floor and then took the stairs to the eighth floor, where Sheena was waiting for him.

He dropped to his knees and felt under the furniture. He'd forgotten to check for bugs! Tyler wouldn't have been pleased with his tradecraft oversights. He might have made a serious mistake, but at least the spies listening in couldn't record the meeting if he found the bug now.

All they would catch on audio was him and Sheena testing the limits of the bed frame in the bedroom. His fingers slid across an exposed staple under the couch.

Sheena stepped out of the bathroom wearing a skintight cantaloupe-colored dress, flattening her dress and adjusting her hair. She tilted her head and rested an arm on her hip. "What are you doing?"

He jumped to his feet. "Nothing. I dropped my...watch." He followed her eyes down to his finger and grabbed his handkerchief to absorb the blood.

Sheena looked bewildered as she approached him. Her eyes seduced him as she hugged him and kissed his neck.

"You should go now." He led her to the door, sexually spent and at peace with the world. "Remember, this is our secret."

"Of course, Minister Hernandez," she said, "I never tell anyone about our sex life. Your wife would get very upset."

He shook his head in amusement. He looked at the disheveled sheets in the bedroom and pulled the door shut. The plan also had been a perfect opportunity for an afternoon tryst, which he admitted to himself honestly had played a key role in deciding to have the meeting in a hotel room. "I mean being in this room with me." He held her and looked into her eyes. "Listen to me carefully," he said. "We weren't here today, understand?"

She nodded nervously.

He kissed her forehead and then made his way down to her lips and neck, suddenly aroused again. "Good, now—"

Two knocks on the door interrupted him.

"Listen to me carefully," he whispered, "you're my assistant. You're here helping me with some important business matters."

She nodded knowingly, and seemed to understand that it was time to put on her game face and play her role.

Two more knocks made his heart race. He cleared his throat. "Be right there," he called. He reached for the doorknob and smiled at her until she smiled back.

"Welcome, Colonel Dupree," Victor said, impressed to see the military man wearing a gray business suit, although it could have used some tailoring. "Come in," he said and gestured to Sheena. "My assistant, Sheena, was just on her way out."

"Pleasure to meet you, Sheena," Colonel Dupree said, assessing her body with a grin.

"I'll arrange the meeting and fax these documents," Sheena said with a priceless reaction to Colonel Dupree's creepy stare.

"Excellent," Victor said. "Excellent," he repeated and gestured for Colonel Dupree to have a seat on the couch, not impressed by the colonel's lack of decorum.

"Mind if I use your bathroom?" Colonel Dupree asked.

"Of course," Victor said and gestured to the door. "I'll call you later," he whispered to Sheena with a wink and closed the door. "I'm glad you could make it, Colonel—wait!"

Colonel Dupree lifted his hand from the doorknob. "What?"

"The bathroom," Victor said, "is over here." He opened the other door and gestured inside. "I'll pour us a drink," he added.

Victor waited for the bathroom door to close before hustling into the bedroom to tidy up the bed. An American was involved, so he had to run things differently. The gringos didn't understand the mistress concept and judged it in moralistic terms. Gringos, both men and women, often equated sexual gratification with the love that holds families together, and therefore often opted for divorce rather than do the honorable and civilized thing of sustaining the relationship for the sake of the children. Victor, being the refined gentleman he was, could have absolutely euphoric sex with Sheena and go home to his lovely wife and family without missing a beat. As long as the working class was obsessed with erotic love, which often resulted in broken families, his family's dynasty wouldn't be threatened.

Two knocks interrupted him as he finished with the bed.

"Is somebody here?" Colonel Dupree asked from the bathroom.

Victor scurried to the front door. He pulled Manuel Espinosa inside without a greeting and looked both ways to ensure no one had followed him.

"Good to see you, too," Manuel said sarcastically and pulled a pack of cigarettes from his shirt pocket. "I hope this is important."

Victor gestured to the couch. "Please, have a seat." He took a deep breath to calm his nerves as Manuel sat and lit a cigarette. He focused his thoughts on the meeting, but the opening of the bathroom door broke his concentration.

Colonel Dupree looked at Manuel. His eyes narrowed as he finished drying his hands. "Who the hell invited him?"

"Please," Victor said, "have a seat, Colonel."

Colonel Dupree plopped himself on the couch with a heavy breath, leaving an empty cushion between him and Manuel.

Victor sat in his chair, which he had positioned strategically to control the meeting, and crossed his legs. "Gentlemen, you're probably wondering why I called you here today." The plan was under way. He was finally the Minister of Foreign Affairs. His confidence returned. "Have you ever heard the expression, my enemy's enemy is my friend?"

The recruits nodded.

"We have a common enemy," Victor continued, "someone we can each profit from destroying."

"I doubt he and I have anything in common," Colonel Dupree said, looking down his nose at his couch companion.

Manuel shook his head in disgust. "Cowboy."

Unfazed, Victor gestured to the wet bar. "Let me offer you a drink." He had expected animosity, but the plan would unify them. He filled the tumblers with ice and Scotch. Colonel Dupree and Manuel joined his silent toast.

Manuel set his drink down. "What's this about?"

"Cesar Gomez," Victor said, enunciating both names.

Colonel Dupree nodded knowingly and lifted his drink. Manuel didn't look convinced.

"I don't have to tell you what he has done to my life," Victor continued. Two people he loved dearly, Helena and Tyler—dead. "I know you want him behind bars," he said to Colonel Dupree.

"I want him in an electric chair," Colonel Dupree clarified.

"I also know your views on Panama," Victor said. "We're pragmatic men. We believe in order and stability. We know that—"

"What the hell is this about?" Manuel interrupted.

"You, however," Victor said to Manuel confidently, unfazed, "probably don't consider Cesar an enemy. In fact, I know you work for him."

Manuel scoffed. "I don't work for him," he said, then looked at Colonel Dupree and shook his head in disgust. "I'm not a drug dealer."

"You work for a cocaine trafficker," Colonel Dupree said.

"Gentlemen," Victor said, "allow me to patch up your differences. Colonel Dupree, can you confirm that the operation to arrest Cesar Gomez was put on hold?"

Colonel Dupree groaned. "I didn't get all the details, but they put the investigation on hold after Tyler Broadman was murdered. No offense," he said apologetically, with a deferential gesture to Victor, "but his murder should make us turn up the heat, not cancel the damn operation. Not to mention, I blame him for the death of Helena, and I don't care about his stupid alibi. Her blood is on his hands."

Manuel leaned forward. "Excuse me, what investigation?"

"I agree," Victor said, putting Manuel on hold. "I propose we start our own operation and eliminate this son of a bitch once and for all." He gestured to them with a circular motion and leaned forward to look them in the eyes. "Are you with me?"

There, he said it—no turning back. He could feel his heart pumping again after so many days of unbearable pain. Tyler had asked him a similar question the previous year when he asked him to spy for the CIA. With hindsight, his acceptance had been hasty. He would have said yes, eventually, but Tyler had made him feel it was now or never—*strike while the iron is hot*. This time, however, he was the spy, and this was his operation.

"The investigation might have been put on hold," Colonel Dupree said, "but I've dedicated every asset I have to interdict Cesar's cocaine shipments."

Victor grinned. "With the right information, Colonel, you won't have to search for his shipments." He looked at Manuel. "We will know where they are, right?"

Manuel lifted his hands defensively. "Wait a minute. Cesar doesn't tell me that kind of information. You're out of your mind."

"But you could get that kind of information," Colonel Dupree said, warming to the idea. He gulped his drink and grinned like a cat with a mouse under its paw.

"I am sure he could," Victor said confidently. Colonel Dupree certainly had intelligence sources but probably no one like Manuel.

"No way," Manuel said. "If he suspects anything, he'll kill me. He doesn't fuck around. If you want me to stop meeting with him, no problem." He leaned back and folded his arms. "Why should I risk my life for you two?"

Victor chuckled to himself. He had anticipated Manuel's response! Panama wasn't a player on the world stage, and his position as Minister of Foreign Affairs up to this point had been a pathetic string of compromises and ribbon-cutting ceremonies. For once, he was going to dictate the rules. A surge of energy rushed through him as he prepared to make a man bend against his will. The sensation of power was energizing!

"Manuel," Victor said, "we both know your rice business relies on tariffs to prevent competition from imports, tariffs that I supported."

Manuel shook his head in disbelief.

"I wonder what would happen if those tariffs were reduced," Victor added and rubbed his chin, "or even eliminated?"

Manuel jabbed an accusing finger at Victor. "I employ thousands of people in Panama. If you destroy me, you'll destroy them. That would be political suicide."

"The issue is on the agenda for the economic summit," Victor said, proud of the perfect timing. "I'm sure the panel will weigh my opinion heavily."

"Look on the bright side," Colonel Dupree said with a grin. "Consider it an opportunity to eliminate a corrupt Colombian piece of shit from your country."

"He'll kill me," Manuel said and puffed his cigarette nervously.

"Listen to my plan," Victor said. "We will destroy a few of his cocaine shipments and wipe him out financially. Without money, he cannot manipulate the legal system."

"Or we just kill the son of a bitch," Colonel Dupree said. "Our people will protect you," he promised Manuel, "until Cesar is behind bars. We'll even put you on our payroll."

Victor tensed up. Manuel was a millionaire who loathed cowboy Americans. Colonel Dupree shouldn't have spoken without doing his homework.

"Only a scum would spy for the Americans," Manuel said.

Victor gulped his Scotch. He didn't consider himself a scum for spying for the Americans. He didn't feel patriotic, either, but the calculus of his decision was complex. "Well then, consider yourself my employee."

"I'll consider that," Manuel said, "but I won't be a CIA spy."

"I don't work for the CIA," Colonel Dupree said.

"Keep your money," Manuel said and lit another cigarette.

"I'll accept that as a yes," Victor said authoritatively.

Manuel exhaled a smoke cloud and rubbed his forehead. "Cesar is getting to be a pain in the ass." He looked up. "Why not? Let's get him."

"You're doing the right thing," Victor said and lifted his glass. "Colonel Dupree, Manuel, to a good team."

"No more bullshit about rice tariffs," Manuel said.

Victor shook his head assuredly.

Manuel leaned forward to speak, suddenly a team player. "Cesar's next shipment is leaving tomorrow night."

"When?" Victor asked. This was too good to be true!

"I don't know," Manuel said, "but I'll find out tomorrow. He's working with a new guy, but I didn't get his name."

Victor looked at Dupree. "Will your men be ready?"

"You bet your ass," Colonel Dupree said and grabbed the bottle of Scotch to provide a two-finger dose to each Musketeer.

Victor leaned back and smiled. He suffered so many sleepless nights hoping that the Americans or the Panamanian justice system would solve the problem for him, and all this time it was within his own power—*Cesar Gomez is finished.* As he imagined the end of Cesar's reign of tyranny, an image of Helena flashed in his mind. Her radiant smile sent a shudder through his body as he longed to reach out to her. He coughed, held his hand to his chest to control it, and then coughed uncontrollably.

"Minister Hernandez, are you OK?" Colonel Dupree said and rushed over to slap him on the back and look into his eyes.

Victor, startled, looked into the genuinely caring eyes of Colonel Dupree as the cough faded. He held his chest and took a deep breath. With a profound exhale and a gesture to signal he was all right, he managed a smile.

The three raised their drinks for a toast.

Chapter Fourteen

Nicholas tugged the lapels of his sport coat as he left the El Panama Hotel lobby and walked to the adjoining casino. He could have used the inside corridor, but he wanted to breathe the night air before the next move. A torrential rain had fallen, and the humid air smelled of dust. The words "La Fiesta" flashed in colored lights above the doorway. The security guard opened the door with a smile and wished him well.

Noisy slot machines and intermittent cheers cultivated an I-feel-lucky mood. Waiters and waitresses with paisley vests, white shirts, and black bow ties carried trays of drinks. Security guards wandered the narrow aisles with walkie-talkies. The carpet was appropriately gaudy, but the room lacked the spaciousness and thematic decor of a Las Vegas casino.

Money. Nicholas could smell it. Ritzy couples stacked chips on the tables as if they were building blocks. They looked entertained, probably wasting interest earned on interest from the family fortune. A dozen Japanese men smoking and drinking Scotch with loosened ties were crowded around a table watching the spinning wheels, bouncing dice, and sliding cards. Money was transferring from one person to the next and back to the casino in the blink of an eye.

Nicholas walked past the noisy slot machines and spotted the buyers, Willie and Daisy Holland, standing near a craps table. They looked just as Tyler had described them: eccentric. Willie, mid-sixties, wore a salmon linen shirt and a tan straw hat. His face was ruddy with a whiskey nose. Daisy, a spicy redhead, mid-fifties, wore a teal dress with a white scarf tied loosely around her neck. A cigarette in a long black holder dangled from her left hand. A waiter handed Willie something on the rocks. Daisy accepted a glass of champagne. Nicholas thought of two words that didn't describe them: drug dealers. The buyers for the first two shipments ended up in jail after the first two seizures were made, so now they had found the third victim. The promise of easy money motivated many people to take on risks that were disproportional to the expected gains.

Nicholas accepted a Scotch from a passing waitress and approached the craps table. He lifted his drink to Willie and offered a cordial smile. Willie returned the gesture and nudged Daisy. She lifted her champagne mechanically and puffed her cigarette; but after making eyes with Nicholas, a lascivious smile filled her face.

"An exciting game," Nicholas said.

"My sentiments exactly!" Willie said.

Nicholas gestured to a distant table. "I prefer blackjack."

"A counter," Willie said. "I always lose, which is why I enjoy the excitement of pure chance. Daisy, here," he said and tapped her arm, "is a blackjack player."

"I love to count," she said with a devilish grin and sipped her champagne.

Nicholas nodded, amused.

"Don't look so serious, you handsome young man," she added and pinched his cheek.

Nicholas extended his hand to Willie. There was no need to say his name.

"The pleasure is all mine," Willie said with a jovial handshake. "This is my wife."

"My pleasure," Nicholas said and kissed her hand, blinded by the three-carat diamond. He concluded that Willie and Daisy resembled two-dimensional stand-ins for a *Love Boat* episode. He gestured to the exit. "Perhaps we could go"—more cheers from the craps table—"somewhere more private."

Willie gestured to the exit and led the way. They strolled down the inside corridor to the outdoor swimming pool area. The tables under the thatched-roof restaurant were mostly empty, but a few people drinking at the bar laughed and toasted merrily. Underwater lights illuminated the pool under the starlit sky, a beautiful contrast with the pink hotel. They walked across the concrete deck, still wet from the earlier storm, to a row of two-story cabanas.

"Here we are," Willie said and opened the door.

Daisy sank her fingernails into Nicholas' arm as she entered and sat in a chair near the window. Nicholas stood in the middle near the bed and watched Daisy's reflection in the mirror as Willie set the keys on the dresser. She crossed her legs and fondled her breasts to enhance her exquisite, augmented cleavage.

"Anyone care for a drink?" Willie asked as he opened the fridge. He poured a glass of champagne for Daisy and apologized for having drunk all the Scotch before the casino excursion. Nicholas accepted a beer.

Nicholas waited for Willie to sit in the chair next to Daisy. "I'm here to assist with the delivery of goods."

"I thought we'd made all the necessary arrangements," Willie said and looked at Daisy for concurrence.

"Tyler was a thorough man," Daisy said. "A very thorough man."

They knew Tyler's true name. Willie nodded, but he suddenly looked bushed.

"The plan changed," Nicholas said. Willie and Daisy had to know about Tyler's death—the story was in the newspaper with his photograph, and the shipment hadn't gone as planned—but he didn't want to take anything for granted. "I'm afraid I have some bad news." Daisy held Willie's hand. "Tyler was murdered."

Daisy closed her eyes and shook her head. "How tragic."

"Tragic," Willie added.

Nicholas cleared his throat. "The shipment, the one that was supposed to have gone four days ago, was canceled," he said, hoping to catch them off guard. No response.

Daisy put a cigarette in her holder. Nicholas lit it and returned to his seat.

"I arranged for another shipment in two days," Nicholas said.

"Saturday, you say?" Willie asked and looked at Daisy.

She nodded curtly, puffed her cigarette, and crossed her legs the other way. "I can't wait to get out of this dreadful country."

"It's not bad," Willie said and looked at Nicholas with a shrug.

"You love the horny women," Daisy said and turned to Nicholas to whisper. "He drags one back here every night, you know. The pill changed my life as a young woman, but Viagra changed this guy's life in retirement." She looked at Willie. "This godforsaken country is utterly hopeless without the Americans."

"You're exaggerating," Willie said; Daisy rolled her eyes and sipped her champagne. "This is a fun culture. They'll survive."

Nicholas watched them, bemused. "I arranged for five hundred kilograms for five million dollars." Those had been the original terms.

Willie and Daisy nodded.

"I only need to know the drop site and payment method," Nicholas said.

Willie handed Nicholas a small piece of paper with a coordinate written on it. "That location is in the Bahamas. Our men will be there at eleven on Saturday night."

"Be sure the goods are wrapped well and float," Daisy added. "My men won't be in any mood to catch heavy falling objects."

"That can be arranged," Nicholas said, resisting a smile. He could only imagine what Tyler had thought about them. Their criminal career would last about ten minutes after the cocaine was delivered. "I'll talk to my supplier. Regarding payment—"

"Wire transfer only," Daisy said. "Technology is such a thrill!"

"We need the thrill," Willie added with less enthusiasm and yawned.

"Wire transfer it is," Nicholas said. "I suggest we meet at ten on Saturday night, say, at the bar by the swimming pool."

Willie nodded and yawned. Daisy winked.

"Once my pilot is circling over your boat," Nicholas said, oddly attracted to the cougar, "you'll wire five million to my account, at which time I'll instruct my pilot to drop the well-wrapped bundles that float."

Willie nodded and yawned again. Daisy sipped her champagne suggestively.

Nicholas stood to leave. "I think we have a plan. I'll call you—"

"Are you an adventurous man?" Willie asked.

Nicholas sat. "I like a good adventure now and then."

"That's good," Willie said, deep in thought. "Tyler didn't seem the adventurous type." He looked at Daisy for her opinion.

96

Daisy exhaled a cloud of smoke and shook her head. "Tyler was a very serious man. Unlike you; you seem the adventurous type."

"Tyler was under a lot of stress," Nicholas said.

"He wasn't Helena's type, either," Willie said, ignoring Nicholas.

Daisy concurred. "We come to Panama frequently, you see, which is how we learned about this side business. No one would suspect two old people of moving drugs. We knew Helena and the Hernandez family before she met Tyler." This probably explained how they got Tyler's name, but they never apparently figured out he worked for the U.S. government. "She liked to live on the wild side."

"Perhaps she decided to settle down," Nicholas said.

Willie shook his head. "Not Helena. She kept partying, even after the overdose and rape. I guess they were just too different, from different social classes."

Nicholas didn't like the sound of that. "Tyler was a successful guy," he said. "The Hernandez family would have been lucky to have him."

"He had to work for it," Daisy said, still ignoring Nicholas. "She didn't. The Hernandez family is loaded. Rich people are just different. If you ask me, Helena was with Tyler because he didn't try to control her, unlike her rich Latino boyfriends."

Willie nodded. "I think it's possible one of her jealous ex-lovers killed Tyler after he planned to take her to America."

Nicholas checked his watch, not pleased with where the conversation was going. "I'll see you on Saturday." He stood to shake Willie's hand and kiss Daisy on the cheek.

Nicholas arrived at the Modern Art Museum in a taxi a few minutes late, then paid the driver the fare with a generous tip and rushed inside. Based on cell phone intercepts, Nicholas had received a tip that Lina Castillo planned to attend the opening for an Ancient Greek art exhibit. One of the best ways to establish rapport with people was to arrange chance encounters. Many people believed in fate, not in chance, so these chance encounters often had a disproportional impact in terms of accelerating the relationship.

Another good way to establish rapport with people was to study their lives and artfully introduce topics or themes into the dialog that would resonate with the person and make them feel comfortable, creating the oddly mystical feeling that their meeting was more than just a chance encounter. In Lina's case, she was a walking success story. Based on the limited information Nicholas could find on her in the files, primarily her student visa, she graduated from the University of Panama with honors in journalism. Her studies included a one-year scholarship program in Washington, D.C., which explained her superb English and ambition. A local newspaper, *El Tiempo*, famous for its critical reporting during the Noriega dictatorship, hired her after graduation. Soon after, she was writing headline stories and ruffling some feathers in the oligarchy circles, but she managed to establish a strong relationship with Minister Hernandez. Unlike most single women in Panama, she could probably afford her own car and apartment. Nicholas' research also had surfaced an amusing story about how President Mendoza had proposed decreasing funding for female university students because, he claimed, most of them attended college to earn a "Mrs." degree.

He made his way to the Ancient Greek art exhibit and noticed Lina standing on the other side of the room holding a brochure and admiring a statue of the goddess Athena. He moved to a painting about twenty feet away and waited. He admired the painting of Iphigenia and felt himself drawn into the sublime horror of a beautiful young woman being sacrificed. When Agamemnon and the Greek forces gathered to sail to Troy, the goddess Artemis was offended by some of Agamemnon's actions and stopped the winds, making it impossible to sail. To appease Artemis, Agamemnon offered to sacrifice his daughter Iphigenia in the bay of Aulis, and tricked her to walk to the location by telling her she was going to marry Achilles. According to some versions of the story, Iphigenia was miraculously transported to Taurus on the Black Sea and was replaced by an animal for the actual sacrifice, after which the winds returned. Nicholas was hypnotized by the look of horror on her face as she looked at the knife.

"Nicholas?" Lina said, surprised.

He turned, surprised, having lost track of time, and kissed her on the cheek. "Lina. I didn't know you like Greek art."

"You mean because I'm Panamanian?" she said sarcastically. "I visited many museums in your country."

"Oh," he said, "have you been to the States?"

"I studied there for a year," she said matter-of-factly and eyed him, "but something tells me you already knew that. What about you?"

He held a blank stare and nodded. "I've always been fascinated by Greek art, philosophy, tragedy, you name it."

"Plato or Aristotle?" she asked.

"Aristotle," he said without hesitation, aware that his answer to that question often depended on his mood. "Let me guess, Plato?"

"Plato's dialogs are more poetic and inspirational," she said, "but there's just something soothing about the calm logic of Aristotle."

"I agree, but I'm always a sucker for Diotima in the *Symposium*," he said, beside himself that Lina Castillo loved the ancient Greeks.

"That makes two of us," she said and gestured to the exhibit. "I'm just so excited that they brought the Greeks to Panama. I half expected Athena over there to come alive and help us solve our problems."

He gestured to continue with the exhibit. She checked her watch.

"Unfortunately," she said, "I have something for work."

"Perhaps we could have dinner," he said.

"That would be nice," she said. "Call me. I'm sure you already have my number," she added with a wink and left.

Chapter Fifteen

Minister of Foreign Affairs Victor Hernandez and First Vice President Antonio Romero waited patiently outside the hotel conference room, a safe distance from the media, as audience members filed in. President Mendoza, in one his rare slipups, decided to have an open forum with visiting economists from the International Monetary Fund (IMF) to discuss the results of their most recent research on the Panamanian economy. Transparency, or at least the perception of it, was fine in larger developed countries, where programs such as these would blend in with hundreds of other cable news programs, but this report had generated a lot of interest in Panama, and Victor couldn't rule out the possibility that his business interests would be the focus of attention. Never mind that he had risked his own money to create thousands of jobs over the years; the resentful economic illiterates would find a way to attack him.

Finally, when President Mendoza arrived, hardly aware of Victor and Antonio, they entered the conference room and exchanged greetings with Thomas Rendall, the State Department Political Counselor, and the visiting IMF economists. Brass-encased nametags assigned their seats. Water glasses and microphones rested at each position. The conference room was small—no more than fifty seats for the packed audience—but the live camera coverage would make a permanent record and allow average Panamanians to see what happens behind the curtain.

Victor was still feeling high from the excitement of planning his operation with Colonel Dupree and Manuel Espinosa against Cesar Gomez. Not only was he working with the CIA secretly to help re-elect President Mendoza, which was good for Panama, he was also running his own covert operation to eliminate Cesar. Panama's fate was in his hands, and tomorrow's shipment would be his first test.

Thomas stood at the podium. The lights dimmed. The room fell silent. "President Mendoza, distinguished guests"—he gestured to both tables—"and members of the audience, welcome. The purpose of this session is to discuss the findings of the International Monetary Fund study requested by the Government of Panama. The findings are recommendations to help Panama prepare for World Trade Organization membership and identify ways to generate economic growth." He gestured to the first economist, a disheveled man with reading glasses and a yellow bow tie.

Disheveled Man leaned forward. "Good evening, ladies and gentlemen. Our first item is import tariffs. Current tariffs are too high for WTO membership and strain the Panamanian economy. These high tariffs protect inefficient businesses, limit competition, and ultimately lead to increased prices for consumers."

That was Victor's cue. The comment offended him, but he wouldn't let his emotions get the best of him. His consumer paper goods factory, for example, produced perfectly fine napkins. Imports were a bit cheaper, without the tariff, and maybe the quality could be improved, but most bars and restaurants used his napkins for every purpose imaginable. Sure they made sticky coasters when folded in half; sure they were difficult to remove from the flimsy stainless steel dispensers; and sure they were too small to wrap silverware; but Panamanians identified with his napkins. Why allow imported napkins to ruin that?

"All nations protect certain industries," Victor said. A moment of silence seemed like an eternity as he glanced at the television camera. "A nation must be able to feed itself in case of a national emergency. Some grains, such as rice, are protected by tariffs, but agriculture accounts for almost 25 percent of our employment. We simply cannot open our markets to external competition in one fell swoop."

Disheveled Man flipped through the report. "I was referring to other products," he said confusedly. "We usually make exceptions for agriculture, for the reasons you just mentioned." He set his finger on the report and held it up. "Chapter two addresses that point."

"Of course," Victor said, unshaken, but pleased he had achieved his objective and made good on his promise to Manuel Espinosa. "I was merely pointing out that we cannot make blanket statements about lowering tariffs."

President Mendoza gestured to Disheveled Man. "We would appreciate your help in identifying which tariffs to lower first. We want a balance between progress and stability."

"Good point, Mr. President," Thomas said and pointed to the next economist. "I'm sure the good people at the IMF would be happy to continue their research."

The second economist, a young preppie lad with round glasses, tapped his microphone with his pen. "The second item," he said, "is barriers to competition. Monopolies dominate Panama's economy, which has resulted in decreased innovation, increased prices, and fewer consumer choices."

Victor was beginning to think that the whole world was out to get him and his profitable businesses—first napkins tariffs, and now this? Did Panama really need, for example, another brewery? His company brewed perfectly fine pilsner lagers in a variety of labels. It even brewed other brand names under licensing agreements. Who wanted genuine Irish-brewed beer when you could have the local version? Sure, all Panamanian beers tasted the same; sure, all were watered down—3.0 to 3.8 percent alcohol, depending on the batch—but beer was beer. Besides, his machines were not equipped to increase the alcohol content or to add all the flavors people enjoy in trendy microbrews, and he certainly wasn't about to invest more money to buy modern machinery his unskilled laborers were not trained to operate.

Victor calmly lifted a finger. "In our defense—"

"You're not here to defend yourselves, Minister Hernandez," Thomas said politely. "We're here to discuss the findings of the study."

Victor smiled. Never let them see you sweat. "I only wanted to emphasize that monopolies are often the result of free competition in a small country like Panama. For example, we don't need more than one Coca-Cola distributor," he added, referring to another family industry in which the owners were hidden through cutouts and offshore structures. "The competition phase is short, and the losers move on to more profitable endeavors. I would venture to say that many of the largest cities in the United States, all of which are larger than Panama, often have local monopolies."

"My point, Minister Hernandez," Young Preppie said after an uncomfortable silence, "was that if more efficient competitors entered the market, you could free up some of your limited local resources for more productive projects or investments in infrastructure."

"You mean allow the corrupt, global multinational corporations to take over our country?" Antonio asked.

Victor appreciated the support from the first vice president, but he was terrified what he might say next.

"American corporations, no doubt," Antonio continued and lifted a finger to keep center stage. "I'm all in favor of economic reform, but letting foreign companies dictate our labor rules would not be good for Panama."

Thomas cleared his throat. "As the report states quite clearly, he was referring to internal competition," he said and waited for a nod of approval from the economists, "not foreign multinational corporations. I hope that clears things up." He gestured to the third economist. "And now the final finding."

The third economist was portly with a thick beard and a round, pinkish face. "The third item is labor laws," he announced. "Panama's laws are among the most rigid in the world. Local companies are hesitant to hire and foreign corporations are reluctant to enter the market. Moving the labor market toward a more flexible and competitive model would help Panama decrease unemployment, increase efficiency, and in many cases increase wages."

President Mendoza cleared his throat and leaned closer to the microphone. "As you are aware, I have tried to address this issue."

President Mendoza, wisely, had offered tax and labor incentives to attract foreign corporations to use some of the vacated U.S. military bases because Panama could not afford to maintain them. The masses had protested, however—at the behest of men like Antonio and other communists—and driven away the companies offering jobs. Was that what they meant by dignity in poverty?

"Panama will not become an exploitation hub for multinational corporations," Antonio said. "We will not allow your corporations to put our children to work!" A few members of the audience clapped. "Panama will make changes, but we will do it Panama's way!" he added, shaking a fist. Most of the audience was now applauding and whistling.

Victor groaned and observed President Mendoza shaking his head solemnly. Minimum wage was low, granted, about a dollar an hour, but the average Panamanian worker was inefficient and didn't understand that a business could not survive if expenses exceeded revenues, any more than a fruit vendor could sell his fruit for a lower price than he paid for it.

Disheveled Man shook his head in confusion. "Putting children to work? That would be a national decision, not a corporate decision, and would be in complete violation of the UN convention against child labor." He cleared his throat. "When you say *do it Panama's way*, what do you mean? Our numbers clearly show—"

"A society is more than a bunch of numbers," Antonio interjected. The audience applauded again. "What you are offering is a model for becoming American consumers. Panama's workers are hard working and proud, but they need good jobs. We have to consider Panama's unique challenges and build our own future, one we can all be proud of."

Disheveled Man shrugged with confusion and raised his voice to be heard over the enthusiastic applause. "Per your official request, we specifically looked at Panama—population, education, public sector, private sector, micro and macroeconomic factors. Without these changes, your proud workers will not have any jobs."

Victor was embarrassed but relieved. Antonio didn't have enough education or refinement to get beyond his crude populism. Unfortunately, though, democracies often elected guys like him, and the re-election of President Mendoza depended on his voter base. The good news was that Victor could finally relax, knowing that his vision for Panama's future was the right one: Panama was not ready for radical economic change.

"You can't shove this down our throat," Antonio continued. "Panama has a lively culture. We enjoy life, unlike you boring Anglo-Saxon prudes." He jabbed an accusing finger. "We must fit the changes to our culture, or not at all."

Young Preppie raised his hands defensively. "With all due respect, sir, you asked us to complete this study, which has been peer-reviewed by a respectable panel of economists from around the world." He waited for President Mendoza to acknowledge his point. "We *did* consider culture," he continued; "but don't you see that economics *is* culture?" Silence. "The way you conduct business, your work ethic, your level of trust—that *is* your culture. Panama's economy already fits its culture."

Victor cringed when he filled in the unspoken conclusion: *and that's the problem.*

"For Panama to progress," Young Preppie continued, "the culture must change."

The audience gasped.

"If you want to grow GDP and lower unemployment," Young Preppie continued, "if you want to move toward a system that is based on rule of law, if you want to promote innovation, we offer some solutions, but there will have to be some structural changes."

President Mendoza leaned forward before Antonio could say another word. "We all agree that changes are necessary. You have been most helpful. Your time and research are greatly appreciated." He stood and clapped. The others followed his lead.

"Who does that son of a bitch think he is?" Antonio muttered through gritted teeth. "How dare he tell us how to live?"

"Not now," Victor said and rested his hand on Antonio's shoulder. The economists had some nerve telling Panama to change its culture. What did ivory tower IMF bureaucrats know about culture? Victor watched Antonio seething with anger and the audience members clapping and shaking his hand. Not one person looked Victor's way or recognized him, or paid him the usual mechanical respects he was used to receiving. Oddly, he wasn't surprised and didn't feel slighted. For the first time in his life, he wondered how his life would have turned out if he had not inherited a fortune or had lacked the money to buy his way into power. As much as it scared him, it also brought a smile to his face.

Chapter Sixteen

Nicholas parked his car a few blocks from Cesar's condominium tower in Punta Paitilla, a ritzy high rise in an upscale neighborhood overlooking Panama City and the Pacific Ocean, and walked the rest of the way. Tropical weather aside, the neighborhood resembled a posh Midwest enclave: German-engineered cars obeying the speed limit, children wearing private school uniforms, and a well-dressed granny walking a groomed poodle. Outside Cesar's building, he winced when he imagined Helena falling to her death, the thud of her body hitting the ground. Strewn violet petals and footprints in the grass near the entrance indicated a mourning site.

"Cesar Gomez," Nicholas said to the security guard in the lobby.

The security guard inspected him. He stood about four foot ten of pure Kuna Indian descent. "Please, your name," he said.

"Nicholas," he said. "He's expecting me," he added and gazed up to see an oscillating security camera, then looked away casually.

The guard picked up the phone. After a few seconds, he spoke, nodded, and hung up. He turned to Nicholas and pointed toward the elevators. "Penthouse," he instructed.

Nicholas pressed the button for the penthouse as the elevator door closed. The plan was simple: the pilot Tyler had contracted to move the third shipment, later contacted by Nicholas, would fly toward Santa Marta in northern Colombia and then break off northeast to landing strip BORNEO in the Guajira Peninsula, where Cesar's men would load the cocaine for a controlled delivery in the Bahamas. After the money was collected from the buyers, the Coast Guard would seize the drugs in the Bahamas, based on a tip from the CIA, and the traffickers would be arrested. At the end of the day, things never worked out perfectly as planned, but the plan had to be simple to have any chance of success. His heartbeat rose with the progressing LCD numbers for the floors. Anxiety about the mission, hatred for what Cesar had done to Helena, his own future—they all clumped together in his throat.

He felt relieved when the gravitational force reversed and the elevator stopped. Cesar was waiting for him when the door opened.

"Welcome to my humble home," Cesar said.

Nicholas admired the plush palace: polished marble floors, leather furniture, a colorful display of Inca artwork, and a wall-to-wall window providing a panoramic view of the city and the Pacific Ocean. Wealth, it appeared, civilized even the vilest of men. "I spoke to my pilot," he said. "My plane arrived and your men are loading the goods. If you're ready, I'll send the money."

"Gloria," Cesar said. She turned the corner and lowered her face to hide the scar. "Could you please turn on my computer to confirm the wire transfer?" She nodded, smiled cautiously at Nicholas, and excused herself.

Nicholas glanced at a man smoking in the living room. "Who is that?"

Cesar turned to look. "That's Manuel Espinosa. He provides information to help my shipments get past the American and Colombian airplanes."

Nicholas shook his head in disappointment and moved toward the kitchen. "I don't want him to see me. I'll wait in there until he leaves."

Cesar waited until Nicholas was out of sight to call Manuel over. Nicholas was able to watch them through the side edge of the swinging door.

"You're confident this shipment will get through?" Cesar asked.

Manuel nodded. "If your men can load the plane and get it airborne in less than half an hour, the Americans and the Colombians probably will not have enough time to react—no AWACS on the schedule. U.S. Customs will have P-3s and the Colombians will have A-37s, but they probably won't detect the aircraft until long after it takes off, well after you collect your money." He extracted a cigarette from a pack in his shirt pocket, lit it, and took a puff. "The rendezvous is at BORNEO, right?"

"I don't know how you do it," Cesar said. "You always have the best intelligence. According to my guy, we're loading as we speak."

Manuel looked around. "If you're working with a new guy, I can investigate him if you give me his name, but I know you won't. You never do."

Cesar nodded confidently and slapped him on the shoulder. "Let's just focus on making sure this shipment gets through. I'll be in touch."

Manuel puffed his cigarette, casually looked around, perhaps sensing Nicholas in the kitchen, and then stepped into the elevator and pushed the button. Cesar clapped once and gestured for Nicholas to follow him into the living room.

Nicholas dialed his cell phone and gestured to Cesar. "I'll send the money." An electronic voice answered and led him through a sequence of steps to process the transaction. He entered the numbers, confirmed his options, and then just like that, $1.5 million transferred from one account to the next. "Done."

"You can wait on the patio while I verify receipt," Cesar said.

Nicholas nodded as two bikini-clad beauties with caftans walked past. The blonde wore a leopard-skin G-string, the brunette a mauve bikini.

The brunette touched her chin inquisitively. "Who's your new friend, Cesar?"

Cesar cleared his throat nervously. "Ladies, this is a friend." He turned to Nicholas. "Allow me to introduce Adriana and Maria, the loves of my life."

Nicholas kissed their cheeks.

"Show him to the patio," Cesar said to the ladies. "And no touching," he added to Nicholas with a nervous chuckle.

"That could be difficult," Nicholas said, seeing through Cesar's forced laughter. He offered each an arm. "Ladies, I hope you didn't get dressed up for little old me."

The ladies led Nicholas to a poolside table. Maria poured him a Scotch on the rocks. He admired the swimming pool, the stocked bar, and, well, Adriana and Maria. Their flirtatious smiles, however expensive or phony, were nonetheless flattering.

"How long have you been the loves of Cesar's life?" he asked.

"Please," Maria groaned as Adriana rolled her eyes. "I don't know how much longer I can put up with his shit, even with all the money he pays us."

"Ladies," Cesar said from behind with a loud clap, "the men need to discuss business."

The ladies said good-bye with seductive winks and the "call us" gesture. Nicholas waved to them and admired the setting sun as Cesar arrived.

"I verified the wire transfer," Cesar said, all businesslike. He gestured to the skyline. "I love the view from up here."

Nicholas didn't acknowledge him. He had a job to do, but he had a few words to say first. "I doubt Helena Hernandez thought the same thing before she fell to her death."

Cesar lifted a finger in anger but managed a smile. "I wasn't responsible for that, as the police are well aware. I went to a bar with my friends two hours before she fell. She was here alone when it happened."

Nicholas remembered the photograph of Helena and wondered why a beautiful woman with such a bright future would jump to her death.

"Tyler was murdered soon after her death. How do you explain that?" He'd just violated an important rule—don't get personal—but seeing Cesar living in luxury while two people were dead was an injustice he couldn't ignore. "And Helena was raped—here—during your party. How do you explain that?"

Cesar whistled at Gloria and gestured with both hands as if swinging a baseball bat. He walked to the ledge and gestured for Nicholas to follow.

Nicholas rested his arms on the ledge and observed the cars below.

"I won't bullshit you," Cesar said. "I gave cocaine to Helena, but the truth is she tracked me down. I never offered it to her."

Gloria handed Cesar a wooden baseball bat and waited for Cesar's nod of approval before returning to the penthouse.

"The irony," Cesar continued, "is that I refused to give her cocaine two times. The first time was the day she was raped." He stepped back and swung the bat forcefully.

"What's with the bat?" Nicholas asked, stepping back to a safe distance. "I used this bat to bust open the skull of the man who raped her," Cesar said and swung it again. "I refused to give her cocaine. So she asked my friend, who got her high and raped her in one of my bedrooms during a party. I killed him and rushed Helena to the emergency room. No one tells that version of the story, but I saved her life."

Nicholas scoffed. "You addicted her to cocaine."

Cesar nodded repentantly. "And that was the day I quit trafficking cocaine, six months ago. I won't waste your time with explanations, but the only reason I'm working this deal with you is to quit the business and retire."

Curiosity compelled Nicholas to ask a question. "When was the second time? You said you refused to give her cocaine two times."

Cesar folded his arms and took a deep breath. "The day she died. She came here asking for cocaine, even offering sex in return, as she had once in the past. I refused and begged her to quit. Imagine saying no to having sex with Helena Hernandez." He gave Nicholas a suggestive glance. "To my surprise, she agreed. I thought it was safe to leave her alone. She seemed happy about her decision and said she wanted to sleep."

"Then how did she fall off the building?" Nicholas asked.

"I don't know," Cesar said, choked up. "I swear on my mother's grave. What I can tell you is that the security tapes from the lobby are missing for the whole week. I don't know about you, but I don't believe in coincidences. And I want you to know I wasn't responsible for Tyler's murder. Given our arrangement, I stood to gain nothing from his death. He was my ticket to freedom and retirement."

As much as Nicholas resisted the notion, Cesar might be telling the truth. He wanted Cesar to be a caricature of evil, an easy target of his hatred...but he had forgotten one important detail. "Let's suppose Tyler was planning to have you arrested or killed. After all, you slept with his fiancée and gave her cocaine. In that case, you would have had a motivation to kill him."

Cesar shook his head seriously. "I have every judge and politician in this country paid off. He knows there was no way anyone was going to arrest me, and I don't think he had it in him to kill in cold blood, which

I mean in a good way." He turned to look at the Pacific Ocean. "I'm sure Tyler blamed me for his problems with Helena, but he was in over his head, with her and with this operation."

Nicholas glared at Cesar, who lifted his hands defensively.

"Don't get me wrong," Cesar said. "Tyler was a good man, perhaps too good."

Nicholas' first impulse was to hit Cesar with the bat, but he checked his anger and decided to let the clues speak for themselves.

"I recognized your name when we met the other night," Cesar said, "so I made a few phone calls—very interesting."

Nicholas shrugged indifferently, suddenly curious.

"You had quite a reputation in El Salvador about ten years ago," Cesar said. "Many people knew you and still say good things about you."

Nicholas resisted a smile as he remembered his special unit of soldiers in El Salvador. He'd trained them and suffered with them through many bitter battles against the FMLN guerillas, always following the rules of war. They were passionate men who sang songs of love and courage around the campfire at night while cooking whatever food they'd scrounged during the day in the mountains of Chalatenango. Each night ended with a solemn remembrance of those who'd died fighting the communists. One evening, after a particularly bloody battle, they invited him to this sacred event, called him one of their own, and offered him a drink of wine from a dented tin cup. The flavor still lingered in his mouth when he thought of them.

Those were the good old days, though, the stuff of legend, until K and Dylan told him the Order wanted to start killing the senior leadership of the FMLN, something Congress would never approve, which resulted in Nicholas recruiting the notorious spades assassin, which resulted in several high-profile massacres after Nicholas lost contact with him, which resulted in the Congressional testimony by Dylan that ruined his chances with the Order and Julia. And just like that, ten years of sublimated anger surfaced in an unwelcome way.

Cesar continued: "My friends in El Salvador said that of all the Americans, only you showed a genuine interest in the regular soldiers. The FMLN guerrillas feared your unit the most precisely because you cared, the exact opposite of the oligarchs the FMLN was fighting. Are you sure you were on the right side?"

"We both know some innocent people got caught in the crossfire," Nicholas said, "but we also both know the Soviet menace had to be defeated. I assume you didn't support killing tens of millions of people in the name of communism."

"I never gave a damn about the Bolsheviks or the Maoists," Cesar said. "They were no different than the tyrants who run the Order and care only about money and power. They're all bastards—Dylan, for example—so I did more research and learned you're not a member. That made sense, given your moral fiber, so I asked myself why do you associate with them? Why do you want to be a part of them?"

"It sounds like you need to find some better sources of information," Nicholas said, surprised that Cesar knew so much.

"Do you know why I left the jungles of Colombia?" Cesar asked.

Nicholas shrugged indifferently, intrigued.

"The FARC commanders, men I once admired," he said, "asked me to wipe out a village of innocent people who refused to pay taxes, and then blame it on the right-wing paramilitaries with staged photographs for the media."

Nicholas glanced inside and saw Gloria talking on the phone. "I hear many women from these rural towns became drug addicts or were forced into sex slavery."

Cesar looked back at Gloria, nodded, and then turned to Nicholas. "Why do you work for those bastards? The Order doesn't care about justice or the common man like we do." He gestured to the horizon. "How many people have they killed in the name of progress? How many more must die?"

Nicholas looked at him. "Spoken like a good communist."

Cesar was suddenly calm. "I'm serious."

Gloria stepped outside and hurried over. "Excuse me, Cesar, we have a problem."

Chapter Seventeen

Captain Tony Price, U.S. Air Force, the Senior Watch Officer, gestured across the operations floor to the intelligence NCO and the weather officer to come front and center. He stared at a computer monitor showing a map of Colombia as the two officers approached. He had tracked many suspect aircraft during his tenure at the 24-hour operations center at Howard Air Force Base, Panama, but that wasn't possible with a blank screen. "What's the status of this shipment departing from the Guajira Peninsula? My airplanes and radars are not picking up any activity in that area." He pointed to the blank screen. "We had one suspect plane approach Santa Marta, but the tower said it landed."

Staff Sergeant Chris Collins, the J2 (intelligence) NCO, nodded assuredly. "We received a report that Cesar Gomez has a shipment departing the Guajira Peninsula tonight," he said. "We don't have an exact take-off time or location—it's a large area—but the aircraft is probably carrying five hundred kilos of cocaine, probably to a drop site in the Bahamas, if previous shipments are any indicator."

Captain Price made some mental calculations about whether to launch more planes, how long it would take for them to arrive, how much fuel would be required, and how these decisions would affect his ability to respond later in the evening to other confirmed suspect aircraft—the opportunity cost. "What's your source?"

"I can't disclose that, sir," Staff Sergeant Collins said, "but it's from a reliable source." As his security clearance demanded, he was protecting sensitive intelligence sources and methods. The intelligence guys did not trust the operations guys with their secrets, and the operations guys were reluctant to take action without understanding the intelligence.

Captain Price concluded the report probably had come from a human source or a communications intercept, unless they had a photograph of a runway being prepped, but then why not provide the location? He had worked with intelligence guys long enough to learn their lingo and long enough to realize that the world of espionage possessed an element of intrigue. Waiting four years to be denied a cockpit hadn't made for a thrilling career, but at least he'd found a productive job working with airplanes.

"How confident are you?" Captain Price asked calmly.

"Very reliable," Staff Sergeant Collins said.

Captain Price shrugged skeptically and pointed at the computer monitor. "And yet we still have a blank computer screen. The navy P-3, call sign Viper, is patrolling the north coast of Colombia looking for this plane, but I don't want to get everyone spun up and start launching more airplanes if this turns out to be another bogus tipper. I don't care how you do it, but we really need a more precise location to focus our radars. Otherwise, for all we know, the plane has already left."

Captain Price gave Staff Sergeant Collins a thumbs-up and faced Second Lieutenant Andrew Atkins. "I need up-to-date weather photos with details—wind speed and direction, humidity at the airport café, everything, to the point of absurdity. The Colombian pilots freak out about flying in storms."

"Yes, sir," Second Lieutenant Atkins said and hustled to his desk.

Price pivoted smartly on his left heel. "I need you to work some magic," he said to Bruce Devlin, the U.S. Customs Service representative. "We have two Citations ready to launch from Barranquilla to vector in the Colombia A-37s, but we're going to need your boys to keep searching for this needle in the haystack."

"We're on it," Bruce said. "These guys are almost impossible to detect until after they take off. As you know, the Citations will need Colombian Host Nation Riders, so you might want to get them spun up as well."

Captain Price knew the rules. He had to. Federal laws and regulations delineated the role of the military in law enforcement-related activities.

The Posse Comitatus Act made it illegal to use the military to enforce civil law. Title 10, United States Code, prohibited the military from directly participating in arrests, searches, or seizures. The Foreign Assistance Act prohibited U.S. personnel from performing law enforcement activities overseas. Because of these restrictions, Colombian nationals, aka Host Nation Riders, rode aboard U.S. aircraft to coordinate with the Colombian military or law enforcement agencies for endgame operations. This transfer of power ensured that Colombia acted as a sovereign nation when shooting down aircraft suspected of carrying drugs.

Captain Price pivoted on his left heel and gestured crisply to Master Sergeant "Skip" Higgins, his trusty Senior Watch Technician. "Call our guys in Bogota; tell them we need two Host Nation Riders ASAP. And check if the A-37s are ready to launch."

Master Sergeant Higgins nodded and picked up the phone. "Sir, should I call Colonel Vasquez as well?"

Captain Price nodded. "I have to see our friends in the next room about an airplane," he said and walked to the adjoining room.

Inside the room, airmen were crouched over glowing green radar screens scrutinizing radar data and punching keys on their computers. The idea was simple: if a plane wasn't on an official flight route, if it hadn't filed a flight plan, if it was flying too low, if it was flying too slow, then the verdict was guilty: a bad guy.

Ground and airborne radars vacuumed the skies around the clock and blew raw data through computer servers that filtered out legitimate air tracks to create a visual display of potential bad guys, which now was blank. The bad guys learned to avoid some radar sites and flew past others with impunity, but many also knew the filtering criteria and planned accordingly to avoid detection. The battle seemed hopeless at times. Like many service members, Captain Price considered the war on drugs a noble concept, but many people complained that billions of dollars were being wasted to stop two steps short of accomplishing the objective.

Despite the war on drugs, cocaine flowed unabated into the U.S., roughly 300 metric tons a year, enough to fit on one ship but account for a visible sliver of GDP. The drug cartels spent millions of dollars on technology and bribes, and had evolved into an efficient network of interdependent nodes along a supply chain, from the seeds in the fertile Andean soil, to the cocaine laboratories, to the speedboats in the Caribbean, to the black Peso market to launder the profits through banks, to the white powder on an addict's nose who just died of an overdose in an emergency room. Money was the name of the game, and the counterdrug warriors had a difficult time competing with the criminals who were satisfying an insatiable demand they played a significant role in creating.

The airmen stood their watch, taking pride in the few times their efforts led to an arrest or the destruction of an aircraft. They were on the front lines, fighting someone they could call an enemy: criminals intent on selling addicting drugs to the citizens of their nation. So they sat, watching their radarscopes, looking for the next bad guy.

Captain Price leaned over Senior Airman Phil Andrews' shoulder. "Have your radars picked up anything in the Guajira Peninsula tonight?"

Senior Airman Andrews looked back. "No, sir. The intelligence guys told us about the tipper, but we haven't seen anything."

"I have some concerns about the plane that landed in Santa Marta," Captain Price said and stood tall, "but we have to find this plane. Can you do that?"

Senior Airman Andrews grinned. "I'll find that son of a bitch! I mean, I mean—"

"No, you got it right the first time," Captain Price said. "Find that son of a bitch." He slapped him on the shoulder.

On the operations floor, Master Sergeant Higgins set the phone down. "Sir, the Colombians have two A-37s ready to launch."

Captain Price gestured to Bruce. "How does it look?"

"My Citations are fueled and ready to go," Bruce said and held a small headset to his ear. "The Colombian Host Nation Riders are heading out to our planes now."

Captain Price picked up the radio. "Viper, Viper, any luck with finding this airplane?" He waved at Colonel Vasquez, the Colombian liaison officer, when he entered.

"This is Viper…that's a negative," a voice said on the radio speaker. "Request you consider getting us diplomatic clearance to enter

Colombia airspace, which would improve our chances of detecting the aircraft. How copy?"

Captain Price nodded and gestured for Master Sergeant Higgins to make a phone call. "Viper, we are working the diplomatic clearance. Do not, repeat, do not enter Colombian airspace until advised. How copy?"

"Good copy...Viper standing by."

"That just might work," Captain Price said to Master Sergeant Higgins. "See if they can make that happen two minutes go." He gestured for Colonel Vasquez to approach.

"Captain Price," Bruce said, "we're ready to go."

Captain Price gave Bruce a thumbs-up and focused his attention on Colonel Vasquez. "Sir, we have a report indicating that Cesar Gomez has a shipment departing tonight from the Guajira Peninsula, but we don't have a specific location, so our radars are having a difficult time locating it. We have two Citations and two A-37s on deck in Barranquilla. If we launch now and patrol the area, we might get lucky and find them."

"How's the weather?" Colonel Vasquez asked.

Captain Price gestured to Second Lieutenant Atkins, who rushed over with a pile of satellite photographs.

"Everything looks good on the north coast," Second Lieutenant Atkins said and handed the photos to Colonel Vasquez. "That small storm is out of range and dissipating. Cloud coverage is minimal—"

"I think it's obvious," Captain Price cut in, "the weather is fine." He gestured to Colonel Vasquez. "Sir, it's your call."

Colonel Vasquez analyzed the photo and nodded. "I'll recommend to my people that we launch, but they will be reluctant to do so without a specific location."

Captain Price resisted a smile and nodded professionally. He handed Colonel Vasquez the phone and pressed the auto-dial button for the operations center in Bogota.

"This is Viper...interrogative, status of our clearance?"

Captain Price picked up the radio. "Viper, the clearance is still pending. Please remain at least 12 nautical miles from the coast."

Colonel Vasquez analyzed the weather photos as Master Sergeant Higgins called for an update on the diplomatic clearance. Captain Price and Bruce moved to the computer to calculate how long it would take to arrive at the Guajira Peninsula.

Master Sergeant Higgins set the phone down, obviously not pleased. "Sir, they'll have the diplomatic clearance soon."

"Soon?" Captain Price asked and gestured to Colonel Vasquez. "Sir, it would really help to have the P-3 on the scene. Can you help?"

"I'll see what I can do," Colonel Vasquez said, "but it might be difficult at this hour. Next time, you should request it earlier in the day."

Master Sergeant Higgins and Bruce looked eager to speak but Captain Price pre-empted them. "Sir, you have A-37s ready to launch and credible intelligence about a cocaine shipment for Cesar Gomez. Isn't the next logical step to grant diplomatic clearance? It has never been denied, so it should be a formality."

"This is Viper...due to rough weather, we have moved farther away from the coast, which is limiting our radar coverage...interrogative: status of diplomatic clearance?"

Captain Price grabbed the radio. "Viper, still working the clearance. If the plane launches, please be prepared to track it to the delivery site."

Captain Price turned to Colonel Vasquez. "Sir, we are going to launch the Citations."

"Without the A-37s?" Colonel Vasquez asked.

"We have to locate and destroy this aircraft before it takes off," Captain Price said. "We can vector in the A-37s later."

"Hey, you need our permission to launch the Citations," Bruce said.

Captain Price glared at him. "Do you have any objections?"

Bruce grinned and chuckled. "Hell no."

Captain Price groaned and grabbed the radio. "Magic Zero One, Magic Zero Two, be advised: you are cleared to launch."

"This is Magic Zero One," the voice on the radio said. "Good copy."

Bruce pumped his fist and returned to his desk. Master Sergeant Higgins sat and typed journal entries in the computer logbook.

Soon after the two Citations launched, two blue dots appeared on the map near Barranquilla, Colombia, heading in the direction of the Guajira Peninsula. Captain Price checked his watch and shook his head doubtfully. The minutes dragged as the two blue dots moved across the screen one millimeter at a time.

Colonel Lance Dupree entered the operations floor dramatically and strode toward Captain Price and Colonel Vasquez. "Who's ready to destroy an aircraft full of cocaine?"

Captain Price didn't appreciate unannounced visits, especially from Colonel Dupree, but he liked his energy. "Sir, we have all of our radars focused on the Guajira Peninsula but have had no luck finding it."

Colonel Dupree grinned smugly as he removed a piece of paper from his pocket and unfolded it to reveal a coordinate. "This is where the plane is," he said and handed the paper to Bruce. "Vector your Citations to this point." He turned to Colonel Vasquez. "And let's get those A-37s in the air now."

Colonel Vasquez nodded, walked to the other side of the room, and picked up a phone to make a call.

"We're going to lay some hate on launch site BORNEO," Colonel Dupree said.

Captain Price shook his head in disbelief. "I knew it. The plane that approached Santa Marta earlier gave the call sign BORNEO. They're paying off people at the tower to lie about their location."

Colonel Dupree tapped his head. "They're smart bastards, but not smarter than us."

Colonel Vasquez hung up the phone and gave a thumbs-up. Soon after, two more blue dots appeared on the digital map heading toward the Guajira Peninsula. The minutes ticked by slowly as everyone gathered around the computer monitor to watch, the closest thing to silence on the operations floor.

Finally, the silence ended.

"This is Magic Zero One," the voice on the radio said. "We have spotted a suspect aircraft on a remote dirt runway preparing to take off…The A-37s have been vectored in by the Colombian controllers."

Captain Price quieted the cheering airmen and picked up the radio. "Magic Zero One, good copy. Standing by."

"This is Magic Zero One…We got word the A-37s have been cleared to fire…I say again, the A-37s are cleared to fire."

All eyes fixed on the computer monitor. The snail-paced action was the most exciting video game in town. Captain Price stood aside and watched patiently. He'd done all he could—vector in Colombian fighters for the kill. Unfortunately, the staff weenies would judge his work a success or a failure depending on whether the Colombians destroyed the aircraft, which was beyond his control. A part of him suddenly felt comfortable chasing drug dealers in Panama, but his days were numbered. If this job taught him anything, it was that there was a much bigger world out there.

"This is Magic Zero One...The A-37s have fired on the aircraft...A direct hit...The aircraft crashed at the end of the runway in a ball of flames...I say again, a direct hit...This guy is history!"

Captain Price smiled as the others cheered and slapped high fives.

"Good work, Captain Price," Colonel Dupree said and slapped him on the shoulder. "Good work, boys!" he added and pumped his fist. "You did us all proud tonight!" He pointed at the computer monitor. "Fuck you, Cesar Gomez."

Chapter Eighteen

Nicholas Lowe paced in Dylan Dirk's office with a satellite phone. The coffee and morning sunlight couldn't deceive his biochemistry any longer. He needed sleep. With no real expectation of success, bordering on delirious masochism, he dialed the number again. The feminine digital voice said the phone he was calling was not currently active and asked him to leave a message. He recognized he wasn't thinking clearly when he theorized that the feminine digital voice might respond with a different prerecorded message if he raised his voice. Finally, he acquiesced: the pilot was dead and the shipment was lost, along with the 1.5 million dollars paid to Cesar Gomez.

He pounded the table. Perhaps the pilot was with Cesar's men and had turned off the satellite phone and hidden the cargo? The Guajira Peninsula was a dangerous and remote place that even the Colombian military was reluctant to patrol. He called Cesar.

"Cesar," he said. Gloria told him to hold. He resorted to drumming his fingers on the desk. "Have you heard anything about last night?"

Cesar had heard from his men.

"What the hell's going on?" he asked.

He manipulated Cesar's response to salvage a sliver of hope, but no luck. From what Cesar understood, a Colombian A-37 had shot down the plane as it was taking off and the entire cargo was destroyed in the fire.

"I see," he said and hung up.

Dylan entered the office. "Rough night?"

Nicholas shrugged and rubbed his coarse stubble. "It's not looking good. Any news from the meeting at the embassy?"

Dylan set some folders on his desk and sat in his chair. He cleared his throat and leaned back. "JIATF-South confirmed a Colombian A-37 destroyed the plane as it was taking off. I doubt the pilot survived." He didn't look angry. "What do you think happened?"

Nicholas lifted his hands in defeat. "I don't know," he admitted. "This was the plan for Tyler's third shipment. The pilot checked out. Given the timing and the precision of the strike, I'm inclined to say there might have been a leak."

"Have you ever heard the term BORNEO?" Dylan asked.

Nicholas closed his eyes and shook his head to reverse engineer the events. "God damn it. Is Manuel Espinosa working for them?"

"JIATF-South had exact details about the shipment," Dylan said, "to include the take-off time, place, quantity, and so on. When I asked Colonel Dupree about the source, he privately told me it was," a gesture to Nicholas, "Manuel Espinosa—very good."

Nicholas sat and took a deep breath. "He works for Cesar and was in his penthouse last night when we finalized the deal."

"Did he see you?" Dylan asked.

Nicholas shook his head. "No, but if he's working for the military, it's only a matter of time before they figure out who's working with Cesar. Along those lines, couldn't we avoid this potential problem by just telling other agencies?"

Dylan had a puzzled look. "Tell them what—that we're violating the 1977 treaties to keep U.S. military bases in Panama post-1999? If you want to join the Order, you have to get used to running operations off the books for the greater good. I'm not even sure the president knows what we're doing. We can't risk attribution to the U.S. government."

Nicholas nodded knowingly, still adjusting to the idea of running operations off the books, no matter how cool it seemed. "Just so you know, Cesar told me he has recorded all of his meetings with us, in case we get any ideas about betraying him."

"I can't say I blame him," Dylan said. "Was he reacting to the editorial?"

Nicholas nodded. "I don't blame him, either. Can you think of any possible way Lina could have gotten that information? I'm not convinced she wrote the editorial, but I find it hard to believe a journalist just made it up and got lucky."

Dylan shrugged. "Your guess is as good as mine. Listen," he said with a coach's enthusiasm, "plan the next shipment. I recommend you change the mode of transportation and feed Manuel some bogus information to make JIATF-South look in the wrong place. We can't afford another mistake. The referendum is next week. I scheduled a tour for you at JIATF-South. Learn how they do business so we can avoid this problem the next time."

Nicholas nodded, ready to go. "How did this operation originate?"

Dirk appeared to be collating memories. "After the Canal negotiations failed—there was a last-ditch effort to keep a few military bases post-1999—the Order decided to make a new plan. The problem was we weren't sure which Panamanian politicians supported us." He rolled his eyes. "Everyone was playing the 'I hate gringos more than you do' game."

"That's when Tyler recruited Minister Hernandez," Nicholas said.

Dylan nodded. "We knew Hernandez wanted us to stay, and he helped us understand the political calculus among the elites." Chuckling, he added, "The problem was many of the politicians were neither for nor against our staying. They wanted money, bribes, something our negotiators refused to offer. Hernandez helped us understand that President Mendoza would approve a deal for military bases if we helped him win re-election. After that, K and I called a meeting of the Order and here we are."

"K was involved?" Nicholas said.

Dirk grimaced as if caught in a lie. "K flew here to ask Tyler to run the operation. He even offered him a promotion back in Washington for him and Helena to settle down for a few years and start a family."

Nicholas gestured for Dylan to continue.

"K spoke with President Mendoza at his ranch," Dylan said, "and Tyler and I spoke with Cesar. We made them offers they couldn't refuse."

"Why was Tyler supposed to return to Washington?" Nicholas asked.

Dylan paused and glanced at the ceiling. "Tyler and Helena were having problems. I offered him time off to help her—everyone knew she was using cocaine—but he was obsessed with blaming Cesar and others for her problems. I'm not blaming Tyler, but I think he could have done more to help her. Her father, Minister Hernandez, was no better. He spoiled her and looked the other way, even after people told him what was really happening." He paused and stared out the window. "Anyway," he turned to Nicholas, "getting back to our original discussion, at the JIATF-South operations center you'll meet the watch officer who was on duty last night when the plane was destroyed."

Nicholas stood.

"I hope you arranged to see Lina Castillo soon," Dylan added. "If she has proof of our financial links to President Mendoza and Cesar Gomez, you have to steal it from her—God and country, right?"

With the exception of loud music and a few shouts at the NCO club, Howard Air Force Base was quiet as the sun was setting. During the roughly three-mile drive from the front gate, Nicholas recalled fond memories from his assignments during the 1980s in Central America to fight the communists. This return to the field triggered feelings his desk in Washington had stifled during the past ten years. He realized now just how much he missed those days, and how good he felt to be back.

Building 705, known as the Pizza Hut building because of the shape of the roof, had earth-toned semicircular roof tiles and white plaster walls, which was the architectural standard for the base. At the front door, Nicholas picked up the phone, dialed the posted number, and waited patiently. Captain Price said he was on his way out. Boot marks about knee high smudged the wall where soldiers leaned back for smoke breaks. A security camera stood 24-hour watch. A sign warned that the use of deadly force was authorized.

"Welcome," Captain Price said as he opened the door, looking fit and disciplined in his camouflage uniform. They shook hands with a firm professional grip. "You must be Nicholas Lowe. We received the request from Mr. Dirk."

"I'm here for the tour," Nicholas said and offered his passport, pleased that the young Captain Price had not said "CIA."

Captain Price opened a three-ring binder and flipped to a fax sent by the embassy. He rested his finger on "Nicholas Lowe" and slid it across the social security number to his security clearance, "TS-SCI," the highest security clearance granted by the U.S. government. (Nicholas was cleared for other special access programs, but that fact was classified.)

Captain Price pressed a sequence of buttons on the cipher lock and pushed the door open to the operations floor. It was about the size of a three-car garage, inversely proportional to its impact on the war on drugs. The room was cold enough to protect the computers from the tropical weather and to engender a Protestant work ethic. The raised tile floor hid the tangled web of cables below. Maps of Latin American countries and photographs of airplanes covered the walls. A black-and-white photograph of a destroyed aircraft was taped to one of the computer monitors—Nicholas' plane, no doubt, along with his 1.5 million dollars. Three sergeants stopped typing on their computers and stood at attention.

"I heard you guys got one last night," Nicholas said and gestured for them to sit.

Captain Price nodded as the sergeants returned to their computers. "We received confirmation that a Colombian A-37 shot down the aircraft as it was taking off."

"Are shoot downs common?" Nicholas asked.

Captain Price nodded. "The Colombians normally strafe the planes after they land, but this time we had excellent intelligence."

"That's great," Nicholas said.

"We receive many intelligence reports," Captain Price said. "I ignore most of them because they usually lack specific details—not actionable, as we say. Last night, however, we had an exact take-off time and location. Fortunately, our air assets are based in a great location to respond to air shipments departing from the Guajira Peninsula."

"Interesting," Nicholas said. It was time to learn how to avoid a repeat for the next shipment. "Why don't you tell me about your mission?"

Captain Price clicked the mouse for a PowerPoint slide.

The drug trade began in Bolivia, Peru, and Colombia, where most of the world's coca leaves grew, in part due to the choice of the drug traffickers, but also due to the unique combination of altitude, soil, and climate that made it difficult to grow in other locations. From there, the cocaine was transported, mostly to the United States and Europe, in general aviation aircraft, speedboats, commercial ships, or over land.

Different federal law enforcement and intelligence agencies disrupted different transportation modes or money laundering networks. One of the more controversial ways to attack the problem was eradication, attacking the root of the problem, so to speak, but local nationalists and farmers protested against the eradication programs as a violation of national sovereignty. People in the Andes have been chewing coca leaves and making tea for centuries.

"You're responsible for the airspace over Panama and South America?" Nicholas asked. "That's a large area to cover. What do you consider your strong and weak areas?"

Captain Price gestured to a map on the desk and pointed. "As I said, based on the location of our air assets, our best place to operate is the north coast of Colombia. Our sister operation in Key West is best positioned to disrupt drug shipments in the Caribbean."

Nicholas nodded, not pleased to hear his first shipment's profile had matched JIATF-South's competitive advantage.

"Our mission often overlaps with Key West's mission," Captain Price continued. "We control the land and they control the water, but airplanes fly over both land and water."

Nicholas made a mental note as Captain Price pointed at a map.

"The coastal waters between Colombia and Panama are difficult to monitor," Captain Price said with a sweeping motion.

"Drugs are moving through there?" Nicholas asked.

Captain Price nodded confidently. "The Colombian navy and the Panamanian National Maritime Service have a limited ability to patrol those waters." He pointed at Colon, the city at the northern end of the Panama Canal. "Drugs move along the northern coast of Panama and are often shipped out of the Colon Free Zone in containers."

"Do many drug shipments depart Panama by air?" Nicholas asked.

"That we don't know," Captain Price said and shrugged. "If I were a drug dealer, that's how I'd move the stuff, at least until we figure out how to stop it."

Nicholas checked his watch and extended his hand. "Captain Price, I'd like to thank you for your time." He gestured to the others. "Have a good evening, gentlemen, and congratulations on your endgame last night."

Chapter Nineteen

As the taxi approached the entrance of the El Panama Hotel, Lina Castillo checked herself in a compact mirror, reapplied her lipstick, and sprayed on some perfume. She got out and leaned forward to pay the taxi driver through the open passenger window and noticed he was wearing a T-shirt supporting re-election for President Mendoza. She gave him a nice tip, "Thanks!", and shook her head in disappointment.

Work had been another chaotic day. Her computer crashed before the deadline, the IT guys couldn't fix the problem right away, and the editor was worried that some of the language might offend some of the advertisers and oligarchs. Was it any wonder Panama was still struggling to take even the most basic steps that would lead to economic growth and social prosperity? What Panama needed was the equivalent of a First Amendment to give journalists and every citizen the right to pursue the truth without fear of retribution; nay, that the government would actively protect journalists and citizens who have the courage to shake up the system with hard-hitting investigative reporting or other dissenting acts of free speech that were deemed subversive. Even *El Tiempo*, which was founded with the noble mission of revealing to the world the horrors of the Noriega dictatorship, seemed to be succumbing to the institutional malaise of serving as a mouthpiece for corrupt elements within Panama or shaping the tone of the newspaper to attract advertisers. Unfortunately, she had no idea whether *El Tiempo* would step up to defend her if the chips were down, which could happen with her story about President Mendoza taking drug money to fund his re-election campaign.

Lina entered the pool area and saw Nicholas sitting alone at a table below the stars, wearing a classy oxford shirt and tan dress slacks. He looked up, stood with a friendly wave, and waited for her to arrive, greeting her with a Latino hug and a kiss on the cheek that was reminiscent of someone who had done it hundreds of times before. Many gringos struggled with this somewhat simple yet graceful exchange. The kiss on the cheek could vary from an air kiss with limited facial contact to a more familiar kiss where the corners of the mouths touch ever so slightly. She was pleased that Nicholas met her halfway with a perfect dose of cologne. And he wore nice shoes.

"I love this place," she said and allowed him to slide her chair back like a gentleman before sitting. "Work was crazy as usual. Just as I was finishing my story, the computer crashed and the IT guys couldn't figure it out, and then," she continued, realizing she was probably talking too much, "you know, problems with graphics and other boring stuff that you probably don't care about."

"Not at all," he said, "I'd love to hear about what you're writing. But I can tell you from my own experience that IT guys are all the same, am I right? They're always there when you don't need them..."

"And never there when you need them," she said and laughed with him, until the waiter arrived with a notepad.

"Would you like something to drink?" he asked her.

"Let's see," she said, perusing the wine menu. There were so many wines, some she liked, some she didn't like, some cheap, some expensive, some red, some white, some from Spain, some from Chile, but the ritual of selecting the wine was an important part of the process that most people fumbled through and it usually ended before you knew it.

"I'll have a glass of the Brunello, please," Nicholas said confidently.

Lina set her menu down, relieved and pleased to hear that the expensive wines on the bottom of the list were in play. "I'll have the same."

"*Una botella, por favor,*" Nicholas added with the slightest American accent that made it all the more charming.

The waiter nodded smartly and walked away.

"According to your newspaper, President Mendoza is moving up in the polls," Nicholas said. "Looks like he might win re-election after all."

"Can you believe it?" she said, suddenly flustered yet eager to talk substantive issues. "He's flooding the streets and the media with advertising, and people are changing their vote. I mean, give a taxi driver a T-shirt and he'll vote for you."

"Lots of campaigning," he said, "lots of money, I'm sure."

"No kidding," she said, cognizant that Nicholas was probably eliciting information from her about her editorial about the president and drug money, surprised and curious that the CIA had not yet confronted her more directly. "I wonder who's funding him."

"You're the expert," he said and glanced around the restaurant casually. "I tell you, T-shirt prices are outrageous these days."

She appreciated the humor. "I'm sure he'll lose," she said. "I can't wait to see him out of office. He's destroying Panama." Probably no one at *El Tiempo* wanted President Mendoza to win, but the poll numbers were troubling.

"Destroying Panama?" he asked. "Is Panama worse off now than it was when he started almost five years ago?"

She set her menu down and looked up, careful to not let her feelings on the subject appear too transparent, which would hurt her credibility as a journalist. "He and his friends are making the rich richer and the poor poorer. Did you know that GDP growth has dropped to less than 3 percent? After the invasion in 1989, the growth rate was closer to 8 percent. Things are getting worse."

He looked puzzled. "I heard the growth rate after the invasion lasted until the economy had returned to its pre-invasion size—the result of filling a void, not of actual growth."

"Other developing countries are growing at 8 percent," she said, pleased to be talking to someone who could discuss numbers coherently and push her to refine her own arguments to new levels of clarity.

"You blame the president for that?" he asked. "Do you really think one person has the power to make those changes?"

She didn't really believe it but nodded anyway. At a minimum, the president could remove obstacles to progress or stop lining his own pockets.

The waiter set two crystal glasses down and poured a sample of the beautiful crimson wine that formed a layer of translucent bubbles on the surface. Nicholas touched the stained end of the cork and lifted his glass. He swirled the wine under his nose and whiffed the bouquet. "Politicians are like ancient priests who punished the masses for preordained seasonal changes." He sipped the wine again and nodded approvingly. "I think economic forces are more powerful than any one man."

"That's because you live in a developed economy with over 300 million people," she said. "Panama has great potential, but we have to make changes. Our economy should be based on equal opportunity for all, not on inheritance for the few, but the rich families maintain their grip on power because our country is so small—only three million people. Once someone owns a small segment of the economy, competition is almost impossible."

He gestured in an offhand way. "The president favors democracy and free trade, and is even pushing for Panama to adhere to World Trade Organization standards. That sounds like positive change to me."

"So he says," she said, hoping he wouldn't view this discussion as too academic or argumentative, "but he's only helping himself and his friends. He doesn't want to help the poor or fund any social programs." Although she couldn't promote it publicly, it seemed clear to her that if a group of disinterested professionals were to take over the administration of Panama, progress would come quickly and many vested interests would see their empires crumble.

"What, specifically, would you do?" he asked and held her stare with comforting eyes that didn't seem to be assessing her as a potential sexual conquest.

"They could spend more on education or basic preventative medicine," she said, feeling the pressure of shifting from the emotional abstract to the concrete particular. "Companies will not open factories here if our workers lack skills. And without good jobs, the consumers will not have disposable income. The rich here don't seem to realize that their businesses would make more money if the people had more money."

"Then why do Panamanians vote for these guys?" he asked with a reluctant smile that radiated in a gentle and soothing way.

"Because they're mostly uneducated and susceptible to propaganda," she said, disappointed with her answer and feeling her heart race a little faster.

He raised an inquisitive eyebrow. "It sounds like you don't think too highly of your fellow citizens. I thought the ideal was to let the people govern themselves and use the ballot box to hold politicians accountable."

"Only when they're ready," she said, making a move on a chessboard, pleased with the direction the conversation was moving, but unsure whether he was speaking from conviction, playing devil's advocate, or steering the conversation to his own ends.

He looked confused. "The U.S. was a democracy from the beginning. We found a way to work it out, which included a bloody Civil War. The dirty little secret of democracy is that it is often painful and requires a lot of trial and error. There is no magic template that you can simply impose on a people."

So true! She resisted a smile, thrilled that he was engaging her as an intellectual equal, without the slightest hint of machismo arrogance or brutish sexual innuendo, the same way things had been with Tyler and unlike the way things were with every Panamanian man she had ever met. "Your country wasn't founded on democracy—unless by democracy you mean limiting suffrage to white men over twenty-one who own property. Many people in America were not allowed to vote until the twentieth century, which had many benefits. There is such a thing as allowing universal suffrage too early. America," she continued as a smile filled her face, enjoying this moment to speak freely, "was created by a small group of people with a vision for the future, and a first president who voluntarily gave up power to go back to his plow. President Mendoza's plans for change—to include keeping U.S. troops and liberalizing trade without protecting labor—won't work."

"A small group of people are making decisions for Panama," he said, "and they seem to have at least a modest vision for the future, which includes some of the key chapters of the IMF and the World Bank play book. There's no need to completely reinvent the wheel. Panama will improve with time, no?"

She shook her head, still unsure whether he was speaking from conviction, but enjoying his rhetorical skills nonetheless. "Positive social change is always the result of action, not of the passage of time. In fact, this is precisely the problem with Panama. The rich believe the poor suffer from laziness, and the poor vote for the rich person who makes the most empty promises—a frustrating, vicious cycle."

"Then what hope is there for progress?" he asked.

Almost taken by surprise, she found herself in the perfect place to explain in clear words what has been plaguing Panama all these years and what no one seemed to understand, no matter how many stories she wrote for the newspaper. "The only hope for positive change is an elite class of people with a noble and selfless desire to build a prosperous nation." She leaned back and looked at him, unable to avoid the oddly comforting conclusion that he had led her to this point. "Unfortunately, Panama lacks such a class of people, and such a class of people is unlikely to rise to power within our democratic system."

"A toast," he said and raised his glass as the waiter arrived to take their order, "to noble ambitions."

"To noble ambitions," she said, feeling her heart beat a little faster.

Nicholas downshifted the car to maneuver past the potholes and turned left as Lina gestured to an unlit street. The headlights showed the way as they entered a less affluent part of town. During dinner, she mentioned in an offhand way that she had taken a taxi, knowing full well that a gentleman like Nicholas would offer to take her home. Men were so predictable in their DNA-coded desire to feel like a protector of women, which could be a wonderful thing if done the right way. The truth was she had a car and could drive but wanted to see how things would play out this way. If things didn't work out, she could always kiss him on the cheek and enter her apartment alone.

"I was thinking about our discussion the other night," she said, ready to test the waters. "I heard Tyler was found killed in his car in a shady part of town." The information contained in the documents she took from Tyler seemed to indicate some sort of CIA operation, but there was no proof in the documents, only mention of President Mendoza, Cesar Gomez, and a company called Enterprise Associates. "What I don't understand is why he would go to a place like that, because when he stopped by to see me earlier the same night—"

"Tyler stopped by your apartment the night he died?" he interrupted.

"Yes," she said, pleased with his reaction, because it suggested surprise and doubt, "to tell me he'd received an offer to move back to Washington." She had repeated the lie many times in her mind to make sure she remained consistent.

"If you don't mind my asking," he said with a vague gesture, keeping his eye on the road as the headlights wove down the dark street, "were you and Tyler, you know, seeing each other again after Helena died?"

She shook her head innocently. "No. He was depressed after Helena's death and needed someone to talk to, so I tried to be there for him."

He slowed to look both ways and glided through a red light, which were optional at this time of the day in this part of town. On the side of the road, three homeless men stood around a roaring barrel fire and watched them drive by.

"Did Tyler say anything about where he was going?" he asked.

She shook her head, keeping her responses to a minimum to protect her false claim that Tyler had visited her, which was the best way to obscure the truth. If Tyler visited her, there was no plausible way for her to get the documents.

"So what have you been writing these days?" he asked. "I've been reading your paper, but I haven't seen your name on many stories."

She shrugged, knowing full well that his more aggressive pursuit of the truth was about to begin. She was frightened but at the same time she realized this would have to play out one way or another. "Different things."

"Different things—like what?" he asked.

She shrugged. "Mostly politics, some economics."

"There was one particular editorial that has caused quite a stir," he said. "It made some bold claims about President Mendoza and drug money."

She tilted her head and scrutinized him, surprised that he had opted for such a direct approach. "If you're wondering whether I wrote it, the answer is yes." It was clear that Nicholas and his government already knew. At this point, the best she could do was obscure how she got the documents because that was clearly a sticking point for the Americans.

He nodded nonchalantly and followed her gesture to turn right. "That was a provocative piece, because if what you say is true—"

"Of course it's true," she said. "Do you think I would write lies? Do you think I would risk my career as a journalist?"

"No," he said and turned to her defensively. "I was only suggesting that you must have proof or something."

She gestured to an apartment complex, ready to end the date and never see him again. He entered the parking lot and found an open space. She reached for the door and then turned and looked at him.

"I had a wonderful time," she said and leaned forward to kiss him on the cheek.

"I hope we can do it again," he said with an irresistible smile.

For a silent moment, the weight of the world seemed to be lifted from her shoulders, just as it had with Tyler. She closed her eyes and kissed him on the lips.

Lina set her keys on a table next to the day's edition of *El Tiempo*. She didn't live in the nicest part of town, but she kept it clean and did her best to give it a woman's touch: a floral arrangement on the coffee table, plants hanging from the ceiling, and the lingering smell of incense. She was saving some money and would be in a good position to move into a nicer place after the next promotion.

She opened the fridge to eye the water, juice, and wine. "I have to use the bathroom. You're welcome to anything in the fridge."

She kissed him on the lips, smiled, and turned to enter the bathroom. She closed the door and looked in the mirror with a deep breath. When a board creaked near her bedroom, she moved to the other wall and pressed her ear to the wall to listen. It was not clear, but she heard the muffled sounds of movement—papers, clothes, and so on. She waited a few moments to calm her pounding heart and then flushed the toilet and turned on the sink to wash her hands. She stopped at the door with a mental count of three to avoid seeing him in the wrong place—*please don't be in my bedroom*. When she opened the door, he was leaning against the kitchen counter with two glasses of white wine. Part of her wanted to believe he wasn't in her room, that it was all in her imagination.

"I see you found something to drink," she sai, and stood next to him and accepted the glass of wine.

They toasted and sipped the wine. If he was in her room, he sure had a good way of not showing it. She caressed his arm. "Is something wrong?"

"Not at all," he said and smiled as they stared into each other's eyes. "Do you like classical music? I hear there's a concert this week."

"I love classical music," she said and rested her head against his chest.

He wrapped his firm arms around her and kissed her on the forehead. The steady pulse of his heartbeat was comforting. She looked up at him, kissed him passionately on the lips, and then walked over and locked the front door.

Chapter Twenty

Minister of Foreign Affairs Victor Hernandez accepted a Scotch on the rocks from the bartender at Club Union and walked to the patio of the club to escape the crowd. Outside, the breeze was cool. The view of the city was fabulous.

Despite the progress he had made with the referendum and attacking Cesar Gomez, to include working with Manuel Espinosa to destroy his last shipment, the pain in his heart remained, and he could trace it back to that fateful event. He had planned a family vacation to a beach resort, hoping to recharge his batteries before the campaign season. As a pleasant surprise, they had met Dylan Dirk and his wife Ellen at the swimming pool. The trip was superb, until Dylan mentioned in private that he had reason to believe Helena was using cocaine and that Cesar Gomez was probably her supplier. When the CIA speaks, you listen. Unfortunately, Dylan had been right. Victor found a stainless steel case filled with cocaine in Helena's purse. She threw a tantrum when he confronted her, saying he didn't respect her privacy, insisting she was only experimenting, but she agreed to flush the cocaine and quit.

Like most fathers, he believed her, needed to believe her during the following hectic months. The party's potential loss of the presidency and the imminent departure of the U.S. military were threatening Panama's future. Only two things could save Panama: finding a candidate to win the next election and an agreement to maintain a U.S. military presence post-1999. No one seemed capable of helping the party accomplish those objectives, except the Americans. In hindsight, the Americans seemed to have orchestrated the events, but he believed they offered the only hope. And when a young diplomat named Tyler Broadman asked him to provide classified information to the CIA, he agreed.

The word treason didn't enter his vocabulary until weeks later, but he eventually realized he was an agent, a spy, on the payroll of the CIA. This awareness coincided with the second time he found Helena with cocaine. His unthinking reaction was to yell at her and cut off her allowance until she agreed to seek help. His wife, always the more insightful one, thought of a better solution and played Cupid. After a classical music concert, she introduced Tyler and Helena and practically planned their first date. She had no idea Tyler was a spy—to this day—but considered him a gentleman, which was what Helena needed.

The plan worked, at least initially. They fell in love, and Victor had never seen Helena so happy, like the little girl he loved so much, which was why her rape and overdose during a party at Cesar's penthouse came as such a shock. He and Tyler were having a discussion in a discreet venue when the news arrived. He instinctively blamed Cesar but eyewitnesses testified he had refused to give her cocaine and even killed the man who had raped her. Helena had a miscarriage, Tyler's child. The doctor said she probably would have died if Cesar hadn't helped her. Nonetheless, Cesar was to blame for her cocaine addiction. He realized then that destroying Cesar was more important than all his other plans.

For all he could tell, things improved. Helena stopped using cocaine, or found cleverer ways to hide her addiction, and Tyler asked for her hand in marriage. He hated to lose his little girl, but he knew she would have a better life outside of Panama. Their formal announcement was one of the happiest days of his life. Helena was his little girl again; the sight of her laughing and crying with joy at the engagement party was forever painted in his memory. Improving matters more, the CIA told him about a plan to arrest Cesar. He had thought of ways to eliminate Cesar on his own, but the CIA plan offered a better chance of success. He placed his trust in them. However, everything changed with the death of Tyler and the CIA's decision to put the operation to arrest Cesar on hold.

"Welcome, Mr. President," someone said inside the club.

Victor looked inside the club as a bevy of loyal supporters greeted President Mendoza. He finished his drink and waited outside, needing more time alone.

He had no regrets about his plans for Panama; the means he employed, however, were biting his conscience. By accepting the post of Minister of Foreign Affairs, he swore an oath to protect the people of Panama and to promote its national interests. No one had given him permission to pass secrets to the CIA.

Tyler had been clear: he wanted nonpublic information about the Panamanian political calculus. Who supported maintaining a U.S. military presence in Panama post-1999? Who was opposed? Who was willing to change the 1977 treaties? With the departure of President Mendoza, the party was battling within to find a candidate before the next election. The opposition was not open to renegotiating the 1977 treaties. He had considered the situation hopeless, but Tyler showed his brilliance by recommending that they change the constitution to allow President Mendoza to run for a second term in office. The president would sign any deal in exchange for re-election, any chance to remain in power. The referendum would unify the party and guarantee victory in the election.

Mr. Dirk and his boss, a most distinguished gentleman named K, arranged for a meeting to discuss the idea. Victor attended the meeting with President Mendoza and acted surprised by the proposal, to keep his relationship with the CIA a secret. President Mendoza, a true leader of men, analyzed the idea from many angles before agreeing to the terms. He used prudent skepticism to weigh the proposal against Panama's long-term security objectives. However, the possibility of re-election undoubtedly weighed on his decision. The plan was good for Panama, but Victor felt like a traitor the day he manipulated the president's decision. After that, his meetings with Tyler were less frequent. For the first time, he felt used; but the guilt subsided when the plan went into effect with immediate results. The inflow of money initiated an advertising campaign that pushed the polls above 50 percent. Now only time would tell.

"Why aren't you enjoying the party?"

He turned to see President Mendoza. "Hello, Mr. President." He looked up at the stars. "Just getting a breath of fresh air."

President Mendoza stood next to him and set his drink on the ledge. "We're making good progress in the polls," he said and inspected a cigar.

"Allow me, Mr. President," Victor said and lit the cigar. The dancing flame forged a bond between them that double-breasted suits never could.

President Mendoza puffed a rapid succession of gray smoke clouds. "Thanks," he said and inhaled deeply. "I spoke with Mr. Dirk earlier. He said the next payment would be delayed a few days. Not sure what happened."

"Should I call to see what the problem is?" Victor asked. As the architect of this plan, he would assume full responsibility. "You heard the good news about one of Cesar's drug shipments being destroyed?"

President Mendoza nodded and inspected the glowing coal on his cigar. "We have enough funds for a few days." He offered a cheerful wink. "This advertising campaign for re-election was brilliant."

Victor didn't consider President Mendoza a social equal, but no civilized man could ignore the words of a sitting president who had received a mandate from the people. "Panama will be fortunate to have you in office for five more years, Mr. President."

President Mendoza rested his hand on his shoulder. "You've always been a great source of wisdom for me. I look forward to serving with you again. Would you do me the honor of being my Minister of Foreign Affairs?"

"It would be my honor, Mr. President," Victor said.

President Mendoza gestured inside. "The Minister of Government and Justice briefed me earlier. We're closer to a final agreement regarding how to change the 1977 treaties. Convincing the others to approve it will be an uphill battle, but we're on the right track."

"I'm right behind you," Victor said.

* * *

Typically, Club Union would be empty this early in the week, but the president had taken advantage of a lull in his schedule to hold a fundraiser. This type of event usually attracted established families with disposable income and a charitable bent. Now, mostly because of upward mobility, Club Union was flooded with *nouveau riche* who loved to network and flash their cash in vulgar ways.

Speak of the devil, he thought as First Vice President Antonio Romero entered with three cronies. Antonio was a commoner par excellence who had received instant social status from the election. Victor gestured to the bartender for another drink.

"Mr. President, Minister Hernandez," Antonio said jovially, obviously drunk, "what a turnout!" He gestured to his three cronies. "I think I've convinced a few old friends to make a nice contribution."

"Excellent," President Mendoza said. "We need all the help we can get."

Victor focused on the men and recognized them as lacking **wealth** and political clout. In fact, one was Antonio's ally from his leftist activist days in college. Panama was a small country and memories were long.

"How much have they pledged?" Victor asked casually.

"That depends on how well we treat them," Antonio said as if nudging fraternity brothers. "That's what I wanted to talk about. With all this money flowing in, I thought maybe I could take a small advance. The more I wine and dine them, the more they'll give."

Victor cleared his throat. "Funds are limited for the moment." He waited for President Mendoza's nod. Antonio obviously wanted some party cash to burn on his friends, which was not uncommon in politics. "I'm sure their donation will more than cover your expenses. In fact, just keep whatever they give you."

Antonio gritted his teeth. "You know I can't afford to entertain people. My salary is all I have, unlike you two."

"We were expecting a large sum of money yesterday," Victor said, "but for right now we are low on cash. You understand."

The bulging vein on Antonio's temples indicated he was about to make a scene. President Mendoza cleared his throat and gestured to Victor. He took a deep breath, removed the wallet from his coat pocket, and handed Antonio a score of hundred-dollar bills.

Antonio, surprised, slid the money into his coat pocket with a finger pistol and nodded respectfully before returning to his friends.

President Mendoza leaned closer to Victor. "I know you don't like him—no one does—but he's got us by the balls. If his party doesn't support us, we'll never win re-election. And if we do not start spending more on social programs for the poor, our days as a political party will be numbered. Just keep him happy."

"Of course, Mr. President," Victor said. He agreed that avoiding conflict was prudent, but to what extent would the party dilute the leadership with people like Antonio? They were sadly approaching a day when they would choose candidates and a platform that reflected not the party's traditional values, which were required to sustain society, but the whims of the masses, which inevitably resulted in decadence and decay.

Victor sat at the bar. Sheena, sitting on the opposite side, gazed at him seductively. She ate a maraschino cherry, tossed the stem behind her like a piece of discarded lingerie, and then stood and discreetly gestured for him to follow her to the exit.

Victor eased the front door shut. The lights were out. Silence. He breathed a sigh of relief, set the keys on the table, and walked to the kitchen to pour a drink.

"How was the party?" Ivonne asked from the living room.

Victor cringed and took a deep breath. She was sitting on the couch in a bathrobe looking at a photograph by candlelight.

"I thought you were sleeping." He sipped his drink and approached her cautiously.

She set the photo aside and stood to hug him, and then immediately backed off. "I was right. The perfume you bought was for her," she said coldly and walked away.

He smelled his suit coat and followed her to the kitchen. "Honey, I was at a fundraiser tonight greeting many people."

She turned on the light and looked at him. "Do the people you greet normally leave lipstick on your neck?"

He touched his neck and looked at the oily red smudge on his fingers. "I can explain—"

Treaty Violation

"You don't have to explain," she said, rubbing her temples. "I know about Sheena. Everyone does. You'd make a terrible spy." She almost smiled but instead shook her head sadly. "Just the other day, my friends asked me about the perfume you bought for me, the bottle they saw you buy at the department store."

He reached for her, but she stepped away.

"I bought a bottle for myself so no one would gossip," she continued and looked at him. "I come from a respectable family, but you seem intent on making a fool of me. I know all about the mistress culture, trust me, but I thought you would be different."

"Honey," he said, "I never meant...I swear, I'll never—"

"Save your promises," she said and tugged his lapels. "Sheena's a beautiful woman. You would be crazy not to want her."

He was unsure how to respond. Was she giving him approval? Was she setting a trap? "I've acted like a fool, a total—"

"No," she said and forced a smiled. "You've been acting like a healthy man. I'm happy to see you looking so virile." She looked away and took a deep breath. "I only wish I still aroused those passions in you."

He rested his hands on her shoulders. "You're the only woman I love," he said and wiped her tears. "The only one."

"Am I not beautiful anymore?" she asked.

His heart melted as he gazed into the eyes he fell in love with so many years ago. "My God, you're more beautiful than ever." He kissed her gently on the lips. "I've been a disgraceful fool. You deserve better."

She smiled and kissed him back. "Perhaps you can act like a disgraceful fool with me sometime. You don't know how jealous I've been. I want us to be happy again."

They embraced. He thanked God for his blessings. "What do you say we take a romantic vacation after the referendum? Just the two of us—"

A pain shot through his heart as he hugged her. Without Helena, life would never be the same. Her death couldn't have been more tragic.

He had rushed to the emergency room when he heard the news about Helena falling from Cesar Gomez's penthouse. He couldn't describe the pain he felt when he saw her lifeless body on the operating table—the white robe soaked with blood, her limbs broken from the fall. She died instantly, but the doctor found scratches on her neck where her necklace had been, the pearl necklace Tyler had given her. Everyone assumed Cesar had done it, but the scratches were only minutes old. Eyewitnesses saw Cesar in a bar two hours before she fell, and the security tapes for the lobby were missing, which most people had concluded was due to the security guards failing to keep them running.

To his horror, the police initially ruled her death a suicide. With no additional evidence, he could not prove otherwise, but he convinced them to declare her death an accident. She didn't kill herself, he knew it, and he wouldn't let the Catholic Church condemn her soul. Her funeral made matters worse. Nosy journalists probed for details and wrote stories full of lies. They had no respect for their privacy. Hundreds of people who probably never knew her laid flowers—violets, her favorite—at the site of her death.

"I can't believe she is gone," he said with tears in his eyes. He allowed the pain to permeate his body. "We should have done more to help her."

She leaned back, surprised. "Helena couldn't have asked for a more loving father. You did everything you could. She adored you."

He wiped his tears. "I know, but sometimes I feel like—"

"Like what?" she asked.

"Like we should have been stricter with her," he said. "We could have isolated her in a treatment facility or done more to help."

"Honey, you can't feel guilty. Helena was an independent woman. That's what made her beautiful." Her smile reversed. "The cocaine, that's what got her into trouble. If all the love we gave her didn't save her, nothing would." She dried his tears. "Just make sure you put that monster Cesar Gomez behind bars."

He nodded as they embraced. "I love you so much."

"I love you, too," she said.

"Starting today," he said and wrapped his arm around her shoulder as they walked to the bedroom, "we're going to turn this marriage around." They stopped at the door. "Mrs. Hernandez, would you do me the honor of having dinner with me tomorrow evening?"

She sighed. "Mr. Hernandez, I'd be honored." She kissed her index finger and touched his lips. "Wait here," she said and arched her eyebrows suggestively. "I have a surprise."

He felt the spark that had been missing for years. He was wasting his time with Sheena and the other mistresses. The woman he really loved all along was standing before him looking more beautiful than ever. Despite the pains of life, their love was the bond that held him together and gave him the strength to live.

She returned with a pillow and a blanket. "Enjoy the couch," she said.

He flinched when she slammed the door in his face.

Chapter Twenty-One

A Panamanian National Police officer wearing a shabby khaki uniform waved Nicholas past the front gate of Fort Amador. The former U.S. military base had been a jewel of the former Canal Zone: plush base housing, a nine-hole golf course, an officers' club, and a yacht club overlooking the southern entrance to the Canal. Now, however, preventative maintenance didn't reign supreme. The buildings needed paint, the grass was uncut, and tree branches littered both sides of the roads.

As Nicholas waited for an oncoming car to pass through the single-lane gravel road detour, he noticed the row of abandoned white cement barracks wounded with bullet holes from the U.S. invasion in 1989. AC-130 gunships had blasted the buildings before U.S. tanks forced out the Panamanian Defense Forces. Farther down the road lay the tomb of Omar Torrijos, the dictator who participated in the *coup d'état* on October 11, 1968, then a lieutenant colonel. As Panama's beloved "benevolent dictator," he initiated massive public works projects with loans that made Panama per capita the most heavily indebted country in the world. Torrijos also invited a flood of illicit activities—drug trafficking, money laundering, weapons smuggling, whatever the mind could imagine, activities that fathered Panama's persistent notoriety. And of course the United States took advantage of his hospitality to establish a staging base for fighting the communists throughout Central America during the 1980s.

Torrijos' greatest achievement was snatching the Panama Canal from Jimmy Carter in 1977. The Republicans were still bemoaning this act of treason when Nicholas joined the Agency. Some reputable thinkers had decreed the 1977 treaties unconstitutional, noting that the president lacked the authority to cede sovereign territory to a foreign nation, but Carter won the day. The two treaties—one for operating the Canal, the other for the defense and neutrality of the Canal—made Torrijos a national hero. The prospect of controlling the Canal lifted the spirits of many Panamanians, but the reality of low profitability and high maintenance costs would quickly shatter their hopes for a free lunch.

Torrijos died in a plane crash. Rumors inevitably surfaced that the CIA was responsible, but the rumors were discordant with the fact that Torrijos for the most part had been a cooperative puppet, to include allowing the United States to use Panama as a staging base for covert wars. Nicholas never met Torrijos, but he met his successor, Manuel Noriega, who had been Torrijos' Director of Intelligence, responsible for the dirty work, like killing those who were fighting to re-establish democracy in Panama. More than one American diplomat spoke out against this violation of American principles. Noriega was on the CIA's payroll, as well as those of other intelligence agencies.

Nicholas remembered the meeting with Noriega well. K and Tyler were also there. They'd met farther down the road past the causeway at one of Noriega's homes on Flamingo Island, an old World War II artillery site. K had assigned Nicholas and Tyler to transport weapons and supplies to the anticommunist guerrillas in Nicaragua and El Salvador. Nicholas admired the way K arranged the deal and manipulated Noriega—Pineapple Face, as he was called, because of his pervasive acne scars. K was a master at making people feel good about the fact that they worked for him. Noriega was no exception. He looked powerless in his khaki uniform, even behind his pugnacious frown, as he grunted obscenities and downed glass after glass of Scotch. Noriega did what he was told, until he didn't do what he was told, at which time he was removed.

The mission was a success—the United States eliminated the Soviet influence in Central America, although a communist legacy remained—and Tyler took the lead after K reassigned Nicholas to El Salvador. Nicholas never saw Noriega again, but he remembered him as a vile yet romantic creature. Despite his cruelty and failures as a leader, Noriega understood that Panama was an oppressive society where the fair-skinned oligarchs would never allow the dark-skinned masses to participate in the power structure, except under the barrel of a gun.

A dust cloud from an oncoming car forced Nicholas to roll up his window, a fitting metaphor for the dust that had settled long ago on Panama's stage. Even though the play had ended years before and Panama was no longer on the front pages of the newspapers, a few actors remained, performing a sequence of disjointed scenes in pursuit of a satisfying conclusion, without any heroes to save the day. Nicholas' cue began after he passed through the bumpy detour, parked at the Balboa Yacht Club, donned a baseball cap and sunglasses, and descended the stairs to the pier.

"Cesar sent me," a swarthy man said from his taxi boat.

Nicholas nodded and hopped in. Waves from a passing cruise ship gently rocked the boat as the driver throttled the engine. He waved at the tourists on the cruise ship. The boat driver ignored them and spat in the water. The single engine revved as the boat bounced over the waves toward the sailboat anchored about one hundred yards from shore. At the destination, Nicholas stood and handed the boat driver five dollars.

"Greetings," Cesar Gomez said and stroked his mustache, wearing a tropical shirt and sunglasses. "Welcome to paradise," he said and shook Nicholas' hand.

The yacht was exquisite. The varnished wooden deck led to a pilothouse filled with advanced communications and GPS equipment. The cabin below probably slept twelve comfortably. Nicholas looked up at the sun and felt the penetrating rays on his face. Drug trafficking aside, this wasn't a bad way to live.

"Gloria," Cesar yelled below, "a cold beer for our guest." He looked at the empty bottles on the table. "Make it two."

Gloria ascended the stairs holding a tray with two beers and wearing a bikini, flip-flops, and an unbuttoned silky shirt tied in a knot at her midriff. Her long wavy black hair was resting over her face to hide the scar. Cesar hardly noticed her as they sat and received the beers.

"Thank you," Nicholas said and sneaked a peek of Gloria's shapely behind as she walked to the front of the boat and removed her shirt to catch some rays lying on a towel. He gestured to Cesar.

"I'm perfectly content with Adriana and Maria," Cesar said. "Besides, we have a long history; it's a long and complicated story."

"I'm just saying," Nicholas said. He couldn't care less about Cesar's personal life, but the case officer in him couldn't help taking some time to build a rapport to help him get what he wanted. It was like breathing. "I'm sensing a lot of chemistry."

"How can I help you today?" Cesar said, ready to move on.

"You mentioned having the fourth shipment ready by Wednesday night," Nicholas said, getting down to business.

Cesar nodded with a smirk. "You guys sure recover from failure quickly."

"A minor complication," Nicholas said.

Cesar assumed a serious demeanor. "What did you have in mind? I can take steps to ensure delivery to you, and for payment to me, but the rest is up to you."

"Why don't we try the same thing?" Nicholas asked. "You can pick a location close to site BORNEO and my pilot will arrive at the same time. Something tells me lightning won't strike twice." He glanced at the cruise ship entering the Canal as his deception plan took shape. "You should give Manuel a heads up to see if he has any information."

"I would ask why you don't just coordinate this with your own government to avoid these problems; but then again, I probably wouldn't like the answer." Cesar grabbed his cell phone, dialed a number, and sipped his beer as he waited. "Hey, it's me. I was thinking TAHITI on Wednesday night. How do things look?"

The cold beer hit the spot as Nicholas admired the scenery around him—palm trees, blue skies, the roar of the ocean, the wind in his hair, and the gentle rocking of the yacht. All things considered, Cesar was living a good life. The absence of a time sheet, the freedom to do what you want, when you want, knowing you had more than enough money to dedicate your time to what interested you, all criminality aside, had a certain appeal.

"Call me back," Cesar said and hung up the phone. "He's looking into it and will let me know later, but it shouldn't be a problem."

"Shall we say same size shipment and same price?" Nicholas asked.

Cesar eyed him and nodded pensively. "You asked me before why an idealistic guerrilla like me would transport drugs. Would you like to know?"

Nicholas sipped his beer and took a deep breath. "Why not?"

"It's gets a little esoteric," Cesar said, "but here it goes. Is it safe to say that you have a good understanding of evolution and Marxist theory?"

Nicholas nodded with a circular gesture to get things moving, assessing that what Cesar was about to say would probably be ridiculous but oddly insightful.

Cesar nodded. "My *raison d'être*, if you will, stems from the premise that a series of genetic mutations long ago severed our link with the subconscious and created certain tribes who enslaved other tribes through violence and oppression."

Nicholas leaned back and prepared for the worst. The Marxists had a peculiar way of concocting phony histories and then viewing them through their own modern lenses to serve their own purposes.

"The problem was the tribes that maintained the link were unwilling to submit to the authority of the violent tribes," Cesar said. "They were bad citizens."

"I thought you said the link was severed?" Nicholas asked.

Cesar nodded slowly. "The genetic mutations affected some tribes more than others, you see. Some tribes maintained the link, mostly through the use of meditation, chanting, or mind-altering substances."

Nicholas sipped his beer and gestured for Cesar to continue. It was always interesting when people tried to argue that regressing to a more primitive stage of existence could be viewed as evolutionary progress.

"The diseased tribes that raped and pillaged to build empires," Cesar continued, "prohibited any drugs that allowed the masses to fuse the link with the subconscious and to tap into the universal consciousness. They also discovered that other drugs were conducive to good citizenship, such as alcohol, caffeine, nicotine, and sugar. These drugs turned the masses into docile, slavish workers."

"I would argue that any responsible and caring government should promote a strong work ethic among the citizenry," Nicholas said, "even if that means prohibiting certain substances in a paternalistic way. Lazy nations tend to die out or become enslaved."

"As a means of national survival," Cesar said without missing a beat, "the program was effective, despite the disastrous effects on the human psyche, evidenced by the explosion of the pharmaceutical industry today. Once nations matured, however, the corrupt leaders decided to profit by selling the bad drugs to the lowest stratum. They made fortunes and created a dependent class of drug addicts."

"Why do you sell drugs if they're so harmful?" Nicholas asked. "And how did we make the transition from tribes to modern nations?"

Cesar chuckled. "I'm beating the corrupt bastards at their own game," he said. "A nation addicted to bad drugs can't survive. With a bunch of drug addicts, the rich bastards won't have anyone to work in their factories. Their fortunes will shrivel, what you call civilization will crumble, and people will return to their natural state." He smiled and sipped his drink. "By destroying civilization, I'm saving humanity."

Nicholas nodded as if intrigued. "Out of curiosity, how many innocent people are you willing to sacrifice for your cause of resurrecting the noble savage?"

Cesar's eyes narrowed. He lifted a finger to speak as Adriana and Maria ascended the stairs in their bikinis with drinks in large plastic cups.

"We came here to get some sun," Maria said, with a wave to Nicholas, which Cesar seemed to notice and didn't seem to like.

"We're not sitting down there another minute," Adriana added.

Cesar gestured to the two lounging chairs. "Enjoy. Just don't bother us while we're discussing business."

Adriana and Maria removed their bikini tops, which Nicholas pretended not to see as he sipped his beer. Their hands caressed their firm bodies with suntan oil until their bronzed skin glistened with the smell of coconut. Pierced bellybuttons adorned their taut abs. Maria's ribs protruded ever so slightly as she inhaled and pulled her silky black hair back in a ponytail. Adriana ran her fingers along the inside of her leopard skin G-string and snapped it into place, tight up into her ass and riding the curve of her hips. As if orchestrating their moves, they slid on sunglasses and sat. Adriana arched her back and shifted her buns to get comfortable. Maria looked up at the sun, adjusted her angle, picked up a copy of *Cosmopolitan*, and flipped through the pages. In unison, they grabbed their tropical drinks in perspiring plastic cups, wrapped their lips around the straws, and sucked. Nicholas and Cesar were hypnotized.

"My feet are sore," Adriana pouted and wiggled her toes.

"What would you like me to do about it, dear?" Cesar asked.

"You could rub her feet, asshole," Maria retorted with another smile to Nicholas. She sipped her drink and returned to her magazine.

"Watch how you speak to me!" Cesar said.

They flipped him off in unison.

"You know I love you," he said nervously, and gestured to Nicholas to suggest he was in control. "You're the loves of my life!"

"You aren't going to rub my feet?" Adriana asked.

Cesar's cell phone rang. He stood to excuse himself and walked to the front of the yacht, standing near Gloria.

"I'm sure Nicholas wouldn't mind," Adriana added. She lowered her sunglasses with an inviting smile.

Nicholas finished his beer casually and slid his chair closer to Adriana. She cast another inviting smile as he approached. He didn't want to appear excited or prudish, rather as someone who treated rubbing the feet of beautiful women as a fine art.

"Finally, a real man," Maria said and returned to her magazine.

Nicholas rubbed oil on his hands and worked his fingers firmly along Adriana's feet, rubbing out knots as beads of sweat dripped down her thighs. She closed her eyes and moaned with clenched fists. Maria lowered her magazine to watch. He rubbed harder with long, firm, smooth strokes. Adriana flinched with pain.

"Behave, Nicholas," Maria said lasciviously.

Nicholas managed intermittent glances at Cesar. He finished talking on the phone and leaned over to talk to Gloria. She was crying. Cesar kissed her on the forehead and caressed her head as she rested it against his chest.

Chapter Twenty-Two

Nicholas arrived at Paitilla Airport as the sun began its descent. The afternoon tropical heat and humidity had blended for a steam room effect. Exhaust sputtering from bumper-to-bumper traffic permeated the air and fed the smog obscuring the skyline.

He entered the terminal. A young woman with chocolate skin and cherry-red lipstick looked up. Her highlighted hair was combed straight and her baby blue uniform was ragged but her eyes effortlessly seduced him with the allure of a Hawaiian Tropic model. He asked her about a pilot named Alfredo, a name he'd obtained from a reliable insider. She gestured outside to a hangar. He grabbed two ice-cold beers from the cooler and left her a five-dollar bill with a friendly wave.

Outside, passengers boarded a small passenger plane while sweating men tossed luggage into the storage bins as another plane sped down the runway and took off. Heat radiated from the baked concrete and simmered the turbid air. Nicholas stopped at the hanger where a man was working on an aircraft engine. A wrench slipped loose and clanked the side of the plane.

"*Carajo!*"

"Sounds like you could use a beer," Nicholas said.

Alfredo slid from under the engine and wiped his brow with a rag. "Thanks," he said and took a swig. "Alfredo," he added and looked at his grimy hands. His cropped hair, manicured hands, and gold crucifix didn't suggest working class.

Nicholas admired the twin-engine aircraft. He had consulted experts from the DEA and U.S. Customs Service to plan this mission, which included identifying someone who was not on anyone's radar. He'd considered the obvious aircraft variables—speed, range, reliability, and so on—but he also looked for a pilot with a good reputation, someone new enough to the business to not attract too much attention.

"That's a beautiful plane," Nicholas said.

Alfredo slapped the wing. "She's a beauty."

Nicholas gestured to the hangar. "Perhaps we could talk in the office."

Alfredo wiped his hands on the rag and led the way.

Tools and aircraft parts cluttered the hangar. Alfredo's cordoned-off spot was modestly organized. An expired calendar hung on the wall, and the digital clock was a few hours behind. Perhaps the G-string-clad Brazilian twins showering under a jungle waterfall from June 1994 had altered his sense of time. Alfredo shoved some papers and folders aside and gestured for Nicholas to sit.

"Do you know anyone with a speedboat on the north coast?" Nicholas asked.

Alfredo nodded. "I have a friend in Puerto Obaldia. What size boat?"

"About thirty-five feet, capable of twenty-five knots and holding at least a ton of goods," Nicholas said, defining the ideal speedboat for moving cocaine in the Caribbean.

Alfredo arched his eyebrows knowingly.

"When can we leave?" Nicholas asked.

"Ready when you are, *jefe*," he said and stood.

"I'll also need you to fly some goods for me tomorrow evening," Nicholas added.

Alfredo sat and cleared his throat. "Goods?"

Nicholas removed a stack of crisp hundred-dollar bills from his pocket and set it on the desk. "That's five thousand dollars for the flight today. You'll get fifty thousand tomorrow and fifty thousand more upon delivery."

Alfredo fingered the cash and nodded.

Alfredo tightened the last bolts and they climbed into the cockpit. Nicholas watched everything Alfredo did to get the plane airborne—

knobs, rudders, switches, throttle, etc.—recalling his own limited flying experience from college.

The flight was smooth and comfortable. At 7,000 feet, Nicholas could see the Atlantic and Pacific Oceans. Grasping the width of Panama in his field of vision helped him appreciate the creation of the Panama Canal. Below was the land the Spanish had traversed during their conquest of the New World. Before genius and technology made the Panama Canal a reality, the Spanish had built a mule trail, *El Camino Real*, to cross the isthmus between old Panama City and Portobelo. Geography was Panama's destiny.

Alfredo gave Nicholas the controls. His flight lessons during college were a distant memory, but it was almost like riding a bike. A feeling of freedom accompanied flying. He tested the stick and rudder to assimilate the plane and soon felt the thrill of the open air. From this perch, the green solitude below looked majestic, a lost world untouched by the forces of history. The mountainous terrain extended to the eastern horizon. Roads and villages spotted the landscape, but there were few signs of human existence. Soon they were over Darien, the forgotten region of Panama, and closing in on San Blas. Alfredo pointed to a coastal village and took the controls. Nicholas prepared for a bumpy landing, but Alfredo managed only minor jerks and pulls as the plane slowed and taxied.

Nicholas hopped out of the plane and fanned the dust from his face. Puerto Obaldia wasn't civilization, more like something from a pirate movie, or one of the many villages he had visited during the 1980s throughout Central America. He half expected to see frantic chickens running loose or burly Spanish conquistadors drinking rum and fighting for the right to sail the next gold shipment home. Reality was less romantic, however. Swarthy men, the kind who could make a living only in a place like this, did inhabit the place, but no gold bullion or Spanish galleons. He cleaned his sunglasses and surveyed the area, keenly aware that he was probably the only white person for many miles.

Alfredo led Nicholas to an open-air cantina near the beach, where they ordered two beers and sat on stools. Nicholas handed the bartender a twenty-dollar bill. The bartender smiled and grabbed two dripping bottles of beer from an ice-filled cooler and whacked a fly with a towel.

His Jamaican laugh bellowed. Nicholas turned when he felt the weight of many eyes; caught staring, the stolid customers looked away and returned to their drinks.

"Is your friend here?" Nicholas asked.

Alfredo gestured to the beach. "He's over there."

Alfredo swigged his beer and strolled to the dock as Nicholas waited behind to watch. The bartender grabbed some crumpled bills from a cigar box and set them on the bar. Nicholas grabbed the change and left a generous tip. The bartender nodded and pocketed the money.

Alfredo whistled and waved him over. Nicholas gave the bartender five dollars for three more beers and walked to the dock.

I'll be damned, Nicholas thought when he saw Charlie. His old friend was sitting under a palm tree near the pristine white sand beach and turquoise water. He wore a pair of knee-length denim cutoffs, no shirt, and no shoes. His black hair was wavy, his teeth white as polished ivory, his body toned. Charlie hadn't changed in ten years.

"Charlie?" Nicholas said and waved.

Charlie shielded his eyes from the sun and rushed over when he recognized him. "Mr. Nicholas, yesiree!" he said and embraced him. "Long time no see!"

"Too long," Nicholas said. "I hear you have a boat."

Charlie nodded and pointed to a swank speedboat moored to the dock.

"How would you like to work for me again?" he asked and clapped him on the shoulder.

"Charlie always ready to work for old friend."

Nicholas paused and shook his head in disbelief. Of all the places in the world, he met an old friend here—Charlie, no less. Charlie had been reliable, cheap, and took risks, the perfect person to help the CIA.

"How are you keeping busy these days?" Nicholas asked.

Charlie pointed at a wooden crate covered with an olive tarp. "I have my own transportation business," he said and led the way. "You taught me well." He lifted the tarp and slapped the crate, then grabbed a crowbar and pried open the lid. "These look familiar, no?" He removed an AK-47 from the protective wood shavings.

Nicholas inspected the rifle. "I'll be damned," he said, recognizing the AK-47 model they had transported during the 1980s to help the various

U.S.-supported militant groups fight the communists throughout the region. Weapons had been cached throughout Central America, with many of them left behind after the fighting stopped. Charlie would have known where to find them. Now he was selling them, probably to the FARC guerrillas in Colombia. Nicholas appreciated the irony but couldn't concern himself with it now. "You're delivering these today?" he asked. Charlie nodded. "Any chance you could bring back some goods for me?"

"Charlie ready to work. But Charlie not cheap like before."

Nicholas handed him a map. "My men will be here," he said and pointed at the "X" northeast of Riohacha, Colombia. "I'll confirm with a coordinate. After they load your boat, return here and give the goods to Alfredo."

Charlie looked at Alfredo and nodded. "I return tomorrow."

Nicholas handed Charlie $5,000 in hundred-dollar bills. "That's for the trip today. You'll get ten thousand more tomorrow when you deliver the goods."

Charlie looked at Alfredo.

"Don't load his plane until you get paid," Nicholas added.

"I'll give him the money," Alfredo protested.

"And then Charlie will give you the goods," Nicholas said. Trust everyone, but always cut the deck—honor among thieves. "Do we have a deal?"

"Deal," Charlie said. He led Nicholas and Alfredo back to the cantina and slapped the bar. "A special drink for my friend," he said.

The Jamaican laugh returned as the bartender grabbed a corked ceramic jug.

"Do you remember the wacky juice?" Charlie asked.

Nicholas nodded, unable to restrain a grin. He and Charlie had imbibed many moonshine recipes throughout Central America. Each recipe had induced a unique buzz and hangover sequence worthy of tall tales.

"My friend has a special blend," Charlie continued and set one hundred dollars on the bar. "Nothing like you've ever experienced."

The bartender uncorked the jug and filled three glasses with the urine-colored hooch. They toasted to old times. Nicholas downed the drink and looked out at the Caribbean Sea as the alcohol burned his throat. The effect was immediate, a tranquil buzz as the hooch rushed to his brain. He embraced Charlie. For the first time since his arrival in Panama, he really felt like he was back in the game.

The bartender snatched the cash and laughed before refilling the three glasses. Charlie grabbed the jug and led the way to the beach. Nicholas sat under a palm tree. The wacky juice was spectacular, embodying the heat of the glazed pottery and slippery on his tongue.

Nicholas laughed as he absorbed more of the alcohol. A rush of adrenaline, long sublimated, energized him as he thought about working for K again, about the certain success of operation Delphi Justice, about his membership to the Order. Of course he wanted to be a member! He was tired of sitting at a desk all day and narrating world events to the senior leadership, who more often than not already knew what they planned to do. He wanted to be a player, to have a piece of the action. This was his opportunity.

Nicholas filled his glass again and walked to the shore alone. He blinked to focus and stood in awe before the mighty body of water. White-capped waves crashed toward him like monsters in a nightmare. The salty air roused his nose. The rhythmic waves calmed him. He closed his eyes and felt the wind blowing in his hair and the soft cotton of his T-shirt caressing his skin. He reached down, scooped up a pile of hot powdery sand, and felt the grains trickling between his fingers. A cool, swirling breeze chilled his skin as he turned and admired the sun dropping on the silhouetted jungle. He dropped to his knees and dug deeper, to the cool, moist sand, and shuddered as he experienced the direct flow of sensory data. He took a deep breath, humbly, reverently, amid the flurry of raw sensations. A tear trickled down his cheek as he fathomed his new lease on life. Slowly, he opened his eyes. He finished his drink and walked back toward Charlie and Alfredo, who were sitting under the palm tree.

"Charlie, this stuff is amazing!" Nicholas yelled and returned for more. When the soft sand under his feet gave way to the hardened ground near the palm tree roots, the piercing sound of an incoming rocket-propelled grenade alerted him to dive for cover.

"Take cover!" Charlie yelled. He grabbed Nicholas and Alfredo and pulled them closer to the wooden crate as sand rained on them from the explosion.

A uniformed soldier standing in the bow of the boat lifted his weapon and fired another rocket-propelled grenade.

"Incoming!" Nicholas yelled and huddled with Charlie and Alfredo. The explosion hit the cantina. The villagers fled in all directions.

Nicholas grabbed Charlie. "What the hell's going on?"

"The Colombian paramilitary doesn't like Charlie's customers," he said and handed each of them a rifle. "Here," he added and dispensed loaded magazines.

Nicholas slammed the clip in and loaded the chamber. "You two swing around back," he said and gestured. "I'll cover this side."

Charlie nodded confidently. Alfredo kissed his crucifix. Nicholas slapped them on the back. They hustled away.

Nicholas took cover behind the crate. The boat engine stopped as the aluminum hull scraped the sand. Boots splashed in the water as militants ran ashore, chasing and firing at the fleeing residents. The sound of gunfire echoed in Nicholas' mind as he gripped his AK-47. His refusal to launch a pre-emptive attack against a village in El Salvador once had resulted in the deaths of some of his soldiers, but he would fight this battle. He wouldn't let his men die this time. With a jolt of clarity and focus, he pivoted from behind the crate and aimed. A militant spotted him and raised his weapon, but not before Nicholas fired two shots, hitting him square in the chest. Bullets sprayed from his automatic weapon as he fell to the ground.

The remaining militants took cover behind a jeep. Every few seconds one exposed himself to fire at Charlie and Alfredo, who were firing back from behind the cantina. Charlie and Alfredo probably didn't have enough ammunition to fight much longer. Nicholas aimed at one of the militants and fired a headshot. The militant next to him turned and lifted his weapon to shoot, but not before Nicholas fired two rounds into his chest. The remaining two, seeing Nicholas, dashed toward the cantina and fired back at him.

Nicholas pursued them along the cantina wall, swinging his weapon in both directions. Behind the cantina, the militants were yelling at Charlie and Alfredo, vowing to kill anyone who helped the FARC terrorists in Colombia. When the militants loaded the chambers of their weapons, Charlie and Alfredo begged for their lives. Nicholas quickened his pace and stopped at the back corner. After a mental count of three, he pivoted and unleashed hell. The two militants fell dead, but blood was oozing from Nicholas' left arm. A warm sensation permeated his body. He struggled to stay conscious, but the world slowly turned black as he collapsed.

Chapter Twenty-Three

In the plush Presidential Palace conference room, Minister of Foreign Affairs Victor Hernandez rubbed his stiff neck—his punishment for sleeping on the couch. He needed all his wits about him. The last meeting with the IMF officials had demonstrated that his vision for economic change in Panama was the right one; this meeting would show that maintaining a U.S. military presence in Panama post-1999 was the best option.

"Good afternoon," Colonel Lance Dupree said from the podium and gestured to both delegations. "President Mendoza, First Vice President Romero, Minister Hernandez, based on your request to address the issue of maintaining U.S. military bases in Panama post-1999, I've assembled a panel of experts."

"On behalf of the Republic of Panama," President Mendoza said, "welcome and thank you. The twenty-first century is a crossroads. One of the most important issues we must address is the possibility of maintaining the presence of U.S. soldiers and bases on our sovereign territory post-1999. We look forward to hearing your ideas."

"I've read their assessment," Colonel Dupree said. "I'm sure you won't be disappointed." He gestured to a lanky lad with thick glasses.

Lanky Lad pushed up his glasses and flipped to the second page of a report. "I'll begin with an easy one, gentlemen, the Panama Canal. Article Four of the 1977 Treaty Concerning the Permanent Neutrality and Operation of the Panama Canal says that the U.S. and Panama agree to maintain the regime of neutrality in order that the Canal shall remain permanently neutral."

Antonio chuckled. "Article Five says that only the Republic of Panama shall maintain military forces within its national territory. Any attempt to go against that would be a blatant violation of the treaty."

Here we go again, Victor groaned to himself. Antonio obviously had his mind set on embarrassing Panama, yet again.

"There's nothing in the treaty that prohibits a superseding agreement," Lanky Lad countered. "A lot has changed since 1977."

"Except that any changes would require approval by the Legislative Assembly and a plebiscite," Antonio said. "The Assembly will never approve—"

"Gentlemen," Victor said, "perhaps we could first have a philosophical discussion about *why* Panama would benefit from maintaining U.S. military bases post-1999. We can worry about the legalities later." He ended his comment with an extended glare at Antonio, joined by President Mendoza.

Lanky Lad tugged his collar nervously. "I have no fantasies about a conventional military attack on the Canal," he said, "but I would offer a business analogy: the customer is always right. Research indicates that private companies consider the U.S. military presence vital for Canal security. Companies plan for the long term, and any negative adjustment to their income statements to account for future projected accidents or other problems with the Canal might convince them to take their business elsewhere. You can't overlook the competitive advantage of having the unconditional backing of the U.S. military."

Amen, Victor thought and cringed when Antonio lifted a finger.

"We Panamanians could respond to any emergency on our own, thank you very much," Antonio said. "We're proud of our Canal," he added confidently.

Lanky Lad shook his head. "Businesses won't give you a second chance. They have options. You don't. You should assume a preventative, forward-thinking mindset."

President Mendoza gestured to Lanky Lad. "Excellent point. Be proactive. Panama should move in that direction."

Antonio shook his head. "We're betraying our own people. I will not allow this to stand, even if it means losing the election."

"Your report documents your research?" Victor asked.

Lanky Lad nodded confidently.

"Sounds like a solid assessment based on credible data," Victor added as Antonio grumbled to himself and clenched his fists.

"As the colonial creator of Panama," Lanky Lad added, reading word for word from an index card, "the world perceives our presence—"

All eyes clamped on him. He squirmed as the room fell silent.

"What I meant to say was…was that in the beginning—"

"In the beginning," Antonio said, "you shoved the 1903 treaty down our throats and sucked Panama dry. You have oppressed us and made a fortune without giving us a cent. We have fought for our independence and we will soon be free. No troops in Panama!"

Even Victor was shocked by Lanky Lad's effrontery.

Lanky Lad flipped his index card. "First, the Canal has been a nonprofit entity. U.S. tax dollars paid for the deficit years. Second, we paid you a stipend every year, even when the Canal lost money. Third, the 1903 treaty is what gave you your independence from Colombia. No one complained about U.S. troops helping you gain independence."

"The treaty was a national humiliation," Antonio said.

Lanky Lad shrugged. "Blame it on the people who signed it."

"You pricks are so damned proud of building the Canal," Antonio continued. "In case you were not aware, it was not your idea to build the Canal."

"Of course we're proud," Lanky Lad said. "And in case you were not aware, ideas did not build the Canal—we did, with genius and the sweat of our brow."

President Mendoza cleared his throat. "Gentlemen, I think we took a wrong turn," he said calmly to subdue the tension, but turned to Lanky Lad. "For your information, young man, the people who signed the treaty did not represent the interests of all Panamanians. I think we can all agree that the 1903 treaty granted you excessive rights and benefits."

"I suggest we move on," Victor said, distressed by the president's comment. His own grandfather had signed the treaty as an important first step in the nation's history. The signatories had had two options: approve the treaty or condemn Panama to perpetual poverty. The initial attempt to build a canal by the French had failed miserably; the Americans were the last and only option. People loved sausage, but no one wanted to see how it was made.

"Indeed, let's move on," Colonel Dupree said, "but let's also please stick to the agenda." He gestured to the next man, a bitter-looking middle-aged man with a facial tic and acne scars.

Bitter Man tapped his pen dramatically. "Drugs [tap], drugs [tap], and more drugs [tap]. It's an ugly war." He arched his eyebrows, again, dramatically, and looked up as if concluding a public service announcement about drug abuse. "My associate mentioned the perception of security. Now let's talk about reality."

The tendons on his neck tightened like bowstrings as his facial tic put his remarks on hold. He opened his report, cleared his throat, and licked his finger to turn the page. "Let's discuss a little thing called the war on drugs."

Victor had had enough of this guy. *Could we please get to the point?* He looked around the room. No one seemed captivated by Bitter Man's histrionics.

Bitter Man tapped his temple. "Reason, not instinct, ought to guide our actions. Without reason, we are beasts; with it, we are noble." He tapped his heart. "We fight a battle every day, but you won't see it on CNN or read about it in the *New York Times*. The battle is between your virtue and the beast. What your virtue takes a lifetime to build the beast can destroy with a single swipe of the claw." He paused for a facial-tic relapse, perhaps remembering his own fateful wound. "Don't let irresponsible people tell you that drug use is a matter of personal choice. That's a cop-out. Drugs destroy our children's capacity to think, and many people go beyond the point of return before they realize their errors." He cleared his throat. "Ever since Noriega ruled, Panama has been a hub for drug shipments. Drug use is on the rise in Panama, and your families are feeling the pain. Maintaining U.S. military bases in Panama post-1999, gentlemen, is the only way to fight this battle."

This guy has serious issues. Victor looked at the others' blank expressions. The American representatives were not what he had hoped for, not the

A team, but he had to make the best of the situation. "I doubt anyone disagrees that drugs are a problem." Pain attacked him from opposite sides as he thought about Helena and Cesar. He knew better than anyone the kind of damage drugs could do to people and their families. "In fact, I think we should use the recent successful operation against Cesar Gomez as a prime example," he added and turned to Antonio. "The Americans coordinated that successful strike from Panama."

Colonel Dupree managed a subtle wink to Victor. "Yes, indeed. Without our JIATF-South operation center, Panama would be a sitting duck. We need a safe place to launch and control our aircraft that is close to the fight."

"I think we agree on this point," Antonio said, "and yes I was fully aware of the success we had against Cesar Gomez, which I applaud, but I detected an accusatory tone. Are you suggesting that Panama is to blame for *your* drug problem? Because as I recall, Noriega was on the CIA's payroll—"

"Not to sell drugs," Bitter Man said condescendingly. "Let's not start a revisionist debate about Operation JUST CAUSE. Ten years ago, the people of Panama, over 90 percent, considered the operation a liberation of Panama. Now you label it an invasion?"

"Thousands of Panamanians were killed," Antonio said.

"Good U.S. soldiers died as well," Bitter Man said and jabbed an accusing finger. "Don't dishonor their names with petty appeals based on hindsight. We fought the battle the best we could and got results. All remnants of the dictatorship are gone. For all practical purposes, Panama is a healthy democracy."

"Excuse me," Victor said, asserting himself, "but I think everyone agrees that stopping drugs is important." He still had mixed feelings about the 1989 invasion. The attack had been necessary to purge Noriega and the military junta, but the Americans assisted Noriega's rise to power and used excessive military force during the invasion. Stealth fighters? "Let's not waste our energy fighting about this issue," he added and gestured to Colonel Dupree.

Colonel Dupree nodded. "We all feel strongly about stopping drugs. Now for the last point." He gestured to the third expert, an overweight man with smoke-stained teeth.

169

Yellow Teeth rubbed his stubby hands and flashed an uninviting smile. "Cash, gentlemen, money." He leaned back and lifted two fingers. "One, maintaining a U.S. military presence post-1999 will bring money and jobs. Granted, we're not talking the same money as 1990, when we had several military bases in Panama, but money and jobs nonetheless, especially for maids, laborers, and hey, let's be honest, hookers." He leaned forward with a cheesy grin and rested his clasped hands on the table. Only the Americans seemed to appreciate the humor. Even Antonio didn't smile. "Two, and more important, is economic security."

Now we're finally getting somewhere, Victor thought.

"U.S. soldiers," Yellow Teeth continued, "regardless of the number, create a comfort zone for foreign companies. I've talked to many business leaders who have told me that continuing to do business in Panama would hinge on two things: first, the continued use of the U.S. dollar; and second, the stability provided by the U.S. military."

"Amen," Victor said, relieved that someone was finally talking dollars and sense. "Asking American troops to leave is tantamount to asking foreign companies to leave with them. I honestly cannot believe we are even having this discussion."

Antonio groaned. "Who needs them? With the right tools, proud Panamanians can rebuild this country."

He just doesn't get it, Victor thought and shook his head. It never ceased to amaze him how these Marxists could memorize dogmatic talking points and find ways to squeeze them into every discussion, regardless of the context.

"Let's be honest," Yellow Teeth continued. "Your wealthy families want U.S. troops to stay as well. The money they invest in Panama accounts for many jobs. At the first sign of trouble, many of them will pack their bags and leave with their money."

"Now wait a minute," Victor said, "you have no right to make accusations like that. I would never pack my bags and leave, nor would my friends." He realized only too late that his remarks would only work against him—class warfare, us versus them, and so on. "We take great pride in Panama," he added. The fickle masses had no idea how much their relative wellbeing depended on the people they castigated so freely.

Antonio laughed and clapped. "Now look who's getting defensive. Where were you before the invasion? Funny how you took an extended vacation and closed out all your bank accounts a few days before the Americans froze all the other accounts."

"I was on Christmas vacation," Victor said and swallowed hard when he remembered how his banking friends had urged him to empty his accounts and take an extended vacation, which only now seemed like an unfair advantage. Perhaps he had taken advantage of the situation, but Antonio's remark was out of line, a complete embarrassment. What did he know about running a country? Did he risk his own capital to start businesses and create jobs? "This isn't the proper forum to discuss this," he said and flipped through the report. He refused to feel guilty for being wealthy.

"I apologize," Yellow Teeth said. "I was merely pointing out that capital flight could be a problem."

"Point well taken," Antonio said and grinned.

Oh, go get drunk and beat your wife, Victor thought.

Antonio continued: "How unfortunate that we have to worry about our own people removing wealth from Panama, considering that Panamanian society is what provided them the opportunity to earn their wealth in the first place."

Victor tapped his pen and shook his head derisively as he glanced at President Mendoza. As was the case with the last meeting, this one had degenerated into a one-sided attack against wealth. People could be so ungrateful. Many of his friends had studied at foreign universities and returned to rebuild Panama after the invasion. Some made millions in the process, but they put the protesting masses back to work and helped rebuild the country one brick at a time.

"I believe that completes our discussion," President Mendoza said. "Gentlemen, I would like to thank you again for your time and ideas."

"Mr. President, perhaps we should tell them our intentions," Victor said.

President Mendoza nodded and sat up. "I believe that maintaining a U.S. military presence post-1999 is the best option for Panama. I intend to approve the agreement."

"Mr. President," Antonio gasped, "the treaty doesn't give you the authority! That would require approval by the Legislative Assembly and a plebiscite."

"My lawyers will review the agreement tomorrow," President Mendoza said to the smiling Americans, ignoring Antonio. "With overwhelming public support, the Legislative Assembly will have to approve it. The plebiscite will be an easy victory."

"What about the clause for *other operations?*" Antonio asked.

"What *about* the clause for other operations?" President Mendoza replied.

Antonio pounded the table. "That clause gives them the right to stage covert operations out of Panama, even *within* Panama. Do we really want the reputation as the only country in Latin America that supports U.S. imperialistic objectives?"

"Imperialistic objectives?" Colonel Dupree said and laughed. "I haven't heard that phrase for decades." The think-tank buddies chuckled appreciatively. "Let's not beat around the bush here, gentlemen. That clause authorizes us to conduct covert operations— attacking drug labs, things like that. Don't get any crazy fantasies about funding guerrilla groups or insurgencies. Those days are over."

Lanky Lad cleared his throat and pushed up his glasses. "Consider this: you have a problem with Colombian insurgents along your eastern border. In fact, paramilitary forces recently attacked Puerto Obaldia and killed several Panamanians."

President Mendoza gasped, obviously unaware. Victor wasn't about to ask how Lanky Lad knew about the attack, but his brief experience with the CIA had taught him that the safe bet was to assume they knew everything.

"Some day," Lanky Lad continued, "you might need our help to resolve a problem like that. We would like to help, but without that clause, such assistance would be impossible."

Bitter Man tapped his pen. "It's a dangerous world out there. We have to fight some ugly battles. We're offering what most countries can only dream of: an alliance."

Yellow Teeth rubbed his hands and added his two cents. "And don't forget, these operations cost bucks."

Colonel Dupree rested his elbows on the table. He rubbed his hands as if molding a lump of clay. Victor was amazed how authoritative he looked and sounded—no fear or reverence, even sitting next to President Mendoza. "I've talked to our people at the highest levels in Washington, gentlemen. This point isn't negotiable. The agreement contains the clause for other operations or the agreement is null and void."

"In that case," President Mendoza said, "let's act soon." He rapped his knuckles on the table to signal the end of the meeting.

Victor held his chest as he walked down the hall, taking the most direct route to the side exit where his car was waiting. What had started out as a cough had grown into throbbing chest pain. He couldn't speak to anyone in this condition, especially not the press. Unfortunately, a secretary near the side exit stopped him and said a man was waiting to see him with urgent information. He reluctantly followed her to an office where Manuel Espinosa was sitting.

"I had to see you," Manuel said and shook his hand after the secretary closed the door.

"This isn't a good place to meet," Victor said. "Why do you have to see me now?"

"I have information about Cesar's next shipment," Manuel said and handed him a folded piece of paper. "I thought it would be best to avoid cell phone communication."

Victor unfolded the paper to read the words, "Wednesday," "11:00 p.m.," "TAHITI," and a coordinate written below it. He started to cough again and held his chest.

"You want me to call a doctor, old man?" Manuel asked.

Victor shook his head as the pain subsided. "Good work," he said. "Go."

Manuel held his arm and assessed him, nodded, and then discreetly left the office. Victor took a few breaths to give Manuel a chance to get away, and then stood and slowly made his way to the side entrance.

Outside, scores of people were carrying protest signs and walking in a circle. They chanted, "Gringos go home!"

Victor held his chest and stumbled as a sharp pain rippled through his heart. The people in the crowd screamed when he collapsed.

Chapter Twenty-Four

Nicholas opened his eyes to see Lina on top of him, moaning ecstatically. The flickering candlelight cast shadows on her smooth, delicate skin as he caressed her. Her passion spent, she collapsed and kissed his chest, gasping for air.

"That was amazing," she said.

"You were amazing," Nicholas said, bathing in the afterglow. He kissed her forehead and surveyed the room as she pulled the white sheet over their bodies and nestled her cheek against his chest. To conceal his snooping, he pointed at a travel agency poster of Anguilla on the wall. "Have you been there?"

"My friend took a vacation there last year—heaven on earth. What about you?"

"No, but I've been to the Caribbean," he said. "Looks beautiful," he added. "Maybe we could take a trip there after all this is done." He was finding it surprisingly difficult to continue this act of manipulation.

She nodded and kissed him on the lips.

He kissed her back. "We could hang out on the beach, sip some rum, and solve the world's problems." His own playful words surprised him.

She smiled and kissed him again with an innocent smile.

Lina amazed him—no apparent bitterness against "the system," yet probably struggling each day to make ends meet in a world ruled by male chauvinism, refusing to sell out, and no obsessive drive to climb the social ladder to live like the Hernandez family. The pursuit of the truth seemed to be her ambrosia. Unfortunately, however, her aggressive journalism had led her to a story that simply couldn't be published, no matter how he felt about her.

He sat up to look at the digital alarm clock on the nightstand. "We missed the concert."

"I'm glad we missed the concert," she said and sat up with him. "Guess what?" she asked enthusiastically and slapped him on the arm.

He cringed and held his arm as his stomach churned and his vision blurred. The bullet wound was still raw.

"I'm so sorry!" she said and kissed his arm.

Nicholas opened his eyes slowly and took a deep breath. The bullet had passed through his triceps cleanly, so there were only a few stitches, but he told her it was from a previous surgery, which he assessed she didn't believe.

"Guess what?" she asked again and kissed his chest. "I wrote the story today, the one about President Mendoza receiving drug money. Can you believe it?"

Nicholas didn't have to feign surprise—*really?*

"I tried to find more information to corroborate my story," she continued, "but I decided what I had was sufficient. I had to write the story before the referendum. Isn't that great?"

He hugged her to hide his lack of enthusiasm. Convincing her to not write the story was the first step, but this unexpected development would trigger actions he had hoped to avoid.

She leaned back and looked at him with the same enthusiastic smile. "The story will be on the front page tomorrow!"

"I thought you were worried about getting in trouble," he said, fully aware that he was now thinking about her safety as much as mission accomplishment.

"Not anymore," she said. "At some point, every journalist has to take a stand. At a minimum, the president will have to offer an explanation. Just the possibility of corruption will ruin his chance of winning the referendum."

He groaned conspicuously and rubbed his temples.

"What's wrong?" she asked.

He sighed as if reluctant to be honest. "I get the impression you want the president to lose this referendum regardless of the truth." At this point, arguing the reporters' creed was his last hope—to save her and the mission. "I thought journalists were supposed to report the facts and let the people decide. Aren't you manipulating public opinion if your stated goal is to make him lose the referendum?"

"I have evidence," she said defensively. "The people deserve to know the truth, especially before the referendum this Sunday."

Journalists believed people deserved things like the truth, which sounded sincere and less like a sound bite coming from her.

"Have you given the president a chance to comment?" he asked. "Perhaps you could talk to Minister Hernandez first?" He kissed her before she could respond. "Look, I'm happy for you, but I'm also worried about how much trust you're placing in this so-called proof. Are you willing to risk your career?"

She suddenly looked concerned.

"He is the president. You can publish the story on Friday or Saturday after you have more proof or give the government a chance to comment. Even better, you can publish it after the referendum. That way, you'll have more time to do research to back your claim before the actual election." He touched her cheek. "As your friend, as someone who thinks of you as more than a friend," he added with a kiss on the lips to watch her smile, "I think you should consider canceling the story—tonight."

She pursed her lips and shook her head. "I can't do that. The proof I have is sufficient or at least demands an explanation." She smiled and nodded confidently. "It's all about choices, Nicholas. The story will hit the streets tomorrow."

The decision was probably irreversible, anyway. The *El Tiempo* editors were probably sipping champagne as the story rolled through the printer.

"Are you hungry?" he asked to change the tone, as he took a deep breath to prepare to do what had to be done. She nodded. "Let's get something to eat." He spanked her playfully. "Take a shower, and I'll call for a reservation."

She wrapped herself in a sheet and stood to walk to the bathroom, stopping in the doorway to look back. The hallway light cast a resplendent glow on her curves. "I have to wash and dry my hair, so this could take some time—lady stuff. Feel free to read the newspaper or help yourself to something in the fridge."

"Take your time," he said and forced a smile, ready to act. She could always rescue her career or find a new job, but this was the last chance the U.S. government had to maintain a military presence in Panama post-1999. He wouldn't allow his feelings to get in the way of national security.

She closed the bathroom door and started the shower. He dressed quickly and rummaged through the dresser, the bookshelf, and the closet, carefully reading each piece of paper. Finally, while flipping through a pile of jeans in her closet, he found a manila folder. His heart raced as he grabbed it and flipped it open. The contents surprised him. The pages, printed on the fine linen letterhead of Enterprise Associates, had specific names: Cesar Gomez and President Mendoza. Fortunately, there was nothing on the documents linking the financial transactions to the CIA or the U.S. government. The documents were obviously from Enterprise Associates at the World Trade Center, which raised disturbing questions about how Lina had obtained them. She had sufficient proof all right: wire transfers connecting all the relevant parties. This evidence could torpedo operation Delphi Justice. And if she or anyone learned the true identity of Enterprise Associates, all hell would break lose.

He dialed Dylan's cell phone number. "Red alert," he said at a whisper. "Meet me outside the Pavo Real right away." He ended the call, took a deep breath, finished getting dressed, and then knocked on the bathroom door and poked his head inside to see a cloud of steam above the shower. "Lina," he said, "Unfortunately, I have to go."

She slid the shower curtain along the steel rod and poked her head out with a smile. "Is something wrong?"

"A work emergency," he said. "I'm really sorry, but I'll call you later."

"Nicholas," she said. "Bye."

He waved as he felt a lump in his throat. "Bye."

He felt a thorn in his heart as he closed the door and imagined Lina standing under the warm water without a negative thought in her mind. He took a deep breath and tucked the folder under his arm as he left the apartment.

* * *

Nicholas parked outside El Pavo Real, an English pub in the banking district between Via España and Calle 50. Dylan was leaning against the driver's door of his maroon Mercedes Benz puffing a cigarette to orange brilliance. Nicholas grabbed the folder and stepped outside. The old eighties thrill returned as he waved the folder and walked briskly toward Dylan. Music escaped from the bar when the front door opened, but the dead-end street was quiet, and the evening air had dropped to the pleasant low seventies.

"You got the documents?" Dylan asked curtly.

Nicholas nodded—*Nice to see you, too*—and handed him the folder. "I took them from her apartment a few minutes ago."

Dylan inspected them and smiled. He tossed his cigarette to the street and crushed it under his tasseled loafer with a twisting motion. "How did you manage that?"

"We were…together," Nicholas said.

Dylan arched his eyebrows, impressed.

"We're going to have one upset Latina on our hands, though," Nicholas added.

"Why?" Dylan asked.

"She sent the story to the press tonight," he said. "Front page story for *El Tiempo* tomorrow morning."

Dylan groaned. "Shit. We'll have to do damage control and convince President Mendoza that she's an angry journalist with an axe to grind. The good news is she can't trace Enterprise Associates to us. Without this proof, however, without the original documents," he added, "she might be in big trouble—libel, perhaps jail."

"And she knows this," Nicholas said.

Dylan nodded with a smidgen of compassion. "But hey, good work."

Nicholas thought about it. "She'll be pissed."

"What can she do?" Dylan asked. "She can't prove you took these documents."

"Yes, well," Nicholas said, aware that he needed to give the appearance of having no emotional involvement, "hell hath no fury, right?" he added with a smile.

Dylan acknowledged his point. "We would be in deep shit if she exposed these documents. These are the financial records from Tyler's first two shipments."

"That's what concerns me," Nicholas said, finally getting down to business and remembering that it was Dylan who speculated that Lina had written the anonymous editorial. "How did she get these documents? The only people working at Enterprise Associates are Jessica and Nash. I assume you've spoken with them."

"We have," Dylan said. "We're confident they didn't do it."

"So who took the documents?" Nicholas asked, and the conclusion suddenly became clear as he assessed Dylan's suggestive tilt of the head. "Tyler?"

Dylan looked down and nodded. "We believe Lina got the documents from him. You probably know that Tyler and Lina were an item before he met Helena. To be clear, we don't know why he took the documents or how Lina got them, but Tyler took them—stole them. I chose to not tell you this initially because I wasn't sure how you would react."

Nicholas stood tall and looked around, trying to process all the information. "I never saw this coming," he said and paused. "On a lighter note, I'm running the deception plan. I asked Cesar to arrange another shipment from the Guajira Peninsula, which he passed to Manuel Espinosa, but I actually hired a boat to pick up the goods in Colombia and transport them to a pilot who will be waiting in Puerto Obaldia—"

"Puerto Obaldia!" Dylan exclaimed and looked around cautiously. "I heard about the attack. Were you there?"

Nicholas rolled up his sleeve to reveal the wound. "Caught in the crossfire. Sorry for not telling you, but I've been scrambling with this diversion plan."

Dirk winced. "No problem."

Nicholas continued: "The boat captain is our old friend Charlie."

Dirk chuckled. "Charlie? Holy shit!"

"Turns out he's running AK-47s to the FARC in Colombia, the guns we moved years ago to fight communism. Irony aside, the Colombian AUC found out and attacked him to sever his logistics line. Luckily, we won the fight."

"I'm always amazed when these guys who used to work for us back in the day resurface," Dylan said. "Some of them go legitimate, but others find clever ways to profit from the skills we taught them." He stood as tall as nature would allow, signaling the discussion was complete. "Great work," he said. "I'm so glad I selected you for this operation. Your membership vote for the Order will be a slam dunk."

"I like the sound of that," Nicholas said. A painful image of Lina taking a shower flashed in his mind as they shook hands.

"Let's get that deception plan rolling," Dylan said.

Dylan looked pleased and relieved when he sat in his car and closed the door. He set the folder on the passenger seat, slapped it, and gave a thumbs-up before driving away.

Nicholas waved back and dialed his cell phone. "Cesar," he said, "we have to make some last-minute adjustments to the original plan. And whatever you do, do not tell anyone about these changes. Are you ready to copy?"

Chapter Twenty-Five

Captain Price stood before the spread of telephones, radios, and computers holding a piece of paper. "Listen up everybody," he said as the room fell silent and everyone turned to listen, "we're once again fortunate enough to possess a precise piece of intelligence that will help us destroy another cocaine shipment owned by Cesar Gomez. You all know what you're supposed to do. If you don't, please stop by to see me immediately," he added with one clap. "Let's do this."

He grabbed the radio and cleared his throat. "Magic Zero One, Magic Zero Two, you are cleared to take off, destination TAHITI, how copy?"

"Magic Zero One copies."

"Magic Zero Two copies."

Captain Price turned to Bruce Devlin and gave the thumbs-up. Bruce returned the gesture and put on his headphones to get down to business. Moments later, two blue dots appeared on the digital map on the computer monitor, taking off from Barranquilla, Colombia, and heading northeast to the Guajira Peninsula.

Colonel Vasquez entered the floor and approached Captain Price.

"Perfect timing," Captain Price said. "The two Citations just launched. The last I heard, the two A-37s are ready to launch as well."

Colonel Vasquez nodded. "I just spoke with my commander in Bogota. Both planes have already been cleared to launch."

"Sir," Master Sergeant Higgins said and pointed at the computer monitor displaying two more blue dots, "we just got confirmation of take-off for the A-37s."

Captain Price gave a fist bump to Colonel Vasquez, "This will be like shooting fish in a bucket." Colonel Vasquez looked confused. "*Como disparando los peces en un...*we should have no problem stopping this shipment tonight."

Colonel Vasquez smiled. "I understand shooting fish in a bucket."

Staff Sergeant Collins exited the intelligence vault and handed Captain Price a report with a map. "Sir, for what it's worth, some of our other sources are reporting new activity—a boat going from the north coast of Colombia to Panama."

"I appreciate the information," Captain Price said and handed the report to Colonel Vasquez, "but if I've learned anything from this job it's that we have to stay focused. I'm not in the business of chasing bright, shiny objects. We have four planes en route to what appears to be a sure thing, so let's not mess it up."

Staff Sergeant Collins nodded. "I just wanted you to know for your situational awareness. We can't corroborate it, but Cesar Gomez might have changed the plan."

"We'll know soon enough when our planes arrive at the airstrip," Captain Price said and paused to think about it, hoping this wouldn't be one of those *in hindsight* issues. "Even the drug traffickers have a hard time with last-minute changes. Can you imagine the security risk of moving this stuff to the coast?"

No one seemed to disagree with Captain Price's logic, which was comforting.

Colonel Vasquez gestured to the map. "We have reports that FARC guerrillas received a shipment of AK-47s in this location. For the safety of our pilots, we would want to steer clear of that area. In order to strafe airplanes on a runway or boats in the sea, they have to descend to within small-arms range."

Captain Price raised his hands to suggest *well that settles it.* "However, just to be on the safe side," he said, the *in hindsight* mantra throbbing in the back of his head, and grabbed the radio. "Key West, we just received a report about a possible vessel moving from the north coast of Colombia to Panama. All of our air assets are tied up with TAHITI. Do you have any available air assets to conduct a search?"

"Negative," the man on the radio said. "We currently have no air assets that can be launched at this time."

"Good copy," Captain Price said and set down the radio and turned to everyone. "If a boat is indeed moving a load of cocaine to Panama, this is his lucky day. We could tell the Panamanians, but without a specific location, they'll never find it."

"Let's do this," Colonel Dupree said with a loud clap as he entered the ops floor. "How are we looking?"

Captain Price gestured to the computer screen, where the four blue dots were closing in on a point marked "T" for TAHITI. "Sir, all four planes are en route and should be there any minute. We got a report about a boat going from the north coast of Colombia to Panama—"

"Not interested," Colonel Dupree said.

"I only mention it," Captain Price continued, "because one of the reports seems to suggest that Cesar Gomez might have had a last-minute change of plan."

"Still not interested," Colonel Dupree said, paused, then shook his head. "After our planes arrive at airstrip TAHITI and destroy more of Cesar Gomez's cocaine, we can talk about chasing a boat."

Slowly, everyone crowded around the computer screen to watch the four blue dots converge on airstrip TAHITI. The wait was nerve-wracking, especially after all four blue dots seemed to be hovering over airstrip TAHITI.

Colonel Dupree grabbed the radio. "Magic Zero One, Magic Zero Two, request update on airstrip TAHITI."

"This is Magic Zero One, we are confirming the coordinate and returning to the area. The dirt airstrip we saw was empty."

"This is Magic Zero Two, confirm the same."

Colonel Dupree closed his eyes and took a deep breath. "Good copy. Please confirm coordinate and try again."

Captain Price's heart sank as he watched the four blue dots hovering around airstrip TAHITI. He didn't believe in mystical insight, but he had worked enough of these operations and had enough professional intuition to know that something wasn't right. To date, this was the best intelligence they had collected about a specific time and place for a drug shipment with plenty of time to plan the endgame in advance. Most of their successes came from the educated guesses of trial and error, combined with a little luck, following one lead to another in a fluid situation that usually gelled at the end. This information was just too good to be true, but he wouldn't be surprised if they found the planes after all.

"This is Magic Zero One," the pilot on the radio said as the room fell silent, "we have a negative on airstrip TAHITI."

Colonel Dupree groaned and grabbed the radio, "Good copy," he said and lowered the radio to look at the computer screen. "Son of a bitch."

Everyone turned to see a red dot flashing on the north coast of Panama.

"Magic Zero One, Magic Zero Two," Colonel Dupree said, "we have a suspect aircraft taking off from the north coast of Panama heading north. Please move immediately to 12 nautical miles off the north coast of Colombia for further instructions. How copy?"

"Magic Zero One copies."

"Magic Zero Two copies."

Colonel Dupree paced and rubbed his chin as the phone rang. Master Sergeant Higgins answered, nodded, and turned to Colonel Dupree.

"Sir, a Mr. Dylan Dirk would like to speak to you," Master Sergeant Higgins said.

Colonel Dupree grabbed the phone. "What can I do you for, Mr. Dirk?" He nodded and glanced at the computer screen. "Yes, we have confirmation of an aircraft taking off as well." He listened and nodded. "Makes sense. Thanks for the heads up."

Colonel Dupree handed the phone to Master Sergeant Higgins and grabbed the radio. "Key West, regarding the suspect aircraft heading north from Panama, please be advised that the drop site is in the Bahamas and our intelligence community partners are requesting a delay on the seizure by two hours after the drop to protect sources and methods. How copy?"

"Key West copies. We will direct a Coast Guard vessel to the Bahamas and will delay intercept until two hours after the drop to protect sources and methods. However, be advised that choppy waters could delay the arrival of the Coast Guard vessel."

"Good copy," Colonel Dupree said and pulled Captain Price aside. "I don't think our planes will be of much use from here on out, but work with Key West to follow this aircraft to the drop site."

"Yes, sir," Captain Price said, perplexed. "Sir, is it just me or did something odd just happen with this plane from Panama?"

"I think it's more than a coincidence that a few days after we destroy one of Cesar Gomez's shipments we receive precise intelligence on a shipment that doesn't happen," Colonel Dupree said. "He must have put out the bogus information in the hope that we would collect it. Just between you and me, we're running a very sensitive source that just might be compromised."

"I don't like to give credit to the enemy, sir," Captain Price said, "but it looks like he played us. And good on the CIA—looks like they've been tracking this."

"Why do you say that?" Colonel Dupree asked.

"Mr. Dirk asked me to give a briefing to some guy named Nicholas Lowe," Captain Price said. "He seemed curious about this specific scenario—a boat shipment from Colombia to an airplane waiting in Panama."

Colonel Dupree tilted his head, perplexed. "No kidding."

Nicholas passed a mass of suits huddled around a big-screen TV in the El Panama Hotel lobby. *CNN Headline News* was summarizing the financial activity for the day—another banner day on Wall Street.

"Good day?" Nicholas asked an intoxicated gentleman.

"Good?" the man said and laughed with whiskey-soaked grace. "Try amazing!" He rattled the cubes in his drink and raised both hands in celebration. "The NASDAQ is close to 5,000!" he added. "I'm going all in with my margin account."

Nicholas pointed at him. "Good luck with that," he said and walked to the swimming pool **area** where Daisy Holland was sitting at a table listening to a salsa band. She wore a black dress, a tasteful step ahead of the other women, but not excessively formal or out of place. She offered her cheek for a kiss and squeezed his hand.

"Does Willie always dance with the band?" he asked and gestured to the stage.

Willie raised his jazz hands joyfully and gyrated his derriere as the attractive singer rubbed up against him.

She rolled her eyes amusingly. "He loves those vixens." He lit her cigarette. "Thanks, love," she said. "Who wouldn't?" She blew a stream of gray smoke. "Such perky tits. Look at them. Perfect."

"They are nice," he said.

She gestured to her cleavage. "These are nice. Hers are spectacular."

"Magnificent," he said.

The eccentric drug dealers were a nice break from espionage and bullet wounds. He could finally relax, knowing that everything was in place for a successful shipment and a large payday for operation Delphi Justice. Alfredo was only minutes away from the drop site in the Bahamas and the Coast Guard had instructions to delay seizing the drugs.

Nicholas eyed the diced apple chunks in Daisy's wineglass when the waiter arrived. "Another glass of sangria?" he asked.

"Tequila, love," she said.

Nicholas raised three fingers to the waiter.

The spirited song about a man whose homosexual tendencies come out when he drinks, something about paddling a canoe, ended. After the applause, the singer escorted Willie to the table and kissed him on the cheek. She wore a gold sequined dress. Her long black hair, obviously a wig, was combed straight. Willie beseeched her to join them for a drink, but she refused politely and gestured to the other band members. Daisy handed Willie a napkin to wipe his face. He looked exhausted but exhilarated as he plopped onto his chair and took a load off.

The waiter arrived with three shots of tequila and set the salt and lime wedges in the middle of the table. Nicholas licked the soft skin between his thumb and index finger, showered it with salt, and grabbed a lime wedge.

"A toast," he said, "to the good life."

"The good life," Daisy and Willie chorused.

Nicholas licked the salt and lifted the shot glass to his mouth. The tequila vapors cleared his sinuses as he poured the golden potion and leaned his head back. He endured the jitters before sinking his teeth into the lime. The citric acid neutralized the aftertaste as he licked his teeth. He felt the effect immediately: a mysterious adrenaline that drove men to test the boundaries of their tragic flaws.

"Shall we discuss business in our cabana?" Daisy asked.

Willie nodded and stood, still breathing heavily. He told a passing waiter to put the check on his room tab and led the way.

Daisy entered the cabana first and sat near the window. She removed a cell phone from her purse, dialed a number, and held it to her ear. The high-tech gadget clashed with her classical aura. "That's wonderful," she said and ended the call. "We're in business. Your plane is circling and ready to make the drop."

Daisy dialed a different number and pressed a sequence of numbers, as if playing a tune on a keyboard. "Five, zero, zero, zero…zero, zero, zero." She looked at Nicholas as she pressed the send button. "Five million coming your way, love."

Nicholas called the Enterprise Associates computer to verify receipt. "Got it," he said.

The tequila had been a mere prelude to the rush of energy he felt when the digital voice said, "Five million dollars."

Chapter Twenty-Six

Nicholas Lowe grabbed a copy of *El Tiempo* and sat on the couch in Dylan Dirk's office. The headline story title wasn't ambiguous: PRESIDENT ACCEPTS DRUG MONEY. The frenzied media were covering both sides of the story, with each side accusing the other of conspiring to manipulate the referendum. *El Tiempo* and other members of the media and the political opposition were demanding an audit of President Mendoza's campaign finances. The government was discrediting the story and threatening to press charges. Lina's expression on television gave her away, though: she didn't have the proof, at least not the original documents. Photocopies would certainly be dismissed as forgeries.

The most important fact of this chess match was that the story was true, but Lina hadn't presented her proof—the original documents that could be compared to the stationery and printers at Enterprise Associates—and President Mendoza couldn't take legal action against her or the newspaper until he was sure she was bluffing. Of interest, President Mendoza didn't know the origin of the money, which meant the allegations probably had come as a genuine surprise. Even more interesting, Lina's story made no reference to Enterprise Associates or the role of the CIA or the U.S. government, which raised more questions than it answered. To Lina's credit, her story was articulate, but she was too progressive for Panama: relying on objective facts to argue a clear point that was not motivated by personal or political gain. She could have achieved similar results by wafting bromides about corrupt politicians while pursuing the audit option. Either way,

Nicholas reluctantly took pride in his deft manipulation of a small nation, however much it pained him to watch Lina face this public scrutiny and possible legal action. One thing was for sure, though: she knew he took the documents from her room, and he felt terrible knowing that she probably felt he betrayed her.

"Morning," Dylan said as he entered the office.

Nicholas slapped the front page. "Lina has made quite a stir."

Dylan checked his watch. "Yes, well her luck just ran out. My media contact said Lina had until noon to present her evidence. President Mendoza negotiated with *El Tiempo* to retract her story in exchange for no fines. Lina, of course, will probably lose her job and could face criminal charges—to be determined."

Nicholas wished Lina had never tripped over a U.S. national security program that had to succeed at all costs. If Lina were to go to jail, international free speech groups and NGOs would demand her release and lionize her as a champion of free speech and a stalwart against corruption, which was the last thing President Mendoza would want to deal with. There were many scenarios in which this bit of bad luck would work out in her favor.

"Let's hope the president's approval rating bounces back with this new injection of cash," Nicholas said. "The good news is the shipment got through last night and we got our five million dollars. That should help the re-election campaign."

"It got through, all right," Dylan said and rested his knuckles on his desk. "The Coast Guard vessel didn't arrive on time last night, so the drugs were never seized."

Nicholas groaned. "I thought seizing the drugs was supposed to be the easy part. We gave them several hours of lead-time. So we just transported five hundred kilograms of cocaine to the United States?"

"Technically, the Bahamas," Dylan said. "DEA and Customs know about the shipment; with any luck, they'll find it and seize it soon."

"For our sake, I hope they find it," Nicholas said and leaned back. "You know, given that the Panamanian National Police clearly isn't making any progress on the investigation, I'd like to take a few weeks of vacation after this operation to see what I can find out about Tyler's murder. I feel like I owe it to him and his family."

Dylan drummed his fingers on his desk and pressed his fingertips as if playing a solemn chord on a church organ. He grabbed a VHS cassette and an envelope from a desk drawer and gestured for Nicholas to follow him to a room with a VCR and a television. After they sat, Dylan slid a cassette into the VCR and grabbed the remote control. A black-and-white picture appeared after a few seconds of static.

"You probably recognize this place," Dylan said, "the lobby of Cesar's building." He pressed the fast-forward button. "This is the recording from the security camera the day Helena died. Given our equities with Cesar, I had a guy steal it to protect our interests." He hit the play button and pointed. "That's Helena entering the building. Notice she's wearing the pearl necklace Tyler gave her."

Nicholas was intrigued to see Helena. Her class and elegance shone through the black-and-white image as she walked to the elevator.

"The security guard greets her as she passes by," Dylan continued. "Little-known fact was Helena was fucking Cesar to support her cocaine addiction."

Nicholas shook his head in disgust. Unfortunately, despite his best attempts to fight it, a painful conclusion began forming in his mind.

Dylan pressed the fast-forward button until a man appeared on the screen. "That's Cesar leaving the building to go to a bar with some friends. As the timestamp at the bottom indicates, Helena has about two hours to live. Numerous third parties and security cameras corroborated Cesar's story. He wasn't home when she died."

"So one of his goons did it," Nicholas said, unable to deny that the image coming into focus in his mind was of Tyler. He cursed himself for thinking such a thought. "Perhaps she committed suicide. She was a drug addict."

"Possible," Dylan said, "but Helena's neck had fresh scratches. She obviously had a struggle with someone." He looked at Nicholas grimly. "Her pearl necklace was missing."

"Cesar could have choked her and left her for someone else to throw her over the ledge," Nicholas said, hoping for the facts to prove him wrong.

Dylan shook his head. "The coroner said the scratches were fresh when she died, certainly not two hours old." He lifted a finger before

Nicholas could speak. "Up to this point, we can't make sense of what happened. As you said, she could have jumped, end of story. But the tape gets more interesting." He fast-forwarded the tape and suddenly hit the play button. "There, did you see that?"

Nicholas leaned forward to look and shook his head.

Dylan played the event again in slow motion and hit the pause button when Tyler's face appeared on the screen, glancing into the lobby security camera. "As you can see, Tyler's arrival fifteen minutes before Helena's death sheds new light on the case."

Nicholas stared at the image of Tyler in disbelief and anger—disbelief that Tyler could do such a horrible thing, and anger that he had. How could he kill Helena? "This doesn't make sense," he said.

"It makes some sense, right?" Dylan said. "Tyler gets engaged to the most desired woman in Panama only to learn she's fucking Cesar to support her cocaine addiction. He knew she used cocaine—I told him many times—but he did nothing to help her. Tyler had the motive to kill her. He took the pearl necklace he'd given her at their engagement party—forcefully, if the scratches on her neck are any indication."

Nicholas was speechless. How does someone judge a crime of passion, especially when the accused was a good friend?

Dylan opened the envelope and handed Nicholas a piece of paper. "We knew Helena used cocaine. When I noticed Tyler was acting strange, I arranged for a urine sample, taken from the bathroom without his knowledge. As you can see, Tyler tested positive for cocaine. Helena must have given him some hits from what she got from Cesar."

Nicholas dropped the paper on the desk. "Really?" He stood to take a deep breath and looked at Dylan, speechless.

Dylan ejected the cassette and gestured for Nicholas to follow him to his office. As Nicholas sat on the couch, Dylan set the envelope and the cassette in a desk drawer, removed a folder, and handed it to Nicholas. "That's a copy of the Panamanian National Police crime scene report for Tyler." He returned to his desk to sit. "I haven't had a chance to look at it, but feel free to use it."

Nicholas began flipping through the file, mostly photographs of the crime scene and written reports of the evidence and ballistics.

"I'll go ahead and ask," Nicholas said and averted his eyes when he saw a disturbing photograph of Tyler dead inside his car. "We possess credible evidence that suggests Tyler killed Helena. What are we planning to do with it?"

"Good question," Dylan said. "I don't know the legal answer, but I can tell you what the Order has decided, which is all that matters. If, as it appears, Tyler killed Helena, then his own death would obviate the need for a trial. Therefore, the decision was made to do nothing, especially when we weigh this against the scandal of a CIA officer killing a local celebrity in the penthouse of a notorious drug trafficker who is working with us to raise illegal money to re-elect the president of Panama to violate the 1977 treaties."

Nicholas continued flipping through the file. "I can see why we focus on hiring people who are capable of working in shades of gray."

"You'll be a member soon enough," Dylan said.

Nicholas flipped to another photograph of Tyler inside the vehicle, taken looking down over his left shoulder. Nicholas noticed a small rectangular object on Tyler's lap. He lifted the photograph to get a closer look but the quality of the image didn't allow him to identify it. As best as he could tell, it was a credit card, a business card, or a small envelope.

"Did the police find anything on Tyler's lap?" Nicholas asked.

Dylan looked up from his newspaper and shook his head. "Why?"

"There's a photograph here that looks like there's something on his lap," Nicholas said and tilted the photograph to avoid the light reflections.

Dylan set the newspaper down. "As I recall, there's an inventory at the back of the file. If the police found anything, it should be there."

Nicholas flipped to the end of the file and began working his way back one document at a time until he found the inventory document. He started down the list, one item at a time, and then flipped the first page. About half way down the second page, his eyes glided over a word and then moved back up and stopped: "playing card." He leaned back and took a deep breath as his heart pounded. He flipped back to the photograph, and as he stared at it this time, the complex design of woven lines on the back of a playing card slowly came into focus as his mind discerned the pattern he didn't know he was looking for the first time. He set the folder down, walked to the window, and watched the outside world in silence.

Dylan lowered his newspaper. "Anything?"

Nicholas turned. "Unfortunately, yes." He grabbed the folder and walked over to sit by Dylan and handed him the photograph. "What do you see on his lap?"

Dylan donned his reading glasses and squinted. "I don't know, a business card?"

"That's what I thought," Nicholas said and handed him the inventory list. "Check out the middle of the second page."

Dylan flipped the first page and looked, then dropped the list on the desk and removed his reading glasses. "Are you fucking kidding me?" He grabbed the telephone and dialed a number. "Good morning, Captain, it's Dylan." He listened and smiled. "I know you guys are probably swamped with the newspaper scandal and street protests but I was wondering if you could help us with an urgent matter regarding the crime scene inventory for Tyler Broadman." He listened and nodded. "That's great, so you were personally involved in overseeing the crime scene?" Dylan nodded and smiled. "I know you guys always do a professional job when our embassy is involved, so many thanks again. Say, on the second page of the inventory list it says you found a playing card. Do you by chance remember which card it was?"

Nicholas raised nine fingers.

Dylan nodded and moved the phone away from ear in response to some loud sounds. "No problem. I'm sure the crowds are very loud." He nodded again and closed his eyes, definitely not pleased. "No, I don't think it's anything significant. We just wanted to confirm for our own records. Thanks again." He hung up the phone and looked at Nicholas. "The police captain said he personally saw it—nine of spades."

Nicholas shook his head in disbelief, completely clueless about where to start processing this new piece of information. "How is this possible? We haven't heard from the spades assassin in almost ten years, and now he resurfaces to kill one of us, and then gives us the proof we need to know it was him?"

"Maybe he's working for one of the cartels," Dylan said and turned to dial a number on the secure phone. "Either way, you're one of us now, so we're going to take care of you…hey, K, it's me. I have Nicholas here with me but I wanted to give you a heads up on some possible bad news. It looks like the spades assassin from El Salvador was the person who killed Tyler." He nodded. "We'll try to get some more details, but there appears to be little room for doubt. Nicholas also knows about Tyler and Helena." He listened and handed the phone to Nicholas. "K wants to speak with you."

Nicholas grabbed the phone. "Good morning, K."

"Nicholas, I know you just got some terrible news today about Tyler and now the spades assassin, but I'm going to need you to stay focused a little longer until we finish this operation. Can you do that for me?"

Nicholas nodded. "Of course."

"In light of some recent developments, such as the journalist's leak of the information and Cesar Gomez telling you he recorded his meetings with us, we're going to have to make some changes. Cesar must be eliminated."

Nicholas nodded. "Will we arrange to have him arrested?"

"Not exactly. We cannot risk an exposure of this operation. I'm coming down for a meeting with President Mendoza. Can I count on you to see this through to the end?"

Nicholas nodded. "Yes, sir." The phone went silent; he handed it back to Dylan. "K is coming down. I think he wants us to kill Cesar."

Dylan nodded. "I had a feeling things were going to play out this way."

Chapter Twenty-Seven

Nicholas Lowe sat on the couch in his hotel room, reflecting. The thrill of imminent success for the operation and gaining membership to the Order combined with the shock of Tyler's crime and the return of the spades assassin was wreaking havoc on his emotions. His successes would vindicate his name and get his career back on track, which would help make up for ten lost years in Washington, but Tyler's crime against Helena and his death at the hands of the assassin Nicholas had recruited gave him pause. Was he capable of killing in cold blood? Why did the spades assassin choose now to resurface, and what message was he trying to send? What other secrets from the past might come back to haunt him? He purposefully avoided resorting to New Age clichés to find inner peace or to rationalize the terrible events. The path of action was the only way, so he focused his attention on the two beautiful actresses at center stage, Adriana and Maria, who were mixing drinks in the kitchen.

Despite the friendly rapport he had established with Cesar as part of the operation, which was a critical part of being a case officer that many people had trouble understanding, Cesar in the final analysis was a notorious drug trafficker who was responsible for destroying countless lives in the United States and around the world with his toxic substances. The Order had negotiated with Cesar in good faith, with a sincere plan to allow him to retire on a Caribbean island with most of his money, but the partial exposure of the operation in the press and Cesar's implicit threat of having audio recordings of the meetings motivated the Order to reduce the risk of this operation to as close to zero as possible, which for the Order meant removing Cesar from the battlefield. Nicholas had been involved in removing less significant enemies from the battlefield for smaller crimes, such as in El Salvador, but they were people he did not know and had never met, which showed how difficult it was to be involved in killing people you had gotten to know on a personal level. For Nicholas' part, he decided to focus on tormenting Cesar by having him see his two favorite prostitutes with another man.

A blonde curl from Adriana's bangs dangled as she sliced a lime. She wore a red polo shirt tucked into faded Daisy Dukes. Her ass swayed as she squeezed the juice into her Cuba Libre and poked the ice cubes with a straw. Maria poured two glasses of Scotch and soda and approached the couch. She wore a skintight white tank top cut above the midriff with khaki shorts. Her silky black hair was pulled back in a ponytail.

"Nicholas, rub my feet, baby," Adriana whimpered and sucked her straw seductively.

"I don't think so," Maria said. "He's rubbing my feet today." She handed a glass to Nicholas and sat on his lap. "Drink up, baby." She kissed him on the cheek and licked his ear. "You're going to rub me all over," she whispered and snuggled her ass on his crotch.

Nicholas had talked Dylan into giving him extra operational funds, without mentioning that four hundred dollars was for Adriana and Maria. He tapped the cushion as Adriana approached. She sat and kissed his mouth. The taste of dark rum and citrus lingered on her tongue and lips.

"Let me ask you something," Nicholas said. "Do you feel comfortable with me?" They nodded like schoolgirls. "I know you two are close to Cesar—"

"*Por favor*," Maria groaned and hastily drank her Scotch. "You don't know how long we've waited for a real man like you."

"Who could afford us," Adriana added matter-of-factly.

Fair enough, Nicholas thought and sipped his drink. "Cesar is stopping by," he said. "I just wanted to make sure you didn't mind."

"I don't mind," Adriana said and kissed Nicholas passionately.

Maria twisted and slapped Adriana's thigh. "Stop that!"

Nicholas relished the possibility of a catfight, but three knocks on the door dashed his vivid fantasy. He spanked Maria's ass and stood.

Nicholas opened the door for Cesar. "Welcome," he said politely with a handshake and inspected the empty hallway.

"Ladies," Cesar said, "I wondered where you were."

Nicholas gestured to the vixens and leaned closer to whisper. "We had such a good time on the boat the other day. I invited them over. May I offer you a drink?"

Cesar shook his head. "You shouldn't invite them to our meetings."

"Actually, they're here on business," Nicholas said. "I hope you don't mind." He lifted his drink to Adriana and Maria.

"Cesar!" Adriana rushed over and kissed him. "We didn't have anything to do today. We're just hanging out."

"Look," Maria said and bounced to her feet. "This is the outfit you bought me yesterday." She pressed her breasts together to enhance her fabulous cleavage. "I mean, I got it with your credit card, but you, you know, got it for me. Do you like it?"

So much for victory, Nicholas thought.

"Perhaps we should talk in the bedroom," Nicholas said to Cesar and led the way. He closed the door and turned on the radio. "The shipment got through yesterday."

Cesar nodded. "Congratulations," he said somberly. "It also got past your Coast Guard vessels, which means it's probably being snorted by some poor kids in Miami. Now we can officially blame the CIA and the Order for your drug problem."

Nicholas stared at him blankly, irked by his hypocrisy, but curious about how he was privy to that information. "We'll find the drugs," he said.

"I'm sure you'll devise a top secret operation for that," Cesar said dryly.

Nicholas managed a smile. "You remember someone tipped off our first shipment?" he asked. Cesar nodded. "Did you tell anyone about the last-minute change of plans?"

Cesar stroked his mustache and reflected. "I was sitting by the pool when you called. You passed the information and I...no wait, I was with Adriana and Maria—stinking drunk—and Manuel. Why?"

Nicholas nodded. "When we spoke on your yacht, I gave you false information and asked you to pass it to Manuel. A few hours later, the military had the information, just as they had for the previous shipment."

Cesar took a deep breath and nodded. "So Manuel betrayed me? I guess I never saw that coming." He focused on Nicholas again and pointed. "Excellent deception plan. You would have been a good revolutionary soldier. You could have fought for justice with me in the jungles of Colombia. I needed more men like you."

Although Nicholas couldn't care less what Cesar thought, his comment strangely felt like a compliment. "If we can pass bad information to Manuel again," he said, "we can run a huge shipment on Sunday to close out this deal, the fifth and final shipment."

"What do you have in mind?" Cesar asked.

Nicholas couldn't discern Cesar's mood. Perhaps he was feeling guilty for his past crimes, or perhaps he felt humiliated that his whores were in the next room. Regardless, something was bothering Cesar, and the more he seemed defeated or repentant, the more difficult it was going to be to plan his death.

"How about ten tons?" Nicholas asked. "If my calculations are correct, that should just about be the rest of your inventory." Dylan had said many last-minute bribes would be required to turn the tide in the polls caused by Lina's story, but his back-of-the-envelope analysis suggested that ten tons would buy whole a lot more.

Cesar stroked his mustache. "That's a lot of cash."

"Thirty million dollars for you," Nicholas said, mindful that Cesar would never see any of the money. "A wire transfer that large would attract a lot of attention, so I suggest bearer bonds." Actually, Dylan and K had suggested bonds, to avoid the suspiciously large electronic transactions.

"I do have about ten tons stored in northern Colombia," Cesar said. He seemed to perk up. "This is my last shipment. I might as well go out with a bang."

"I couldn't agree more," Nicholas said, amused by Cesar's choice of words.

"How do you want to move it?" Cesar asked.

"By commercial ship from Barranquilla to Colon," Nicholas said. "Put the goods in a sealed container and make it look official with a customs inspection form. I'll run it through a shell company and re-invoice it."

"You'll have to pay extra to ship it to Colon," Cesar said.

"Add five hundred dollars a kilogram and we have a deal," Nicholas said. What did he care? The drugs would be seized, Willie and Daisy would be arrested, and Cesar...well, the Order had already decided his fate.

"Sounds like a good plan," Cesar said. "I get my money, and you spooks can brag about your stupid war on drugs, however much it pains me."

Nicholas gestured and led the way back to the living room, where the women were waiting with anticipation.

"How did it go?" Adriana asked Cesar and hugged him.

Cesar kissed her on the cheek and moved toward the door. "I have some business to take care of," he added and gestured to Nicholas, with a vague gesture to the ladies. "Enjoy the rest of your afternoon."

"Will you be home tomorrow?" Maria asked Cesar. "You said you'd take us shopping. I saw the most stunning dress—"

"Yeah, yeah," Cesar said, "I'll buy you whatever dress you want. Call me, Nicholas," he added cordially and left the room.

Nicholas turned and looked out the window. Cesar was making this more difficult by the minute with his contrition or repentance, or whatever he was doing, with no apparent regard for the fact that the "loves of his life" were with another man.

Nicholas blinked a few times to see the ladies waving for him to join them on the couch, but he was interrupted by a knock on the door. He turned and opened the door to reveal a disheveled Lina Castillo.

She slapped him across the face.

Nicholas rubbed his cheek as two policemen arrived and restrained her.

"You son of a bitch!" she yelled.

"What was that for?" Nicholas asked, feigning ignorance. He glanced at the two policemen confusedly to convey his innocence.

"You stole my documents!" She wiped her smudged mascara and cried. "When the president demanded my proof, I couldn't find it in my room. The newspaper retracted the story and fired me. And now I might go to jail!"

"Maybe you misplaced it," Nicholas said.

Lina swung her arm to slap him, but Nicholas caught her wrist. The policemen inched closer but he gestured for them to stay put.

The president's strong-arm tactics were only meant to scare her. She would probably be out of jail in no time.

"How could you!" she said, suddenly serious. "What about us? Was it all a lie?"

Nicholas embraced her as she cried. He wanted to tell the truth to end her suffering, but this had to play out a few more moves before he could do anything to help her.

"Please," she pleaded and looked up, "just give me the documents."

"Officers," he said and stepped back to a safe distance, "I'm sorry, but I don't know what documents she's talking about."

"No, no, no, no, no," she said and hugged him again. "Nicholas, listen to me. I left the documents in an easy place for you to find in my bedroom and took a shower to give you time to make a choice. I knew you wanted them from the beginning but I thought our feelings for each other would make you change your mind. I was wrong, OK? I realize now how important they are to you. I didn't mention the company's name or Tyler. I did that to protect you, you see?" She wiped her eyes. "Nicholas, I love you, please."

Nicholas leaned away, took a deep breath, and then looked at the officers. "I don't have any documents."

"Let me go!" she screamed and struggled to free herself as the policemen restrained her. "He stole my proof!"

The officers apologized, led her out of the room, and closed the door. The echoes of her screams faded as Nicholas closed his eyes. Adriana and Maria arrived, held him by either arm, and led him to the couch.

"What a crazy woman," Adriana said.

"You must be really stressed out," Maria said. "Why don't you just lean back and let us take care of you, baby."

Nicholas leaned back and closed his eyes as the ladies began kissing his hands, until another knock on the door interrupted them. He gestured to the ladies that it would be fine and then walked to the door and swung it open.

"Julia?" he said.

Chapter Twenty-Eight

Nicholas looked in the bedroom mirror to finish his double Windsor knot as Julia occupied the bathroom. The bellboy had set her Louis Vuitton luggage on the hardwood luggage rack and her matching handbag in the bathroom. She rendered a $20 tip with a crisp bill curved around the middle finger of her outstretched hand as she smiled at Nicholas and touched his chin. He had hoped to avoid wearing a suit during his stint in Panama, but Julia had taken the opportunity to make dinner reservations at the classiest restaurant in Panama City.

"I never did get to ask," she said from the bathroom. "What kind of sophomoric trouble did you have planned for those prostitutes? If I had arrived an hour later, I can only imagine what I might have found."

He smiled as he finished the knot and pulled it tight. "As difficult as this might be for you to imagine, I was planning to send them on their way." She mumbled something resembling *ah huh*, apparently focused on herself in the mirror. "They spend most of their time with Cesar, so we thought it would be fun to hire his own women."

She stepped out of the bathroom wearing a stunning black dress with diamond pendant earrings and smoky eyes, her blonde hair pinned up elegantly with a Greek braid. She turned for him to zip up her dress, and then turned and adjusted his tie. "Honestly, Nicholas, do you really expect me to believe you were planning to send those two vixens *on their way?*" She rolled her eyes and gestured. "Could you pour me a drink?"

Julia had taken the opportunity to order a bottle of top-shelf vodka, which arrived on a silver tray with ice, soda water, and a pack of cigarettes. He poured two drinks, stirred them, and lit her cigarette. However much he tried, no matter how beautiful she was or how stunning she was in bed, his rational mind could never quite get over the cigarettes—the smell, the subtle teeth stains, the unwillingness to even attempt to break the habit, the scientifically proven carcinogenic ingredients. Despite all of that, though, she still managed to make it look as sophisticated as it had been in the 1950s. In fact, he couldn't imagine a Julia who didn't smoke.

She sipped her drink. "I know it's probably driving you crazy that we're already late for our dinner reservation, but I need a few more minutes. I'm sure you have a newspaper or some classified documents to keep you busy."

"I'm on Panama time," he said. "No rush. In fact, when you're ready to go, I might be busy with something important."

She turned, wrapped both arms around his waist, and pulled him close with a seductive smile and then kissed him passionately. "You'll have to excuse my rude manners. I never asked if you wanted me to visit."

All heads turned as Nicholas and Julia strode through the hotel lobby. He reached in his pocket for the car keys.

"Put that away, darling," she said and gently steered him to the black limousine waiting for them at the entrance.

The driver closed the door, sealing them in the splendor of leather seats, soft salsa music, and a chilled bottle of champagne. Nicholas filled the two flutes, and they toasted with the bubbly as the limousine drove away.

"Welcome to Panama," he said.

"I asked the driver to take the scenic route," she said. "He probably thinks were going to have sex, but if I know my Nicholas, I know you have questions and probably want to get some things cleared up before we have a civilized dinner with Jessica and Barry."

"Are you suggesting I would make a scene?" he asked.

"Let's just say that if this is going to work," she said with a smile, "we're going to discuss some issues in private and other issues in public. There's something to be said for keeping up appearances."

He sipped his drink—*fair enough.* "In that case, we can cut to the chase: why did our relationship end ten years ago?"

"Nicholas, I loved you then as I love you now, God help me," she said, "but we have to be clear on one thing: I will never marry outside the Order. This is my life. It's who I am. And you have no right to ask me to give it up for some romantic ideal. Would you have pursued me if it meant giving up your chance at membership?"

He admired the way she turned his own ambitions against him. It's always the person who doesn't have something who demands adherence to a romantic code of honor.

"Besides," she continued, "we both know you could have salvaged your membership if you had checked your ego at the door. The whole thing with Congress was a whitewash for public consumption. Members of the Order never take the fall."

Once again, with crystal logic, she made complete sense. When all was said and done, he alone had made the choice to spend the last ten years complaining in headquarters, hoping that someone or something would miraculously intervene on his behalf, all based on a code of honor he had no right to invoke. On the one hand, he liked the idea of being part of an organization that took care of its own; but at the same time, he couldn't help but sense that the code of the Order resembled that of an organized criminal network. All great institutions achieved success by making discriminating choices toward a desired end, which meant he would have to give up some of his personal code for the protection of another code.

"Nicely said," he said and sipped his drink, reflecting on how the last ten years could have played out differently. "You were recently engaged."

She extended her flute. He filled both flutes, set the bottle in the stainless steel bucket of ice, and toasted.

"Ten years ago," she said, "I agreed to marry you, but I ended it with you not because your membership to the Order was threatened but because you didn't seem to want to fight for it, which meant, to me, that you weren't willing to fight for me."

"I think we established that point," he said.

"I waited almost eight years before agreeing to marry another man," she said. "Some of the delay was, for sure, due to getting over you, but the truth is that it took me that long to find the right guy."

He resisted a smile. "But you ended it?"

"I told him I needed some time away," she said with a smile and shook her head. "Don't you go alpha male on me. The truth is I was perfectly content with him and we were on the right path for a perfectly happy marriage."

"But," he said nonchalantly.

She sipped her drink. "I would be lying if I said your plans to return to the Order didn't weigh on my decision." The limousine stopped. "Let's finish our drinks. It's time to keep up appearances."

The driver opened the door. Nicholas stepped out and extended a hand to Julia. She adjusted his tie and tugged his lapels. "Just remember, it's all about choices, Nicholas."

The laughs continued as Nicholas and Julia shared a mixed berry cobbler à la mode and the four flaming shots of Sambuca arrived with their wine glasses still half full. If the members of the Order were known for one thing, it was holding their liquor. Nicholas raised his shot glass and inspected the single coffee bean floating in the middle. As the blue flame danced, fine trails of brown precipitate descended from the bean. He blew out the flame, cautiously touched the heated rim of the shot glass to his lower lip, and poured the warm anise liquor down his throat, getting the subtle aftertaste of coffee. Julia touched his hand, and he smiled to suggest he had just about reached his limit with the drinks.

"How's work, Barry?" Nicholas said.

In most situations, Barry would come across as a goofy overweight guy with glasses, but with his tailored suit, Omega watch, and northeast accent that could only come from attending one of the finest boarding schools, he packaged himself in a rather respectable way, more than Nicholas would have envisioned ten years ago.

"Oh, you know," he said, "paying the dues at the family bank. Jess and I hope to be out of here in a couple of years. But it's not bad," he added with a slight inflection in his voice, gesturing to the restaurant.

"We have a small network of good friends, and every once in a while we get a taste of culture."

"You two seem to be doing really great," Nicholas said. Julia, pleasantly surprised, reached under the table and squeezed his leg. "I mean, aside from the Tyler document scandal, things must normally be pretty slow."

A painful silence followed. Nicholas looked around, getting the same negative feedback from all three. "I'm sorry, did I say something inappropriate?"

Barry and Jessica looked at each other, uncomfortable, and then turned to Julia, who smiled and sipped her wine.

"Barry, this wine is fantastic," Julia said.

Nicholas smiled with her and then shrugged. "I'm sorry, but why are we changing the subject? I'm more knee-deep in this issue than anyone at this table."

"Honey," Julia said and touched his hand, "remember what we talked about?"

"I know, keeping up appearances," Nicholas said, "but we're among friends. I can't imagine there's some dark secret."

"When the story leaked in the media," Jessica said with a shrug, and then took a deep breath as Barry held her hand, "the original assumption was that someone from the bank must have leaked the information."

"The only people with access to those documents were all members, you see," Barry said. "So, a few precautionary steps were taken to ensure that one of us didn't do it."

"What, like a polygraph or a bright light in your face in a dark chamber," Nicholas asked in a joking manner.

"Nicholas," Julia said.

Barry lifted his hand to take the lead. "Nicholas, membership is something we all take very seriously, and we all hope that you're able to join us one day soon. But until you formally earn that membership, I should like to think that you would respect that certain things should never be discussed in public, especially with people who are not members, just as I hope you would refrain from discussing sensitive matters regarding your work in public." He tapped his ear to suggest someone might be listening.

Nicholas nodded respectfully, with a glance to Julia to say he was sorry, and raised his wine glass. "Please accept my apologies. I would like to offer a toast: to that place where you can check out any time you like." The others endured an awkward silence as they raised their glasses. "But you can never leave," Barry added with a wink.

Chapter Twenty-Nine

January 31, 2010

Dear Leslie Burns,

I was pleased to hear that you liked my manuscript and would like to read the ending, which I have enclosed. As I mentioned before, I initially struggled with writing the ending but sometimes taking a few weeks off makes things clear.

To answer your first question, yes, the events are true! You probably never imagined that someone like me could be involved in such a plot with spies, drug traffickers, presidential elections, and the global economy, but the best is yet to come. At this point in the story, you are probably wondering how Nicholas and I end up getting married, because this was the last thing on my mind as I was sitting in jail. As you can imagine, I struggled with writing the last chapter about Julia, and intentionally left out any sexual activity that I can only imagine took place. I didn't ask any questions, and Nicholas provided no comments. I have since met Julia and can attest that she is larger than life and in many ways reminded me of Helena. From one woman to another, the real reason I struggled with finishing the book was because I struggled so much with writing the last chapter. It is never easy to create in your imagination a scenario in which the man you love loves another woman.

To answer your second question, the Order does exist. Granted, I amplified the mystery surrounding it, but it should surprise no one to know that a loose network of elite families colludes for financial and political gain, and that many of them believe they are acting with the best interests of America in mind. Many of them still live in what they consider to be the golden age of the 1950s, fighting communism and promoting the values they believe made the American Dream possible. You are correct that they could be viewed as being responsible for some of the problems we are seeing today with the American Dream, but I do not see them as monolithic, and I would certainly hope to avoid turning this into a novel that would appeal to the conspiracy theory crowd. If there is any theme I would like the reader to take away from this story it is the importance of every government making the transition from selecting elites based on blood and family to selecting elites based on merit. Needless to say, I would never join such an organization and do not share their values.

I understand that the publishing process moves at its own pace, but I am obliged to let you know that my condition has not gotten better and that my final wish would be to see this project through to publication. Enjoy the rest of the story.

Sincerely,

Lina Lowe-Castillo

Chapter Thirty

Nicholas slalomed the three cement barriers, Dylan and Julia with him, and stopped the Jeep Cherokee at the front gate of Howard Air Force Base. A Military Police airman sporting a pencil-thin mustache and aviator sunglasses inspected the license plate and requested to see their identification. Normally, during duty hours, the government license plate would suffice to enter, but two terrorist attacks by Islamic extremists against the U.S. embassies in Kenya and Tanzania the year before had put many U.S. overseas facilities on a perpetual state of alert. There was a lot of talk in Washington that a group called al-Qa'ida was launching a series of attacks that could lead to a Global War on Terrorism, but such claims were premature in the minds of most analysts. Many doubted whether a few dozen Islamic radicals could cause serious damage to U.S. interests or merit any significant resources to deal with them. The airman wished them a good day and waved them past.

During the drive, Dylan regaled them with funny tales about K and his antics in headquarters. K was the Sun Tzu of tact, but political shenanigans in Washington were approaching absurd levels. Congressmen insisted on exposing budgetary and operational details of the CIA, only to later complain the CIA wasn't as effective as it could be. "Not when we advise our adversaries of our intentions," K had quipped. He decried the cult of mediocrity for peddling feel-good agendas that caused more problems than they solved, despite people's best intentions. He led the charge on opening up CIA hiring to talented and ambitious patriots without Ivy League pedigree, but he warned people to avoid going down the intellectual dead end of turning the CIA into a social experiment to give a more diverse group of people career opportunities at the expense of operational results. As he and his Army buddies used to say during WWII, they were in the business of protecting democracy, not practicing it. Many people in the Beltway were too concerned about job security, political correctness, and keeping the deficit spending gravy train going to worry about defending the Republic. Despite this trend, while the self-proclaimed do-gooders attended yoga class or debated postmodernism over tofu salads, K scheduled cigar and Scotch meetings to take care of business in ways that avoided the watchful eyes of Human Resources.

As they arrived at the JIATF-South operations center, a blue Air Force pick-up with flashing lights pulled ahead of them to lead the way to the airstrip, where a private jet had just landed and was taxiing to a hangar. Nicholas pulled as close as the crew on the tarmac would allow and put the car in park as the plane stopped and the door opened.

Nicholas and Dylan stepped at a brisk pace to see K pause at the top of the steps, take a deep whiff of the humid tropical air, and wave. He descended to the tarmac with a youthful bounce in his step and greeted them both with hugs.

"I love the smell of Panama," K said with a single clap.

"We're glad you could make it," Dylan said. "President Mendoza should be arriving any minute."

"And look who we have here," K said as Julia arrived. He hugged her and kissed her on the cheek as she held Nicholas' hand. "Lovely as ever. The base commander has agreed to keep you entertained during the meeting." K gave Nicholas a firm squeeze on the shoulder and gestured to the vehicle. "Shall we?"

As a new recruit, Nicholas considered high-level political meetings mere forums for the acceptance of the superficial or the inevitable. From his perspective, nations, entrepreneurs, cartels, and other power organisms collided like molecules in Brownian motion. The goal of government was to manage the chaos and the fall-out. However, he inverted his thought process after he learned that these same power organisms strategically manipulated the geopolitical arena, staking their claim to the world's limited resources to create wealth or obtain power, or to destroy wealth and give away power, as the case may be.

This meeting, which was held in the base commander's conference room without any notification to the media, was supposed to include a formal acceptance of the inevitable, which was anything but superficial, with Panama taking the public lead to avoid the perception that they were bowing to U.S. pressure. President Mendoza and Minister of Foreign Affairs Victor Hernandez had made a public announcement of their plan to request that the U.S. maintain military bases in Panama post-1999, which they would submit to the Legislative Assembly for a vote after victory in the referendum. The inflow of cash from the last shipment had returned the president's approval rating to above 50 percent and *El Tiempo*'s retraction of Lina's story also helped, but certain victory would still require a last-minute media blitz and many bribes to convince opportunistic voting blocks to change their vote. Despite the good news, First Vice President Antonio Romero had surprised everyone by publicly threatening to use his influence with the Legislative Assembly to veto the plan. In many ways, this meeting was for him.

After an hour of deliberation, with the six of them sitting in leather chairs around a solid wood oval table, Antonio hadn't budged. The situation was delicate. President Mendoza's own political party was divided regarding keeping U.S. bases in Panama, and the president's recent, albeit temporary, fall from grace had polarized the two camps. The referendum would be the turning point. Until then, savvy politicians were making ambiguous statements, while outsiders like Antonio were making their opinions known in the hope of attracting followers. Even if President Mendoza were to win the referendum, he would still need Antonio's party on his ticket to win the next election.

Just as the situation looked hopeless, K stood and paced behind Dylan and Nicholas before stopping at the head of the table to look at President Mendoza, Victor, and Antonio. "You know what this discussion reminds me of?" he asked and waited for a few shrugs. "Marriage," he said. Everyone laughed. "Except the discussions I have with my wife are more civil," he added, sparking more laughter, even from Antonio. "Marriage because we want to be together, but also because we know each other intimately." He rested his hands on the table. "So intimately that we've spilled each other's blood.

"Let's go back to the beginning," K continued, "to our wedding day, to see whether some marriage counseling is in order. In 1903, our two countries signed a treaty. In exchange for helping you gain independence from Colombia, we received enough land to build and operate a canal in perpetuity." He gestured to Victor. "Minister Hernandez, I hope you are feeling better. I believe your grandfather signed the treaty. Any comments?"

"Some people say my grandfather sold out Panama," Victor said with a restrained cough and a grateful gesture. "With hindsight, perhaps the treaty did give away too much, but any of us would have done the same thing. Panama was in a shambles—an incomplete canal the French had abandoned, rampant disease, and poverty. He did what he thought was best for Panama."

"Did Panama benefit from the treaty?" K asked pointedly.

Victor nodded. "The land we gave you was mosquito infested— useless to us, given our technology—and the inflow of American capital helped build Panama as we know it. I'll also acknowledge that my family benefited, but my grandfather worked hard. He helped build this nation. I'm proud of what he did."

"Proud you should be," K said and turned to Dylan. "Dylan, as our man on the ground, what is your assessment of the territory the treaty granted to the U.S.? Do you think the U.S. benefited from the treaty?"

Dylan nodded confidently. "The land was sufficient to build and defend a canal at a time when the world was very different. American shipping companies have benefited from the nonprofit status of the Canal, but so has the rest of the world. We've used the Canal to position our naval forces, but today's force structure doesn't require it to the same degree, and we've incurred a significant financial burden keeping troops here. Overall, we benefited, but so has the rest of the world."

K gestured to Antonio. "Mr. First Vice President, both sides seem to think they benefited from the treaty. Any comments?"

Antonio chuckled and shook his head. "You Americans like to break everything down into neat little economic transactions, as if all exchanges are voluntary. I'll be the first to admit that Panama benefited from the construction of the Canal, but that treaty was a disgrace. A Frenchman and a few oligarchs negotiated on our behalf. They had no right to give away our sovereign territory, and you had no right to demand so much from us when we were so vulnerable."

K nodded. "Let's suppose you're right. In 1977, we signed a treaty giving the Canal to Panama." He rested his hands on the table and looked at Antonio. "Whatever injustice might have been done in 1903 was undone in 1977, no? I'm not saying I agree with you, because we were under no obligation to sign the 1977 treaties, but the fact remains that the Canal will be yours. What, may I ask, is your gripe?"

Antonio shook his head with disdain. "You can't undo over seventy years of injustice with a treaty. You've intervened in our internal affairs and you treat us like second-class citizens in our own country. Take this meeting, for example," he said and gestured to the participants. "You no doubt expected us to give you what you're asking for in this secret meeting, no questions asked. That's not democracy."

K nodded sagely and gestured to Dylan again. "Dylan, how would you respond to the first vice president's comments?"

"Building on your marriage analogy, I would call us strange bedfellows," Dylan said, which got a few laughs. "As we've discussed many times, factors such as the aggressive actions of the Soviet Union in the Western hemisphere or drug trafficking often require us to act forcefully in the name of national security, which can have profound consequences in a small country like Panama. However, when compared with Panama being taken over by communists or drug traffickers, the steps we've taken seem prudent and reasonable."

K nodded and turned to Antonio. "Mr. Vice President," he said, "is it fair to say you want to be treated as an equal?"

Antonio nodded cautiously.

"Dylan," K said, "could you please explain why we haven't always treated our Panamanian friends here as equals."

Dylan cleared his throat and gestured across the table, with a focus on Antonio. "Whenever we discuss serious issues regarding national security, such as this, you create a political circus. You turn every request into a threat to your national sovereignty, as a way to take advantage of the situation."

Antonio scoffed. "All countries negotiate and make deals."

"This isn't a game," Dylan said.

"Why should we agree to your requests?" Antonio asked. "What's in it for us?"

"A secure future for Panama, Mr. Vice President," K said. "For one moment, don't concern yourself with us—with how much money we have or how powerful we are. Think only of Panama's future—not your future but your children and grandchildren's." The room was silent. "I'll ask again. Do you want to be treated as an equal?"

Antonio looked blinded by his own ambition. The cat's-got-your-tongue syndrome transmogrified into spasmodic shrugs as everyone waited for an answer. "What kind of question is that?" Antonio said. "Of course."

K nodded confidently. "Gentlemen, the recent tragic deaths of Tyler Broadman and Helena Hernandez," a gesture to Victor, "came as a shock to all of us. Given the possible involvement of Cesar Gomez, we put our operation to arrest him on hold, but now it's time to pick up where we left off. Over the past few days, we made arrangements for a large, controlled cocaine shipment with Cesar Gomez. We would like your assistance in taking him down."

"You can count on my support," Victor said and nodded, along with President Mendoza. Even Antonio seemed to approve.

"The drugs will arrive in Colon," Dylan explained. "We would like to deploy one team to seize the drugs and a second team to take down Cesar."

"To arrest Cesar?" President Mendoza asked.

"To kill him," K said flatly, which caused some unease on the Panamanian side. "We recently obtained intelligence indicating that Cesar has details regarding our plan to keep U.S. military bases in Panama and plans to go public with it, which as we both know would be devastating for the referendum and Panama's future."

"Your police will arrest the buyers," K said, "but Cesar Gomez must die. The referendum is that same afternoon. This last-minute success story should help you win."

President Mendoza leaned back and nodded.

"Cesar's death will show the world what happens to cocaine traffickers," K added.

"Amen," Victor said and nodded.

"Fine by me," Antonio said. "Cesar is a criminal, and he corrupts our politicians and our country. As long as our police leads the operation, we can work together."

"This is only the beginning," K said. "Drugs are a threat, and eliminating a threat takes resources. The problem won't go away if we simply react to every Cesar Gomez that comes along. That's why we need to solidify our alliance in this war."

Antonio shook his head. "Which we can do without U.S. military bases."

Victor groaned. "If you read the agreement"—he paused to cough—"you'll see that Howard Air Force Base will be under Panamanian control."

President Mendoza looked at Antonio. "This agreement will allow us to destroy men like Cesar Gomez before they become a problem. This is a great opportunity."

Antonio took a deep breath. "The answer is no."

K, Dylan, and Nicholas shook their heads in disappointment.

K returned to his seat and discreetly gestured to President Mendoza, who leaned over to whisper to Antonio, who listened intently and looked up in surprise. President Mendoza nodded to confirm he wasn't joking.

Antonio resisted a smile and put on his serious face. "In case anyone misinterpreted my comments, as long as the agreement is limited to the terms outlined in this plan, in which Panama maintains control of the bases, my party is prepared to approve the deal. We look forward to forging this alliance."

With that, Antonio excused himself and left the conference room as Nicholas and Victor watched in confusion. When the door closed, President Mendoza walked over and gave K a big hug with slaps on the back.

"What just happened?" Victor asked.

"I just told Antonio that we received a major inflow of cash," President Mendoza said, "and that we were prepared to give him five million dollars to manage his party leading up to the next election."

He turned to K. "I hope you're taking good care of my horse. I plan to visit you for a ride after the election."

"Any time, Mr. President," K said. "And if I could indulge you with one more favor. We think it would be best if you release the journalist Lina Castillo. Her detention is drawing a lot of attention around the world in a way that could risk exposing our important work together."

President Mendoza nodded approvingly. "Of course."

Back at the office, K, Dylan, Nicholas, and Julia were seated on the couches celebrating with champagne. As Nicholas sipped his drink and put his arm around Julia to pull her close, he felt at ease but at the same time oddly uneasy with his newfound satisfaction, which wiped away the frustrations that had plagued him for so many years. He wasn't responsible for Tyler's death, but it seemed highly unlikely that Tyler would be dead if he had not recruited the spades assassin. And he wasn't directly responsible for the predicaments that Lina and Cesar found themselves in, but the way his future trajectory was shaping up certainly wasn't completely detached from their predicaments, which reverberated in the depths of his conscience. They say that every empire begins with a crime, but he would have to take solace in the knowledge that Lina and Cesar had chosen freely and that Lina would be released soon and would probably go on to have a long and successful career.

K continued with his story: "Unbeknownst to Nicholas, his agent had a jealous gay lover who jumped out of the bushes and charged him with a machete, so Nicholas hopped the fence and ran down the street—in broad daylight, mind you—in his swimming trunks with the whole town pointing and laughing."

Nicholas grabbed the bottle of champagne and filled the glasses as Dylan and Julia laughed. "I thought the guy wanted to relax in the sun by his swimming pool and pass me some information. I'm lucky I got out of there alive."

The laughter continued but faded as the others sipped their drinks. Julia checked her pockets and looked around. "Nicholas, I think I left my cell phone in your car. Could you get it?"

Nicholas finished his drink and stood, with a short pause to get his balance. "Be right back." He left the office, made his way down the stairs and out the door, passing by the security guard at the front door who was playing solitaire.

"Hello, sir," he said with a friendly wave.

Nicholas waved back and continued outside to his car, then hopped inside and began searching for the phone. He found it on the floor mat of the passenger seat. He pressed the power button to see that that she had several missed calls. On the way back, he knocked on the door and opened it when he heard the buzzer.

"Thanks," he said to the security guard.

"Not again," the guard groaned, looking at his cards.

Nicholas walked over to help. "What's the problem?"

"I can never win this game," he said and pointed.

Nicholas walked around the table to get a better look. The security guard was close to winning, but he couldn't play the last card in his hand. Nicholas' eyes moved from one column of cards to the next until he found the problem, a lone ten of hearts. The security guard shrugged and showed Nicholas the eight of diamonds in his hand. As Nicholas did the math, his vision blurred. He grabbed the side of the table to help him stand.

"Where did you get these cards?" Nicholas asked, still scanning the cards, hoping to see the nine of spades.

"Found them in the garbage," the security guard said. "Mr. Dirk throws away many good things, so I like to check."

Nicholas gathered up the cards and gave the security guard five dollars. "Mr. Dirk doesn't like people digging around his garbage, so why don't we keep this secret between us and you can buy a new set of cards. Deal?"

"Of course, thank you," he said. "I do not want to anger Mr. Dirk."

Nicholas set the cards in his front pocket and slowly made his way up the stairs to the office, with a long pause before entering. The challenge at this point was keeping his cool while sifting through all the noise when faced with K, Dylan, and Julia. The conclusions hit him like trucks from all directions—Dylan bought the cards to simulate the spades assassin to cover up his own actions, which meant that Dylan was at Tyler's crime scene to drop the card on his lap, which meant that he probably killed Tyler, with the hope that Nicholas would discover it in the file, which would explain why Dylan personally selected him for this operation. None of this helped him answer the big question—why? If it was because Tyler took the documents, then why did Tyler take the documents? Going down the rabbit hole even more, it raised questions about why they selected him to complete the operation and whether they actually planned to offer him membership to the Order. If not, then why send Julia?

Nicholas took a deep breath, opened the door, and forced a smile as he entered the office. "Julia, I found your phone."

Chapter Thirty-One

Nicholas awoke the next morning with a jolt and blinked to focus his eyes in the darkened hotel room. His head was pounding. His mouth was cotton dry. He threw the blankets off his body, sat up, and rubbed his eyes as he looked at Julia sleeping next to him. Rays of sunlight pierced the vertical blinds flapping in the breeze from the air conditioner. He shivered as the cool air raised goose bumps on his damp skin. He rolled to the side of the bed, struggled to his feet, and groaned when an empty wine bottle spun under his foot and smacked against the wall. The clink of the glass sent a sharp pain through his head as he stumbled to the bathroom.

A dull pain in the bullet wound on his left arm throbbed as he twisted the hot water faucet for the shower. The steaming water soothed his chilled skin as he pondered the deck of cards, the spades assassin, and Tyler's death. He had the whole night to think about it, and things were starting to shape up in terms of eliminating the impossible to arrive at the probable. He didn't want to act hastily, but the only explanation was that Dylan was involved in planning Tyler's death or even killing him. Did the agent actually request a meeting with Tyler and then Dylan showed up to kill both of them, or did Dylan lie about the agent requesting a meeting and then tracked the agent down after killing Tyler? Did Dylan act alone? If so, why? Did Dylan act at the behest of the Order? If so, why? Did K know? What did Tyler do to merit someone killing him?

The most worrisome variable was that the Order had selected him to replace Tyler. Had the promise of membership been a trap? Was the Order planning to use him as a fall guy if things went south like in El Salvador? *Am I next?*

As he sifted through the facts and variables, the elephant in the room, which even Nicholas couldn't understand, was Tyler taking the documents from Enterprise Associates and Lina coming into possession of them. Given Dylan's eagerness to get the documents back, it seemed likely that Tyler's death was related to them. It still wasn't clear why Tyler took the documents or how Lina got them, but the Order had other options that didn't involve killing anyone. The Order could have detained Tyler until they found the documents, just as they had harassed Jessica and Nash at Enterprise Associates about the missing documents. Regardless of how Nicholas weighed the facts, nothing explained Tyler's murder except the fact that he took the documents. Had Tyler threatened to expose the operation? What did other documents from Enterprise Associates reveal? The only reasonable explanation was a plot to cover something up, and the only way to discover what that something was, was to check out the computer files for himself at Enterprise Associates.

After toweling off and getting dressed, Nicholas kissed Julia on the lips and caressed her cheek. She opened her eyes and smiled. "If K or Dylan ask, I have some work to do before the final shipment. You can get some breakfast by the swimming pool."

She pulled him closer for a kiss. "Without you?"

"I have to get a few things done," he said and kissed her on the forehead. "After that, I'm all yours."

Nicholas waved, left the hotel, and walked to the parking lot on this quiet Saturday morning to get in his rental car. During the short drive to the World Trade Center complex, the roads were deserted—Panama City looked as hung over as he felt—and he parked a few blocks from the building to approach undetected from the rear. Unfortunately, the security guard in the lobby recognized him. Nicholas handed him a five-dollar bill for working too hard on a Saturday. The security guard winked and said he never saw him.

The elevator opened with a ding. He walked carefully down the empty hall to muffle the click of his heels on the marble floor. As he approached Enterprise Associates, he removed a lock pick from his pocket and looked around to verify that no one was watching as he opened the door. Once inside, he flicked the light on to record the path to Nash's office in his short-term memory. He then locked the door behind him, turned off the lights, and maneuvered to Nash's office, where he picked the lock, closed the door behind him, and turned on the light. The sterile silence was eerie.

He sat at the computer and tapped the space bar. The monitor lit up and displayed a screen with dropdown menus. As he scrolled through the options, he paused and wondered what in the hell he was doing taking a risk like this. He'd never used this computer. If Nash had any brains, he would have protected the programs with passwords or could audit the system to see which files were being accessed. Not to mention, if the Order had murdered Tyler for taking the documents, he was now risking his life, but he couldn't go through life always wondering what happened to Tyler.

He selected the option to create a financial report—no turning back now. A screen popped up requesting information. He entered the inclusive dates and initiated the search. He jumped in his chair when the phone at the front desk rang, the polite ring from the television dramas about lawyers. He peeked outside the office and took a deep breath to calm himself. When he closed the door, the report was ready.

He selected the print option and read the details on the screen as the laser printer finished warming up. He didn't spot anything unusual as the first page spit out on the fine linen stationery, just names and account numbers, but on the second page, which detailed the transactions from the first four shipments, things got more interesting. If he understood the numbers correctly, the Order was sending only a fraction of the money from the controlled drug shipments to President Mendoza's account. In fact, only one million dollars of the five million dollars received from the most recent shipment had gone to the president. The other four million dollars had gone to a numbered account, which Nicholas jotted down. Perhaps Tyler had discovered the identity of that account, contrary to the wishes of the Order. When Nicholas tried to access the numbered account, he was prompted for a password—dead end. He started formulating new explanations for Tyler's murder—why he'd taken the documents, why the Order wanted them back—but after the third page finished printing, he decided to get out of Dodge. He exited the program and turned off the light; but as he opened the door, the dead bolt on the entrance door twisted.

He swore under his breath and eased the door shut. His heart pounded as he pressed his ear against the door to listen.

"This is Enterprise Associates," Dylan said. Heels clicked on the marble floor. "Nash here handles all futures trading for the Order."

Nicholas began to sweat when the footfalls stopped outside of Nash's office. The sound of jingling keys and of a key sliding into the lock felt like a dagger piercing his stomach. He held his breath and slid back against the wall to hide behind the door as it opened, using the tips of his shoes as a doorstop.

"This is my trading computer," Nash said and turned on the light. "As you can see," he continued after making some rapid keystrokes, "we're down about eighty-seven million dollars on our NASDAQ futures contracts. We made a lot of money on the way up, but now we have a significant short position, betting that the market will drop, but the market has continued to rise to new highs week after week, closing in on 5,000. As of now, our account is frozen until we get more cash to meet our margin requirement. The market will eventually tank, as we all know, and we've been working with major hedge funds and pension funds around the world to short the market with us, but the market keeps going up. To be honest, I've never seen anything like this. We're practically balancing the federal budget with capital gains taxes."

Nicholas dug deep with improvised yoga techniques to control his breathing and lower his heart rate. Losing eighty-seven million dollars explained Nash's stress level, but the Order seemed too conservative to speculate in the NASDAQ futures market—intervene to reduce market volatility, perhaps, but not raw speculation, especially when the goal was to work against the market and the pension funds of average Americans. Despite his best efforts, his heart rate spiked again when he realized the margin call was roughly equal to the value of the last cocaine shipment K and Dirk had asked him to run with Cesar.

"This is a complete disaster," a third voice said gravely. It was K. "Christ, eighty-seven million dollars," he added and smacked the door.

Nicholas' eyes fluttered; every muscle in his body tightened. "We've waited too long to make this margin call, but we'll have one hundred million dollars tomorrow. Problem solved."

Nicholas closed his eyes and shook his head. He could believe Dylan or other members of the Order could be involved in something this sinister, but not K.

"As I mentioned earlier," Dylan said, "this is where Tyler came to steal the documents that ended up with Lina Castillo."

"Did he give her the documents or did she steal them?" K asked.

"It's not clear," Dylan said. "When the police went to his apartment later that same evening, it was empty and the documents were missing."

"Can you think of any reason he would take them?" K asked.

"The only explanation I can think of," Dylan said, "is that he planned to expose the operation or use them as leverage against us. I don't know."

"What a complete mess," K said. "And with this spades assassin on the loose, we should all take extra precautions."

"Agreed. Speaking of tomorrow," Dylan said, "have you heard from Nicholas? I called him earlier, but he didn't answer."

"Julia said he's making arrangements for the final shipment," K said. "Nash, need you to coordinate with the banks to deposit the bearer bonds first thing Monday morning so that we can make this margin call."

"Yes, sir," Nash said.

The lights went out as the three left the office. Nicholas stood in silence and breathed a sigh of relief as the lactic acid oozed through his body. As stressful as that was, he gained some important insights about the plot, all of which suggested that Dylan was involved in Tyler's death and that K seemed to know nothing about it. Unfortunately, it wasn't always clear who pulled the strings in the Order, so even though it appeared that Dylan was acting alone and K was unwitting, he couldn't rule out the possibility that Dylan had acted on orders from above and that K was kept in the dark. When all this analysis was done, Nicholas found himself wondering—*to what end?* After ten years of clawing to enter the ranks of the Order, when he pulled the curtain back all he saw was a bunch of self-interested families using their last names and the appearance of an honorable tradition to justify their quest for global dominance—not all of them, of course, but enough to raise questions about their legitimacy. It still wasn't clear why Tyler took the documents, but the mere fact that he had the courage to do something bold suddenly inspired Nicholas to see the only viable path before him: he too would do something bold, even if that meant losing his membership to the Order and Julia. If the Order was going to be part of his life and he wanted to one day look back on his own life with a sense of pride, he would change the Order from within, starting here and now.

Chapter Thirty-Two

Cesar Gomez labored on the stair stepper with a view of Panama City, waiting anxiously as Gloria arrived with a bottle of lime Gatorade on a silver tray, dressed in a bikini and high heels, strutting one sexy step at a time.

"Thank you," Cesar said and chugged the green liquid, gasping for air as he watched her walk to a poolside lounging chair, step out of her high heels, and position herself to give Cesar a good view. He knew what she was trying to do, but without Adriana, Maria, or even Helena to distract him, he had to admit as he looked at her, with her glorious scar for all to see, that he was a fool to have ignored her all this time. The other women had nothing on her, and she and Cesar had shared many experiences in the jungles of Colombia that in many ways defined who they were. His life was about to change.

The cool drink soothed Cesar's throat but his legs felt leaden, his arms leaning progressively harder on the rails to support his seemingly increasing weight. The sweltering heat purged poisonous liquids through his pores. Years of substance abuse had solidified like mineral deposits and had upset his chemical balance—his thoughts, his emotions, his identity. With a few whacks with a hammer and chisel, however, the process of purification had begun.

The next step was retirement, but this time for good.

He ridiculed himself for having believed that Adriana and Maria were ever anything more than conniving sluts. He would stop fooling himself about the finances of feminine delights. "You pay either way," was his new motto, but the old feelings for Gloria that were surfacing again reminded him that the best things in life are sometimes free. He'd paid Adriana and Maria with wire transfers to veil the true nature of their relationship, to sustain the illusion. He'd tried to have his cake and eat it: love and freedom.

Ironically, Nicholas Lowe had woken him from his dogmatic slumber. Seeing Adriana and Maria in his hotel room the other day enraged Cesar, until he evaluated the situation. He sensed that Nicholas was spiting him, but he'd grown to respect the American. He admired the way Nicholas worked in gray areas with humor and class, never losing sight of his objective, and never moralistic. Cesar was honest enough to admit he was jealous of Nicholas—his looks, his charisma, the way women responded to him.

What impressed Cesar most about Americans like Nicholas and Tyler was how they served their corrupt regime with such selfless dedication. He would have been victorious in the jungles of Colombia with soldiers like them. No wonder America was the only remaining superpower: it had an excess supply of highly educated patriots with the material resources to achieve its goals. Despite America's vulgar capitalism, revolutions never threatened the peace, but the gringos were too blind to recognize their blessings or to acknowledge their responsibilities. In the final analysis, America was still an evil empire, regardless of the perceived purity of intent.

Cesar's battle was over. The Americans were too powerful and too corrupt for him to succeed, whether fighting in the jungles of Colombia or selling drugs. Tomorrow's shipment would be his last. He was content after his retirement six months ago, but the Americans had forced his hand. Removal from the Linear target list would make his life easier, but helping the imperialistic war on drugs had been a disgraceful compromise. The Americans were hypocrites, acting with impunity to protect their interests. The only time they preached ethics was to promote their agendas or to stifle economic competition. Globalization, global warming, the "war on" you name it, to name a few, were fraudulent machinations to support their grand plan to convert the world into mindless consumer debt slaves. That was someone else's battle now. Cesar had visions of quietude, a place to contemplate and write his memoirs.

The lobby telephone rang. Cesar, curious about the unannounced visitor, gestured for Gloria to get it. Cesar's muscles approached fatigue as he watched Gloria enter the penthouse. He decreased the stair stepper speed and wiped his face with the towel. Despite the pain and exhaustion, a feeling of euphoria surged through his body. A second wind or some inexplicable energy source seemed to be fueling his muscles.

"Getting your annual exercise, I see," Nicholas said as he walked out to the patio, poised and calm. He wore sunglasses and a navy blue linen shirt with khaki slacks. "The ladies must be shopping," he added and gestured to the skyline.

Cesar laughed and wiped his face with the towel. "I got rid of those bitches. Cesar Gomez is a new man now." Much to his satisfaction, as Gloria returned to the pool, she cast an inviting smile to Cesar without as much as noticing Nicholas.

"Too bad," Nicholas said. "I kind of liked the old Cesar."

Cesar laughed. "You don't have to be kind to me, Mr. Lowe." His muscles were numb now, his pain ecstatic! He slowed the pace, just a bit, but the speed indicator plummeted to the "warm-up" zone. The digital screen flashed to warn him he was stepping too slowly—as if a stupid machine could make such an assessment! No wonder the Americans were heartless: they subjected themselves to the cold calculations of machines.

"If you don't mind," Nicholas said and sat on a patio chair, "I'm going to enjoy the sun. I'm getting tired just watching you."

Cesar looked at the timer: ten minutes to qualify for a successful aerobic workout. But that probably applied to young people. What did the machine know? His body had had enough. He pressed a button to stop the machine. The steps lowered him to the deck.

"Your timing is impeccable," Cesar told Nicholas and groaned as he chugged his drink and stretched. "Let's step inside my office."

Nicholas stood and followed Cesar into the cool air of his office.

"Much better," Cesar said and sat at his desk. "What's on your mind?"

Nicholas leaned back. "I'd like to make a deal."

Cesar set the Gatorade down. "I thought we already had a deal."

Nicholas cleared his throat and leaned forward. "Tomorrow, we will transport a large shipment of goods."

Cesar gestured for him to continue, suddenly eager. Perhaps the two of them could arrange some business deals during retirement.

"I'd like to offer you the chance to turn yourself in and face trial in a U.S. federal court for drug trafficking," Nicholas said calmly.

Cesar read Nicholas' countenance. His initial reaction was that Nicholas was joking, but his face showed no signs of humor. He drank more Gatorade and wiped his mouth to mask his nervousness. "I think I'll stick to the original plan of leaving Panama and moving to a quiet tropical island with all my money."

"Not if you're dead," Nicholas said coldly.

Cesar clenched his fists. The word betrayal sprang to mind.

"They're planning to kill you," Nicholas continued and raised a suggestive eyebrow. "I'm willing to save your life."

Cesar remembered the deal he'd made with Dylan and the CIA and laughed at himself for being so stupid. The Americans were backing out! Nicholas might have something up his sleeve, though; all Americans did. "May I ask you a question?"

Nicholas nodded.

"I know you work for the U.S. government. More specifically," he added and pointed accusingly, "I know you work for the CIA."

"I'm sorry—I missed the question," Nicholas said blithely.

"How do I know you're telling the truth?" Cesar asked.

Nicholas lifted his hands. "You could find out the hard way."

Nicholas was obviously an expert at revealing information on his own terms. Good training; that's what his soldiers in the jungles of Colombia had needed.

"Let's suppose your people are planning to kill me tomorrow," Cesar said. "Why are you willing to save my life?"

"Let's just say I believe in the rule of law and I know that you weren't responsible for the deaths of Tyler or Helena," Nicholas said.

Cesar nodded. Finally, someone knew the truth! He could never kill Helena, even if she betrayed him in the worst way, and he stood to gain nothing from killing Tyler.

"You're right," Cesar said. "I had nothing to do with their deaths."

"I wouldn't go that far," Nicholas said.

Cesar knew he was right, but he refused to acknowledge the point. Rumors had circulated that Tyler was seeking to take revenge against Cesar for Helena's cocaine addiction and death, but Cesar knew the CIA needed him for this operation.

"That's why I think you should face trial for your crimes," Nicholas continued. "The fact remains that the U.S. and Panamanian governments intend to kill you tomorrow. The decision was made yesterday. I can assure you Dylan will do everything—"

"Dylan is a son of a bitch!" Cesar pounded his fist on the desk. Dylan had caused him endless misery by making him a Linear target. Spies had followed him around the clock. He had to pay companies to locate bugs and detect wiretaps. His banks complained U.S. agents harassed them for details about his accounts. The Americans had "turned up the heat." He'd paid his lawyers to hide his assets in complex offshore structures. He even quit dealing drugs because Helena had been raped during a party in his penthouse.

"I figured Dylan would resort to cheap tactics and back out on our deal," Cesar said and shook his head to calm the storm in his mind. "Not that I agree to your proposition, but tell me how you could save my life."

Nicholas folded his arms confidently. "Our current plan is to ship the goods from Barranquilla to Colon. Once in port, my people will re-invoice the container and put it aboard a ship destined for Miami. Simple and lucrative."

Cesar nodded and sipped his Gatorade.

"What you don't know," Nicholas continued, "is a team will seize the container before it leaves port, after we collect the money, of course."

"Of course," Cesar said dryly.

"The buyers will be arrested," Nicholas continued, "and you'll be killed while trying to escape." He gestured randomly. "We'll tell the media you resisted. *CNN Headline News*—you'll be famous around the world for fifteen minutes."

"Sounds dramatic," Cesar said. Dying might be the best way to make the world finally appreciate his revolution, but he refused to be a martyr on the Anglo-Saxon propaganda news network. He wouldn't let the American masses feel safe believing that their government was a stalwart against evil. "And America ends up smelling like roses," he added. "What's the other option?"

"An all-expense-paid vacation to face trial in the U.S.," Nicholas said, "under the condition that you never mention this operation. It goes without saying that even a whisper of this operation will get you killed."

"I see," Cesar said, weighing his options. "Again, not that I'm agreeing to your plan," he said, hoping for another way out though he could see that his options were shrinking, "but how could you stop them from killing me?"

"A journalist," Nicholas said, "Lina Castillo, will be on the scene to cover the story of your arrest as it happens. They won't kill you with her there."

"Lina Castillo," Cesar said, "the one who got arrested for writing that editorial about our operation?" Like any sensible person, he ignored the media in Panama, until this story caused such a stir. "It didn't take me long to figure out that you guys were using the profits from these drug shipments to fund the president's re-election campaign. I guess the more things change, the more they stay the same."

"Lina will make a videotape of your confession to prove that you turned yourself in voluntarily, alive and well," Nicholas said.

Cesar liked that idea. Panamanian holding cells were hardly bastions of civilized behavior or due process; they were places where people "fell" and ended up dead.

"The Panamanian National Police will arrest you," Nicholas continued, "after which you'll be extradited to a U.S. federal court to stand trial."

"How kind of you," Cesar said and folded his arms. Something wasn't right. Americans didn't do selfless things. "I understand everything about your plan except one thing. Why? Why are you helping this journalist? Why are you helping me?"

"I helped Lina," Nicholas explained, "because I felt sorry for her and she got caught up in a complex situation. I'm offering to help you, if you see it that way, because we're a nation of laws. You deserve to be tried for your crimes."

"Crimes?" Cesar asked. "What crimes? I didn't kill Tyler or Helena."

234

"How about killing or destroying the lives of thousands of innocent people around the world with your cocaine?" Nicholas asked. "How many eggs were you planning to break to make your omelet?"

Cesar scoffed. He never expected such banal, sanctimonious nonsense from Nicholas. "Don't make me laugh. How about the Order destroying people's lives around the world with wars, disease, debt, and oppression?"

"Some people have died along the way," Nicholas retorted, "but usually those who profited from oppressing their own people."

"I forgot," Cesar said. "The Order is the savior of humanity. Give me a break." The most ironic claim of those fascists was that they considered their ideology "compassionate," what brainwashed psychologists referred to as "tough love." Nicholas' uncharacteristic comments, however, indicated something was amiss. "How do you know I didn't kill Tyler? And why did that cause you to make a deal with me today?"

"That has nothing to do—" Nicholas said.

"Wrong," Cesar said confidently. "You know I didn't kill Tyler. Who killed him? Why do you feel responsible for the journalist? What are you hiding from me?"

"Nothing," Nicholas said calmly.

Cesar saw through his feigned confidence, but the real face behind the mask remained a mystery. The truth would require more interrogation. "You don't have to play their games anymore. Be your own man, Nicholas. Fight your own battles."

"Who the hell are you to tell me to fight my own battles?" Nicholas scoffed, then leaned back and shook his head. "I don't agree with everything the Order does, but—" he jabbed a finger before Cesar could speak, "you're going to jail."

For the first time, Cesar saw pain on Nicholas' face, which could mean only one thing. "My God," he said and leaned back, "they killed him. They killed Tyler. It all makes sense now." They were more evil than he imagined, even to their own people.

Nicholas shook his head, but his face said otherwise.

"That's what this is about," Cesar continued. He hated to see another victim of the Order's deviant machinations. He leaned forward and extended a hand. "Nicholas, we can work together—"

"There is no we!" Nicholas yelled. He stood and rested his fists on the table. "All the guilty parties will pay for their crimes. That's how we're different."

Cesar stood and shook his head. "We're the same. We're warriors of justice." Nicholas' hostile tone was clearly directed at the Order, not at him. "Why did you risk your life to help those soldiers in El Salvador ten years ago?"

Nicholas appeared deaf to his questions.

"Because you fight injustice," Cesar said. They were alike. They could work together to stop the Order. "We both do. Why do you think I've been fighting this battle?"

Nicholas shook his head in disbelief. "How about I acknowledge that the Order has done some bad things in the past and you acknowledge that your cocaine trafficking activities have been anything but a humanitarian mission. Need I remind you what cocaine addiction did to Helena Hernandez?"

Cesar nodded reluctantly. Nicholas was right. Deep down, he knew cocaine only hurt innocent people and that his plan to unravel the social fabric of the American regime was futile. Byzantine rationalizations led him down this dead end life of drugs and loneliness. He'd spent his adult life attacking bad people rather than helping good people.

"We're going to meet the buyers at Paitilla Airport tomorrow morning at six," Nicholas said, getting down to business.

Cesar nodded, giving the impression of agreeing to the new plan. Nicholas had to be naïve if he thought Cesar would surrender and go down without a fight.

"I'll arrange for the Panamanian National Police to arrive soon after to make the arrests," Nicholas said. "The cocaine will be seized at the port in Colon. In the meantime, I recommend you arrange to have a lawyer on call."

"What will happen to you?" Cesar asked with genuine concern. Perhaps Nicholas hadn't considered the possibility that the Order would kill twice to protect its interests.

"I'll be fine," Nicholas said.

Cesar paused to think. "I agree to your plan. I'll have my day in court, with a lot of money and lawyers. I'll soon be a free man."

Nicholas shrugged indifferently and pointed at him with a serious expression. "Don't try to escape," he warned.

For the first time, Cesar felt the American was really looking out for him.

"I'll see you tomorrow at six," Nicholas said.

Cesar nodded and walked Nicholas to the elevator, and then returned to his office where he grabbed the photo of Helena from the desk drawer. The violet-scented perfume still lingered. Her eternal smile still sent a chill up his spine. The one time they made love, he saw only distance in her eyes, not passion—the only time Helena Hernandez wasn't beautiful. His caresses, his kind words, nothing could make her love him. And rather than refuse to give her cocaine or give cocaine to her without conditions, he'd used the opportunity to satisfy his own desires.

Gloria entered the office and sat on his lap as tears filled his eyes. She gently removed the photograph from his hand, dropped it in the garbage, and kissed him on the lips.

Chapter Thirty-Three

Minister of Foreign Affair Victor Hernandez looked at his wife Ivonne as he lay in a hospital bed, struggling to hide the pain he was feeling. The doctor had some concerns about his health and had requested him to return to the hospital for "more tests," which was probably a euphemism for saying his condition was terminal. Too many years of living the good life had finally caught up with him. He had no regrets, except a few that he had.

She squeezed his hands with love beaming through her eyes. All his happiness and passion for life he owed to this marvelous woman. The happiest day of his life had been the day she said yes to his marriage proposal. He wasn't sure what sealed the deal—his good looks, his money, or his hopelessly romantic antics that nearly resulted in the two of them escaping Panama to elope to Las Vegas, against their parents' wishes—but the one thing he was sure of was that he had acted spontaneously and from the heart, in ways that surprised his family, his friends, and even himself. She was everything a man could hope for, and he wondered what he had done to deserve such a blessing. They had lived a dream life: a beautiful family, a comfortable home, good friends, and his successful career.

The solitude of the hospital bed had given him time to realize he wasn't worthy of her, especially his behavior in recent years. Sheena, the other mistresses, the lame excuses—she deserved better—but from the bottom of his heart he had tried to resist temptation, without success. He tried to keep his affairs a secret, but she knew and surely felt betrayed, even though his behavior was not the exception. Still, his family had always been the most important thing to him. He took care of them, spent lavishly on them, and stayed with them through the good times and the bad times, which was more than many faithful men could say.

She kissed his hands with the look of a saint praying for the soul of a sinner.

He looked at her, paralyzed, afraid of losing her respect. He prepared to speak but coughed and held his chest until the pain subsided. She encouraged him with a smile. He closed his eyes. "I haven't always been a good husband," he said.

"You were a loving father. You provided for us well," she said.

Her past-tense response, without reference to their love, caused him more pain. He held his eyes shut to avoid facing her.

"I forgive you, dear," she added and squeezed his hands.

He opened his eyes, relieved. "I love you," he said. She forgave him! But he needed an answer to an important question. "Have we lived a good life?"

"We've lived a wonderful life," she said.

He wondered whether that was true. Poverty was rampant in Panama, yet he sat atop a pile of wealth he inherited from his father and his grandfather. His success had been largely a function of his last name and his complimentary club membership to the halls of economic and political power. Who knows how well he would have fared in a world of free competition. Who knows how much better others would have performed given the same advantages. He worked hard and paid his dues, as the system required, but he had started the game with a head start and few obstacles in his way. He used his status to prevent competition and to protect his own business interests. However, as he was quickly beginning to realize, death was the great equalizer.

"We could have done more for Panama," he said. "We could have done more to help the poor and the needy."

"You've served Panama with great distinction," she said. "Think of all the jobs you created and all the charities you supported."

He hoped she was right. Perhaps one could never give enough, but at least he had given something back to the people of Panama. He could have stashed the family fortune in offshore accounts and lived off the interest, but he didn't. However, it was now clear to him that it wasn't enough. There was still more to do.

"I want you to do something for me," he said. "First Vice President Romero has been working with a large public school here in the city. I would like you to take one million dollars every year and make the school better—better food, better books, better teachers. We have to give these kids a chance. We can't keep living this way."

She wiped his tears and kissed his forehead. "I think that's a wonderful idea. I would love for both of us to help these children. We'll do this together."

He took a deep breath and managed to smile. "We've lived a good life, right?"

She smiled and nodded. "I wouldn't trade it for anything."

A man knocked at the door. "Excuse me, Minister Hernandez, I'm sorry to bother you, but could I have a word with you?"

Victor looked up as the familiar-looking man leaned inside and waved.

"I'm sorry," Ivonne said. "No visitors please."

"I'm Nicholas Lowe," he said. "Tyler Broadman was my friend. I only need a minute. It's very important."

Victor gestured to Ivonne that he would be fine. She kissed his hands and left the room. Without her touch, however, the spell was broken. He was a sick man. The antiseptic smell repulsed him; the IV in his arm made him feel like a circus spectacle; and the beeping heart monitor reminded him of the flesh-and-blood fate he realized he couldn't escape.

Nicholas held the door open for Ivonne and then approached the bed. "I promise I won't take much of your time."

Victor coughed as he looked up and admired the handsome young man.

"Do you know someone named Manuel Espinosa?" Nicholas asked.

Victor nodded as recognition dawned on him. "You were talking to Lina at the hotel, and you were at the meeting with K and Dylan."

"That's right," Nicholas said. "I was sent here to replace Tyler. Could you tell me about your relationship with Manuel?" He poured a cup of cold water for Victor and held it out to him.

"Thank you," Victor said and took the cup. He managed sips between painful breaths. The crushed ice soothed his throat. "I paid him for information about Cesar's drug shipments." He finished the water and dropped the cup by his side.

"Could you tell me why?" Nicholas asked.

"Cesar destroyed two people dear to me," Victor said. "Mr. Dirk said the operation to arrest Cesar had been put on hold, so I decided to eliminate him myself."

"That was honorable of you," Nicholas said. "Do you have any plans that might interfere with our operation tomorrow?"

Victor shook his head, taking pride in the fact that he was still part of the plot to destroy Cesar. "You seem to have things under control."

Nicholas nodded. "Cesar will be brought to justice."

"I assume you know about my relationship with Tyler," Victor said.

Nicholas nodded and touched his shoulder. "Without you, we wouldn't be where we are today. If our plan works, you will have played a major role in destroying Cesar and ensuring a secure future for Panama."

Victor enjoyed a moment of pride but quickly returned to reality. "Perhaps, but I regret what I did."

"I understand," Nicholas said, "but I think we both agree that leadership isn't easy—it's all about choices."

The true mettle of a leader was having the courage to make decisions contrary to popular consensus, for the good of the country. "But I gave secrets to the CIA," Victor said.

Nicholas smiled. "If our president had asked you directly to help the U.S. maintain a military presence in Panama post-1999, would you feel the same?"

"Of course not," Victor said. Diplomacy and spying were different. "I've had good relations with your president, and I never supported the 1977 treaties."

"The president wants to maintain a U.S. military presence in Panama," Nicholas said. "We just happened to be the agency he tasked to execute his policy decision. Don't worry. You were helping us build a bilateral alliance for Panama's future."

Victor felt relieved. Any great political leader would have made the same decision. Panama needed U.S. troops.

"I promised I wouldn't take too much of your time," Nicholas said. "Thank you, Minister Hernandez. Speedy recovery."

Victor managed a wave as Nicholas left. For a moment his pain subsided, until the door closed and a vision of Helena appeared before his eyes.

"Helena," he whispered and reached out to her. She removed a metal case from her purse, dipped her finger in, and snorted some cocaine. "No!" he begged, trying to yell, but he was in too much pain. She dropped the metal case and cried, reaching out to him, "Help me, Daddy."

Victor trembled as he looked around the room. For the first time, he felt alone. The beep of the heart monitor pushed time ahead in ruthless, discrete intervals. The clear IV liquid dripped from the plastic bag, slow steady drops that refused to synchronize with the beeps of the heart monitor, until the fifth drop, when the cycle started again. He suddenly felt warm and removed the blankets.

"Help me, Daddy," Helena's voice echoed.

"Daddy's here," he said and looked around, but he couldn't see her. He blinked, desperately trying to conjure an image of her. Since the day he learned of her cocaine addiction, he yelled at her and punished her, all in a feeble attempt to make her quit.

"Help me, Daddy," her voice echoed again.

He did everything in life right, except this. His hard work, his career, his money—none of it meant anything without his little princess Helena. She had a problem, and he had been too blind to see that all she had needed was his love.

His heart raced. He held his breath as the pain returned—first a sharp pain around his heart, and then a numbing pain permeating his body. Finally, Helena's radiant face appeared as he closed his eyes.

"Daddy's here...Daddy's...here."

The steady tone of the heart monitor faded away.

Chapter Thirty-Four

Dylan Dirk swirled his Scotch on the rocks to escape the humdrum. Embassy events were usually a waste of time, this one especially, with operation Delphi Justice less than twenty-four hours away from completion. However, K was in town, and protocol dictated that certain formalities be satisfied. He would be relieved when this operation was over, but history would show that the extraordinary measures he had taken were necessary to ensure operational success.

"Dylan, are you listening to me?" K asked.

"Of course," Dylan said and looked up.

K grumbled and finished his drink. "We've completely mismanaged this situation. It's gotten way out of control."

"What do you mean *out of control?*" Dylan asked.

"We should have kept the two operations separate—helping re-elect President Mendoza and making the margin call for our NASDAQ futures contracts," K said. "We should have known this would never end well with Tyler and Cesar working together."

Dylan swallowed hard. "Without Congressional support, we needed the money to fund both operations. You told me—"

"I know what I told you," K said. "I'm not blaming you. You were right to encourage Tyler to continue the operation, as a matter of national security, but we should have been more sensitive to his situation."

Dylan leaned closer to whisper. "In case you forgot, Tyler was using cocaine with Helena before he killed her. He was out of control. I spent many hours talking to him about this, but he let her slip away. Besides, the mission wasn't complete."

"Mission," K said incredulously. "The truth is we've lost our way." He inspected the area and leaned closer. "I'm worried about the Order, Dylan. Historically, we focused on building the great American empire, a place where anyone could succeed by the sweat of his brow, but the new generation of members is only concerned about speculating in the financial markets, and the old generation is only concerned about preserving their wealth. The Order once stood for something. We worked carefully behind the scenes to impose a benevolent rational order on society to build that great city upon a hill." He swirled his drink. "Now we're no different than these Panamanian oligarchs. If we would have told Tyler the truth about the operation and why we needed the money, we might have avoided these problems."

K's tone worried Dylan. For the first time he sensed weakness in his mentor. "We can't disclose those details to outsiders."

"As far as I'm concerned," K said, "Tyler was as much a member of the Order as those spoiled pricks who inherited membership from their fathers and have never worked a real operation." He grabbed a drink from a passing waiter. "Nicholas, too. Luckily for us he has things under control. The future of our Republic depends on people like him, people who naturally rise to the top because of ambition and merit. Who are we to turn our back on them to protect our own interests?"

Dylan disagreed that the Order should accept new members like a country club. Membership had to be tightly controlled to avoid dilution. Members of the Order bred their sons from a young age and taught them the virtues that working-class and middle-class people often didn't embody or couldn't master overnight. The Order needed people with aristocratic virtues who could network with the global leadership in a calm and thoughtful manner, not ambitious people who viewed membership as a way to build a legacy for their grandchildren. Membership was reserved for those who already had arrived. Trust and loyalty were essential for membership, but today's college graduates were for sale to the highest bidder, even to foreign corporations. Duty, honor, and country were nostalgic virtues of a distant golden age for many, but they were the cornerstone for the children raised by members of the Order.

"I just want this behind us," K said. "We can't let reckless speculation in NASDAQ futures contracts make us lose sight of the big picture."

Dylan sipped his drink in disbelief. K was telling him that operation Delphi Justice wasn't important, that they should have quit at the first sign of trouble. The Order didn't conduct operations without careful forethought. The younger generation K referred to couldn't have tampered with Order funds without approval from the senior leadership. Did K think Tyler's happiness was more important than maintaining military bases in Panama post-1999? Did he think letting the Order lose $87 million was trivial?

"Regarding tomorrow," Dylan said, "where's Nicholas?"

K checked his watch. "Probably working. He'll deliver Cesar's head on a platter and clean up this mess. You'll see."

"Excuse me, Mr. Dirk," a waiter said and handed him a note.

Dylan accepted it. It was from Nash, saying he had to see him right away outside the front gate. "I'll be right back," he said.

As Dylan headed outside, he thought about Helena. He couldn't believe a year had passed since they first met. Fresh wounds opened each time he remembered her—one for lost passion, the other for his transgression.

The humid air simmered as the sun hovered in a cloudless blue sky. Dylan and Ellen entered the swimming pool of the beach resort, a cozy escape on the Pacific Coast for wealthy Panamanians. Children played and splashed in the shallow end. Men with round bellies in snug shorts rubbed oil on their tanned skin and strutted while women relaxed in lounging chairs, read fashion magazines, or gossiped. Waiters carried trays of food and drinks to the guests. A listless lifeguard spun a whistle around his finger.

The wet cement deck soothed Dylan's scorched feet as they walked. He focused on the man waving at them in the corner as they approached two open chairs near a patio umbrella. "Minister Hernandez," he said, "what a pleasant surprise."

Victor stood. They shook hands.

"You remember my wife, Ellen," Dylan said.

"Always a pleasure," Victor said and kissed her cheek.

"A perfect weekend," Dylan said as the wives greeted each other. Victor nodded. "Absolutely splendid."

Lying beside the minister's wife was a young woman wearing sunglasses. She lowered her copy of *Vogue* and gestured to the crowd of people. "If you can call this a vacation," she said. "Those screaming kids are driving me insane."

Victor chuckled, embarrassed. "You'll have to excuse my daughter, Helena. She's in one of her moods."

"Daddy," Helena protested. "Pleasure to meet you, Mr. Dirk," she said and lowered her sunglasses with a smile to reveal her hypnotic sapphire eyes. "I'm *not* in one of my moods." She wiggled her toes and looked at her magazine.

Dylan's gaze fixed on Helena as she slid her sunglasses up: tanned skin glistening with coconut oil; firm body with voluptuous curves; full, rounded breasts pressed together by a Corvette-red bikini, sweat dripping into her cleavage.

"Honey," Dylan said, touching Ellen's arm when Victor gestured to the two open chairs, "should we sit?"

"Darn," Ellen said, "I forgot the sunscreen."

Dylan sneaked another peek at Helena as Ellen rummaged through the beach bag. Helena applied lip-gloss and kissed the air as she looked at him from behind her sunglasses.

"We have some," Victor said and held up a bottle of coconut tanning oil.

"Thanks," Ellen said and continued rummaging, "but I need at least factor 45 sun block. My skin is sensitive. Honey," she said and looked up at Dylan, "could you get it?"

"Of course," Dylan said, jerked back to reality. "I'll be right back."

Helena set her magazine aside. "I need my headphones." She stood and rattled the cubes in her red plastic cup. "Daddy, order me another drink, would you?"

"Helena," Victor said, "you'd better slow down—"

"Daddy, *please*," Helena said. "Just one more drink."

Victor nodded and gestured to a passing waiter.

"Love you, Daddy," Helena said cheerfully and grabbed her purse. "Ready?"

Dylan nodded. "We'll be right back, honey."

Ellen looked up and smiled as Dylan gestured to lead the way.

"Don't be so shy," Helena whispered playfully as they walked. "Haven't you ever been with a younger woman before?"

"I, ah, just don't want people to get the wrong idea," he said.

They stepped inside the elevator with an elderly couple.

"The wrong idea?" she said and raised a suggestive eyebrow.

"What floor?" he asked.

"We can stop at your room first," she said.

Dylan pushed the button for the sixth floor. He glanced at the elderly couple and smiled to suggest *nothing going on here*. His heart pounded as her leg rubbed up against his. Finally, they reached the sixth floor.

The elevator door opened.

Helena followed Dylan and stood by him as he angled the room key for the lock.

Dylan paused but couldn't resist a smile when he watched her swaying as she bit her lip. "Right, we'll get my stuff...and then get your stuff." He gestured back to the pool area as he opened the door. "My wife needs her sunscreen."

Helena set her purse on the table near the humming air conditioner and rubbed her arms. "It's freezing in here. Why do you Americans like it so cold?"

Dylan closed the door and allowed his imagination to peel off her bikini. "The sunscreen is in the bathroom."

Helena sat on the end of the bed.

"Right, you have a seat and I'll...be right back." He closed the bathroom door and looked in the mirror. He checked his teeth and sucked in his stomach, then took a deep breath and looked for the sunscreen.

"I found it," he said and stepped out of the bathroom to see Helena snorting a line of cocaine on the table. "What are you doing?" he asked and rushed over. He wiped the white powder into the trash and closed the stainless steel case.

"Oh, playing rough," Helena said lasciviously. "I like that. Relax, stud. I've been stoned all weekend, and now I'm horny."

"That stuff will kill you," Dylan said with a lump in his throat.

She set the stainless steel case in her purse.

"Where did you get that?" he asked and gazed upon her erect nipples.

"From a man," she said playfully.

"Did you get if from Cesar Gomez?" he asked.

"Don't worry, I won't tell anyone," she said. She reached behind her neck and untied the bikini strap. He glanced back at the door. "You won't get in trouble."

He gestured for her to stop as she unhooked the back and let the red bikini fall to reveal her perfect breasts.

"I promise I won't tell anyone," she said. Her hard nipples poked his chest as she wrapped her arms around him.

His arms lifted mysteriously until he hugged her and gently kissed her neck. He ran his hands along her back and felt the curve of her hips, flesh begging him to take a bite. "We should go," he managed to murmur.

"He's blushing," she said. "You Americans are such prudes." She tickled his sides. "Come on, try to relax."

He resisted laughing and grabbed her arms. "We should go."

"I love a man with a firm grip," she said and shivered with delight.

"We should go," he said, but resisting her now was futile.

She stroked his crotch with the back of her hand. "Oh my, someone's excited," she said, and then dropped to her knees. "Something tells me this won't take long."

Dylan exited the embassy compound and approached Nash's black Toyota Land Cruiser parked on the side of the street. He opened the passenger door and climbed in. A can of Budweiser was in the drink holder.

"This better be important," Dylan said tersely.

Nash gripped the wheel. "You remember how Tyler printed the financial documents a few weeks ago?"

Dylan nodded.

"I have a program in my computer that tracks when people use the system and which documents are printed," Nash continued. "I stopped by the office after we gave K the tour today—"

"Get to the point," Dylan said irritably and observed the passing cars.

"Someone else printed documents today," Nash said.

Dylan rubbed his temples and groaned.

"About the same time we were in the office, in fact, and the report that was printed included details about the wire transfers to the futures trading account." Nash released his hands from the steering wheel and looked at Dylan. "I spoke with the security guard in the lobby. The person he described sounded like Nicholas."

Dylan smacked the dashboard and pointed at Nash authoritatively. "You did the right thing. Don't tell anyone about this."

Nash was visibly distressed. "What's going on?"

"I'll take care of this," Dylan said, then exited the car. Nash drove away.

Dylan gazed at the Pacific Ocean and felt the cool ocean breeze as he strolled down Avenida Balboa to calm his nerves. The fact that Nicholas knew about the futures trading account could mean only one thing: he knew about Tyler and the spades assassin. With hindsight, it probably wasn't the best plan, but it was the only way to cover up Tyler's death and make Nicholas share in some of the guilt. It was easy enough to trigger a meeting with the agent and then tell Tyler the agent had triggered a meeting to get them both in the same place at the same time, but the spades assassin was the weakest link. For all he knew, the spades assassin was already dead. Perhaps at some level he always suspected that it would come down to this, which is why he selected Nicholas for the operation. With his history, he was the easy fall guy if things didn't work out as planned.

He nodded solemnly, reflecting on how his life had taken him down this path. His affair with Helena had been brief, three months of blissful sexual trysts. His marriage had seen better days but Helena had satisfied every desire encoded in his DNA. Who could deny her? Why deny her? Unlike the other men in Helena's life, only he had the courage to help her. He never let her get high when they were together. He tried to help her quit the cocaine but his busy career and rocky marriage prevented him from spending enough time with her. "Poor Helena," people had said—people who didn't know her. She had an iron will and took what she wanted when she wanted it, the same way she took Tyler from Lina Castillo. What she needed was a strong man, someone to protect her and keep her safe, something her father had failed at miserably. He had warned Victor repeatedly about her problem, but Victor's scare tactics and threats were a cowardly way of shirking responsibility. How could a father, an aristocratic man raised on traditional values, have been so negligent?

Making Cesar Gomez a Linear target had been the logical decision to stop the flow of cocaine through Panama and into the United States and get him out of Helena's life, but Cesar gave cocaine to Helena and used her addiction to satisfy his own perverse desires, which ultimately resulted in Helena overdosing at a party at Cesar's penthouse and getting raped. In response, Cesar quit dealing drugs and made a mockery of the Linear operation. Cesar could burn in hell for eternity and never pay his debt for destroying her life.

Dylan had hoped Tyler would be a good influence on Helena, but he couldn't balance his personal and his professional life, which is why he never should have been offered membership to the Order. Tyler could have prevented all of this. After all, he was with Helena every day and knew about her cocaine addiction. She would be alive now, pregnant with her first child, happily married, and operation Delphi Justice would have continued without incident. Tyler had the chance to redeem himself, but upon finding Helena at Cesar's penthouse, he chose murder, not forgiveness. In his most disgraceful act, he took the necklace he'd given to her at their engagement party, as the scratches on her neck had indicated. Tyler's death had been a just punishment.

Dylan removed a photograph of Helena from his wallet. He smiled at her radiant face and smelled the lingering violet-scented perfume, a reminder of the soft skin he'd kissed and caressed. Only Helena kindled his passions and satisfied his desires. Despite the faults of Victor, Cesar, and Tyler, he ultimately blamed himself for her death.

"I'm so sorry," he whispered.

He should have swept her away when he had the chance, but he refused her love. He was too concerned about what the other members of the Order might think, for he certainly would have lost his membership if he had chosen Helena. She said she wanted to spend the rest of her life with him, but like a fool he encouraged her to see Tyler, someone closer to her age. He would give up anything to be with her now—the Order, Ellen, everything—and grudgingly accepted the sad reality that was his own creation. His love for Helena was something Ellen and the world would never understand and would forever remain his secret. He took a deep breath and looked at the ocean. Operation Delphi Justice would succeed, and the only way to guarantee that was to stop Nicholas Lowe.

Chapter Thirty-Five

Nicholas Lowe parked down the road from Cesar Gomez's condominium tower as the sun was rising. He stopped the car and looked at Lina Castillo with upraised eyebrow to suggest—*here we go*. Needless to say, she was probably still recovering from the fact that he had stolen her documents, and was in no mood to pick up where they had left off, but she looked charming with her hair up and her intellectual glasses. The neighborhood was quiet, except for a dog that barked as they closed the car doors and made the short trek to Cesar's building.

Keeping the new plan a secret wasn't easy. Nicholas had arranged to collect the bearer bonds from Willie and Daisy Holland at Albrook Airport, with the false promise of a one-way flight to anywhere with Alfredo. At the same time, he was talking to K, Dylan, and the Panamanian National Police as if the original plan at Paitilla Airport was still on schedule, the same place Cesar Gomez thought he was going, in case he got any crazy ideas. At the last minute, he would advise everyone that the plan had changed, for reasons beyond his control, due to a mix-up with Willie and Daisy Holland, which would give him time to get things done his way. Most reasonable bosses knew that things never went as planned, and that the best officers could be trusted to think on their feet as long as the mission was accomplished.

The far more difficult part would be explaining why he brought Lina to facilitate the arrest of Cesar, which would expose the event to the media and make it difficult or impossible to move forward with the plan to kill him. He didn't want to get in the business of extrajudicial killings.

As an added bonus, accurate coverage of the story would discredit any theories about collusion with drug traffickers. The last time he ran afoul of the Order in El Salvador with the spades assassin, which was beyond his control, his membership was denied and it nearly ruined his career. As such, he was betting heavily on the idea that once he presented the facts about Dylan, K would see the wisdom of his ways and reward him, not punish him. Besides, helping the Order fix their $87 million margin account problem would probably guarantee his membership or at least keep him off their shit list.

Nicholas and Lina entered the lobby. The Kuna Indian security guard, who seemed to be expecting them, gestured for them to pass.

"I can't believe we're going to Cesar Gomez's penthouse," Lina said.

Nicholas gestured to the elevator and led the way. Lina was two steps behind and pressed the button for the penthouse.

Besides asking for forgiveness, Nicholas had revealed enough details of the operation to whet Lina's journalistic appetite. As it turns out, her short stint in jail wasn't unbearable and made her a minor celebrity around the world. He admitted to stealing the documents, but her anger subsided when he told her she was part of a top secret national security operation to arrest Cesar Gomez and to end to his cocaine trafficking activities. She seemed pragmatic enough to understand that this story would put her on the map, but she also made it very clear that things between them wouldn't return to how they were, at least not any time soon.

The elevator door opened with Cesar looking down the barrel of a rifle. "Put your hands in the air or I'll shoot," he said coldly.

"Nicholas!" Lina screamed and latched onto his arm.

Nicholas pointed an accusing finger at Cesar. "Where are your manners?"

Cesar lowered the rifle. "There's no fooling you, Mr. Lowe," he said and shrugged apologetically. "Sorry, Ms. Castillo."

Lina looked at him cautiously and held Nicholas' hand.

"What's with the rifle?" Nicholas asked, feeling the pain of her grip. "Are you planning to shoot coconuts from your prison cell?"

"I used this rifle to fight for justice in the jungles of Colombia many years ago," Cesar said, noticing Lina and Nicholas holding hands. He examined the rifle and handed it to Nicholas. "I want you to have it."

"Thank you," Nicholas said, genuinely moved, and checked his watch. "We should go," he added and gestured to the elevator.

As Cesar hoisted a small travel bag onto his shoulder, Gloria turned the corner crying. He hugged her and kissed her on the forehead.

"I'll wait for you," Gloria said. "I love you."

"I love you, too," Cesar said. "Remember our plan."

Outside, the city was still sleeping as the sun was rising. The Pacific Ocean was tranquil, oblivious to the misdeeds of mortals. Nicholas turned left on Avenida Balboa and began the trek to Albrook Airport, with Lina in the passenger seat and Cesar in the back. At the Intercontinental Hotel, he turned right on Avenida Frederico Boyd and headed up the undulating hill.

"The plan changed at the last minute," Nicholas said as he looked in the rearview mirror at Cesar, who looked confused about where they were going. "Even if you had a team in place at Paitilla Airport to help you escape, the Panamanian National Police would have overwhelmed them and killed you. I told you I'd keep you alive."

Cesar looked bemused as he shrugged to suggest he had no idea what Nicholas was talking about. Lina was busy jotting notes. Nicholas assumed the day wouldn't continue without a glitch, so he took advantage of the lull before the storm to clear up a mystery.

"May I ask you a question?" Nicholas asked as they waited at a red light.

She mumbled something that sounded like approval.

"How did you get the documents from Tyler?" Nicholas asked.

She stopped writing and looked up. The light changed to green. Nicholas shifted into first gear and started driving. Cesar leaned forward to listen. Lina glanced back and waited for Nicholas' nod of approval.

"The night Tyler was killed," she said, "he stopped by my apartment and asked me to hold an envelope for him. He said something important was about to happen."

"He wasn't more specific than that?" Nicholas asked.

She shook her head. "My sense was that he was tired of this work and wanted to get out to do something else."

"Did he say what was in the envelope?" Nicholas asked, knowing full well that Tyler would never give her the documents. He could only assume that she was lying because she didn't want Cesar to know the truth or had something to hide.

"He said he would pick it up the next day," she said. "When I heard about his death on the news, I decided to see what was inside," she added with an apprehensive look at Cesar. "So I decided to write the story."

Nicholas nodded to suggest he was satisfied with the story and then grabbed his cell phone and dialed a number. "Good morning, Dylan." He nodded. "Hey, we had a small mix-up with the buyers, so we're moving to Albrook Airport, so if you can advise the police to get there—" He looked at the phone, shrugged, set it down, and checked his watch. "The fun should start in a few minutes."

A security guard at the front gate of Albrook Airport waved Nicholas past. He drove to the small runway about a half mile down the road, past buildings that until recently had been barracks and offices for the U.S. military. He parked near where Alfredo was waiting outside the twin-engine Piper Navajo aircraft. The propellers were spinning as complete window dressing before the arrest, to make Willie and Daisy Holland believe they were about to fly away safe and sound. On the other side of the plane, Willie and Daisy Holland were waiting in a black BMW with tinted windows.

"Hand me the black bag," Nicholas said to Cesar. He removed a video camera and turned on the power. An image of the steering wheel appeared.

"Are you ready?" Nicholas asked Lina and Cesar.

They nodded as Nicholas focused the video camera on Cesar.

"Have my fifteen minutes of fame begun?" Cesar asked.

Through the video camera, Nicholas saw a repentant Cesar Gomez looking back at him. He handed the video camera to Lina. "Start your interview."

Nicholas grabbed a Glock 9mm from under the front seat and loaded the chamber. "Just to be safe," he said in response to Lina's horrified look.

Lina cleared her throat in a ladylike way. "Please state your name."

"My name is Cesar Gomez..."

Nicholas stepped outside, closed the car door, and waved to Alfredo. They shook hands. "Thanks for coming. We won't be flying today, but here's some money for your troubles." He handed Alfredo an envelope with five thousand dollars.

He waited for Alfredo's nod of approval before walking around the plane to the BMW. He knocked on the glass. The power window lowered. Willie removed his straw hat and smiled. Daisy crushed her cigarette in the ashtray and winked.

"How's my favorite couple?" he asked.

"It's God-awful early," Daisy said. "I'm still buzzing from last night."

"We received word that the container with the goods arrived in Colon," Willie said.

Nicholas nodded. "Do you have the payment?"

Daisy gestured to two black attaché cases in the back seat. Nicholas opened the back door, opened both cases, and checked the contents: U.S. bearer bonds with a face value of one hundred thousand dollars. After thumbing through fifty of them—about one tenth of the pile— he extrapolated five hundred per case for a total of a hundred million dollars.

A car speeded onto the tarmac and skidded to a stop. Nicholas, confused, looked to see Dylan's maroon Mercedes Benz.

The driver door swung open. "What are you doing, Nick?" Dylan yelled, then got out and fired a round. The bullet struck Alfredo in the head. He collapsed on the tarmac. Nicholas dove for cover behind the plane as Willie and Daisy gunned it fast enough to make the rear door slam shut as they drove away with the bonds. Dylan fired another shot. This one ricocheted off the concrete and whizzed past the plane.

"You won't get away with this!" Dylan shouted, taking cover behind his door.

Nicholas unholstered his Glock and aimed as police sirens wailed in the distance. He fired a shot at Dylan's door, forcing him to retreat behind the car.

"He had to die," Dylan yelled and blasted a hole in the idling Piper Navajo's tail, barely missing Nicholas. "He failed us. He failed the operation. He didn't deserve her!"

Nicholas cringed when another bullet struck the plane. *What the hell is he talking about?* He fired back and pierced Dirk's windshield.

"Hand over the money, and we'll forget this ever happened," Dylan said. "You'll get your membership. You have my word."

Nicholas aimed to fire again, but Cesar jumped out of the car and fired his rifle, smashing Dylan's right headlight.

"Dylan, you son of a bitch!" Cesar yelled and aimed again as he paced back and forth. "Step out and fight like a man!"

The wailing sirens grew louder as four police cars entered the base and approached the airstrip. Nicholas watched, amazed, as Cesar rolled to the right, dodged Dylan's next shot, and fired his own, which missed. Cesar aimed the rifle from one knee and fired again when Dylan pivoted into sight. Cesar's blast hit Dylan in the chest. Dylan's shot caught Cesar in the left arm, knocking him down.

Nicholas rushed over to Cesar. He was bleeding badly. "You'll be all right," he said as the four police cars with flashing lights and sirens could now be seen.

Cesar pushed him away and gestured to the plane. "Go!"

"Nicholas, let's go!" Lina shouted.

Nicholas started to lift Cesar, but he screamed with pain.

"You can't help me," Cesar said. "I was right about the Order. They'll kill you if you don't leave now."

"You can make it," Nicholas said, struggling to lift him.

Cesar screamed in pain and struggled to breathe. "Nicholas, all my life I've fought for justice. Today I finally got the courage to face my enemy." He pointed at Dylan's lifeless body. "You inspired me, Nicholas. Don't you see, I won...we won."

Nicholas nodded, fighting back an inexplicable tear, feeling a bond with Cesar he didn't want to acknowledge.

"We're warriors," Cesar said. "We're brothers."

Nicholas smiled. "All right, you saved my life," he said. "Now quit being so damned dramatic, and let's get the hell out of here."

With a grunt, Nicholas lifted Cesar onto his shoulder and carried him to the plane. Lina pulled Cesar inside as Nicholas removed the wheel blocks.

Nicholas climbed into the pilot's seat and fiddled with the gauges. He eased the throttle forward as the police cars arrived on the tarmac and skidded to a halt. Some of the police officers stepped out of their vehicles to aim their weapons. The plane taxied past Dylan's lifeless body toward the runway.

Lina screamed as the Piper Navajo accelerated toward the police cars.

"Hang on!" Nicholas instructed and stomped his foot for a full right rudder. The plane spun and skidded to a halt. He paused to listen to the engine hum and then slammed the throttle forward. Two police cars gave chase, the occupants firing their weapons, but stopped as they approached the end of the runway. Nicholas strained to pull the stick back when the end of the runway was in sight. The plane's wheels scraped the weeds and lifted into the air.

Chapter Thirty-Six

Nicholas Lowe stood alone on the beach and gazed at the moonlit Caribbean Sea. Docked sailboats bobbed and listed like drunken sailors as waves splashed ashore. A cruise ship on the horizon sounded its horn; its cabin lights flickered like fireflies. Reluctantly, after painful deliberation, he dialed the number at Dylan's office.

"Hello?" a voice said. It was K. "Nicholas, is that you?"

"It's me," Nicholas said, able to discern Julia's voice in the background.

"All hell's broken loose," K said. "Where are you?"

Nicholas took a deep breath. "Why did you lie to me?"

"Nicholas," K said, "I have to admit that I don't know what the hell is going on—"

"Dylan tried to kill me," Nicholas said, "and he killed Tyler, as far as I can tell. There is no spades assassin."

"Dear God," K said. "Dylan's dead. The police said you flew off with Cesar and the journalist. I need you to tell me what's going on."

"I had to change the plan at the last minute because of the buyers. I called Dylan to advise the police as soon as I knew, but he showed up and tried to kill us." Nicholas looked at Cesar sitting under a palm tree. "Dylan shot Cesar. He didn't survive."

"I guess he got his just punishment," K said tonelessly. "Nicholas, we'll work this out. Do you have the bonds?"

Nicholas felt like he'd been doused with cold water. "Is that what this mission was all about? I know about your eighty-seven-million-dollar trading loss. Why didn't you just tell me, or Tyler for that matter?"

"I apologize for not providing you all the details," K said, "but you know how these things go—need to know. Look, I don't know what's going on, but I'll get to the bottom of it. Do you have the bonds?"

"No," Nicholas said. "When Dylan showed up and started shooting at us, the buyers drove away. Were they captured?"

"We found their car," K said, "but it was empty. Where are you?"

"A senior member of the Order just tried to kill me," Nicholas said. "If you don't mind, I'd prefer to keep my location a secret for now."

"I understand," K said. "Nicholas, you did a great job and this shouldn't interfere with your membership to the Order. I'll return to Washington for a senior-level meeting and tell them Dylan was responsible for everything."

"Was he?" Nicholas asked. "Only him? Are you sure?" He wanted to trust K, but the issue of membership was up in the air. Any attempt to expose Tyler's murder would prove futile, and he'd seen enough of the Order's machinations to know that joining them was tacit consent to conformity to their dictates.

"Nicholas, listen to me," K said. "Things aren't as they seem. The Order is having some serious problems at the most senior levels, and I intend to fix them. There's still hope, but we'll need people like you to get things back on track. Just promise me you'll call tomorrow."

Nicholas decided to respect K's request. "I'll call you tomorrow."

"Stay safe," K said.

Nicholas walked toward Cesar. His feet sank in the soft sand, until he reached the hard roots of the palm tree. "I told them you're dead," he said.

"Cesar Gomez is dead," he said and stood. "I'm a new man now."

"Too bad," Nicholas said. "I kind of liked the old Cesar."

Cesar smiled and took a deep breath. "No more revolutions for me." He folded his arms with a smirk. "At least for now."

"So what's this plan you and Gloria have worked out?" Nicholas asked.

"After escaping from Paitilla Airport," Cesar said with a smile and a pause, "I was supposed to meet her in Colombia. We decided to use all of my money help people, and, who knows, start our own family."

"So what happened between you two?" Nicholas asked.

Cesar paused to reflect. "Gloria was working as a prostitute in a small village, against her will, addicted to drugs. I convinced my FARC commander to allow me to take her as a sex slave, after another FARC member raped her and cut her face, but my intentions were good. When we found out she was pregnant with my child, I told her she had to quit drugs. But she couldn't quit, so she got an abortion. I swore I would never forgive her."

"And now that you have forgiven her?" Nicholas asked.

"For the first time in my life I feel free," Cesar said. "That Lina, she seems really special. Don't make the same mistake I did."

They embraced with firm slaps on the back, and then Cesar waved and walked down the beach, fading into the night.

Nicholas turned and walked down the row of beachside bars and restaurants. A television in one bar caught his attention. *CNN Headline News* was reporting from Panama that legendary drug kingpin Cesar Gomez killed veteran CIA officer Dylan Dirk during a top secret operation that resulted in the seizure of ten tons of cocaine. Despite the tragic loss of a brave American hero, the White House hailed the operation a success and denied accusations it had been conducted without the approval of the Panamanian government. In a related story, President Alex Mendoza narrowly lost a referendum to run for a second term in office. The cameras switched to people waving Panamanian flags and partying in the streets of Panama.

Nicholas paused to consider the news and found it oddly satisfying. In the final analysis, the mission had failed—the U.S. wouldn't maintain military bases in Panama post-1999—but things would probably work out in the end.

He continued down the row of beachside bars and restaurants, filled with an eclectic mix of expatriates and tourists, and then made his way back to the hotel. Inside the room, the bathroom door was closed and the faucet was running. Salsa was playing on the clock radio near the bed. Figuring that Lina was getting ready for dinner, he sat on a chair next to the bed and turned on the television to watch the news.

The bathroom door unlocked. Lina stepped out wearing a stunning black dress and with her hair down. He stood to give her a hug and a kiss on the cheek.

"You look amazing," he said.

"Thank you," she said and then smiled and touched his chin.

"Did you see the news?" he asked and gestured to the television. "President Mendoza lost the referendum." He gestured to the chairs.

"It's for the best," she said as they sat.

"I don't mean to pry," he said, suddenly serious, "but I'm curious about why you said Tyler gave you the documents. I knew Tyler well enough to know he would never ask someone to hold classified documents."

She nodded and looked down. "You're right. He didn't give them to me. I took them from his apartment the night he died." She looked up as if seeking advice. "After Helena died, Tyler and I, how do I say, started hanging out again."

He nodded. "Hanging out?"

She looked down again. "I'm ashamed to admit it, but after Helena died, I took advantage of Tyler." She looked up. "I called him every day, offering my support, but I was really trying to get back together with him."

"Makes sense," Nicholas said, sensing trouble.

Lina shook her head. "No. I knew Tyler was vulnerable, but all I could think about was myself. It must have worked though because the night he died we talked about getting back together again. He said he never should have let me go."

"I'm sure he meant it," he said, encouraging her to talk, but surprised to hear that she and Tyler were so close, so recently. "Then what?"

Lina looked at him as if he'd lost his mind. "Then what? They killed him! He said there were some weird things happening at work, which is why he took the documents. What if they killed him for taking the documents? What if he took the documents as leverage to get out because he wanted to be with me again?" She rested her face in her hands and wept.

"You can't blame yourself for that," he said, consoling her. "I can't give you all the details, and you certainly can't publish this," he added with a smile, "but you weren't responsible for his death. None of this was your fault—Tyler, Helena, none of it."

She looked down and started crying.

"What now?" he asked and wiped her tears.

She took a deep breath. "I...told Tyler."

"Told him what?" he asked.

She closed her eyes. "I told Tyler that Helena would be at Cesar's penthouse." She looked at him, more relaxed. "I overheard Helena telling one of her friends that she was going to Cesar's place to get some cocaine. I told Tyler to go see for himself, hoping he would break up with her as a result."

He grimaced. "The day she died?"

She nodded and wiped her tears as he consoled her with a hug.

"I know," he said. "I saw the security tape."

She leaned back and looked at him. "So you know what happened?"

He looked at her nodded. "The security tape shows Tyler entering the building a few minutes before Helena died. The coroner said her necklace was missing, the one Tyler gave her on their engagement, and there were scratches on her neck."

She nodded slowly. "He admitted to me that he went to see her. The worst part was I was glad when she died. I know that sounds terrible. She could have had any man in Panama, but she took Tyler, even though she knew we were together."

He touched her cheek. "You've been through a lot. I have some issues of my own to resolve with work, so we might be here for a few days."

"Thank you so much," she said and kissed him gently on the lips. "Did I tell you he bought the necklace for me?"

He shook his head, suddenly curious.

"About a month before he met Helena," she said. "I found it in his bedroom. It said, 'with Love, Tyler.' I figured he was waiting for the right moment to give it to me." She wiped her tears, embarrassed.

He leaned closer and kissed her on the lips and held her hands. He had to wonder why she had rushed things with him during the past two weeks, or why Tyler had gone back to her so soon after Helena's death. The one thing he was certain of, however, was that he was in no position to judge. In many ways, he felt like his entire life was a painful and convoluted journey of trial and error just to get him to this point. He kissed her again and looked into her eyes. A smile filled his face because for the first time he truly felt the three words he knew he would one day say to her: *I love you.*

Epilogue

Dear Nicholas,

If you are reading this letter it is because I am no longer with you. The love we shared gave me the strength to fight as long as I could, but the repeated attempts to cure the cancer were not successful. The pain and suffering were at times unbearable for me, but I know that you were suffering as well, and I couldn't bear to see you sitting by my side or discussing the next treatment we both knew wouldn't succeed. In ways that I cannot explain in words, I knew this was the end.

I'm so pleased you had a chance to read the final version of my manuscript for *Treaty Violation* and that you enjoyed it. I imagined you smiling as you read my version of the events with a lady's touch. That is the hopeless romantic in me. In the end, I wanted it to be a love story, our love story, because I wanted the world to know how lucky I was to have lived with and loved someone like you. Something tells me Minister Hernandez never quite saw the error of his ways, as I portrayed in the story, but I certainly hope he found some peace before the end. He was like a father to me, and I knew his heart was in the right place, but I didn't want to live in his world. Something also tells me that Cesar Gomez has a long way to go to leave his past behind, but I was pleased to hear that he and Gloria are still together in Colombia and that he liked the manuscript as well. I assume you're satisfied with my portrayal of K and Dylan, which you assured me was accurate. Please tell K how much I love him!

I never for one moment doubted our love for each other, but you know I was always insecure about your decision to be with me rather than Julia, with all of her beauty, class, and money. (I wouldn't be a woman if I wasn't jealous!) In many ways, for better or worse, she reminded me of Helena. Only true love could make a decision like that, I know, but I also know that our being together limited your possibilities in the Order, and that you were always frustrated with your inability to make changes to accomplish your objectives. I too found most of the members pretentious and arrogant, but we both know that something had to be done, and that the American Dream would eventually become the American Nightmare if the elites continued their path of allowing our values to deteriorate and our financial system to transform into a casino. As we discussed many times, why do the elites refuse to teach average people how to succeed? Why have they allowed this path of destruction to continue?

If there's one thing I regret in life, Nicholas, it was not being able to have children with you. We tried everything and you were so supportive and patient along the way, but I also know it was a source of frustration for you. I saw it in your eyes each time you held someone's child. You know I cannot now in my current state imagine you with someone else, but I am also not so selfish as to demand that this part of your life remain unfulfilled because of me. What I'm saying, Nicholas, is that you should know that I love you very much and that I would smile down on you from heaven knowing that you could spend the many years you have ahead of you with a family. The world would be so lucky to have someone like you as a father.

As we discussed, for obvious reasons, I had to change the ending of the story to portray Willie and Daisy Holland driving away with the bonds. This has been our secret, and I would not want to cause problems for you now with a confession of the truth. You see, even I learned that it's sometimes best to conceal the truth! I was so pleased that you were able to use some of the money for important projects with K, and that K agreed to protect our secret, but now that K has retired and you continue to have so many frustrations with the Order, it might be time to take matters into your own hands. Being a leader of the Order is not a divine right. Once upon a time, long ago, their ancestors were regular people like us with big ideas. As you used to say, every empire begins with a crime. If change is impossible within, you should start your own projects. If and when they succeed, you will inspire others to follow you.

Moving to a more difficult subject, there was another part in the ending of the story that I changed as well, something you might already know or suspect, even though you never let on. When we were talking in the hotel room at the end of the story, you told me you had seen the security tape for the lobby in Cesar's building. It was at this point that I intended to tell you the truth, but when you said you saw Tyler and that you and everyone else believed he killed Helena, I made a decision then and there that my lie would have to continue if there was to be any chance for us to spend our lives together. You see, Nicholas, if you had continued watching the security tape, you would have seen that I entered the building as well. You might not have recognized me with the hat and sunglasses, but it was me. I watched Tyler confront Helena and threaten to end the engagement, but Helena used her usual tricks to convince Tyler that this was the last time and that everything would be fine if he gave her one more chance. He agreed and left, so I confronted her on my own. I yelled at her and grabbed the necklace. (Tyler's manicured nails never would have left such scratches.) To state it clearly, Nicholas, I killed Helena. I didn't intend to kill her, but a part of me knew while we were fighting near the ledge that my final push would have the results that it did, but I was horrified by my actions as I watched her fall to the ground. I could never get the image out of my mind. My original intention when writing this book was to confess to my crime, but the more I thought about it while writing the book, the more I realized it wouldn't be fair to you. The most important part now is that you know. The greatest fear I have is how you might now judge me, but I throw myself at your mercy with the pathetic justification that I didn't intend to kill Helena.

The hardest part is ending this letter because there are so many things I want to say to you. As I said to my editor, I wanted this story to be about the American Dream, and in many ways I think it is. Just as my story had to obfuscate some dark secrets to achieve the desired effect for the reader, America has many dark secrets that have to be obfuscated to achieve the desired effect for all the hopeful people who want to make a difference by living the American Dream. It always troubled me to hear so many Americans complain incessantly about their country, knowing full well that millions of people were lining up for their opportunity. In my case, the American Dream allowed me to pursue the truth as a journalist, without fear of legal repercussions, an opportunity which many people around the world do not enjoy. This is not to say that my career as a journalist was a never-ending blissful journey, which some people now seem to expect from life, but it is to say that as long as I dedicated myself to perfecting the craft of journalism, there were no legal or coercive measures in place to stop me from working. Whether I had success was a different concern because the business is competitive. Many people have succeeded by failing, to the extent that they had the courage and conviction to follow their dreams. The American Dream also allowed me to live in a place that celebrated romantic love, where men (real men) celebrated fidelity and commitment, which in turn gave their wives and children the love and stability they need to thrive and find happiness. I consider myself a "strong" woman, but my strength would have quickly dissipated without your love. One only has to look around the world to see that the biggest challenge many countries face is helping young men make this transition in life. Although many American women view my ideas or this model of marriage as suffocating or archaic, I found it liberating.

I love you more dearly and tenderly than you can imagine, Nicholas. Thank you so much for sharing this journey with me, for which I am eternally grateful. You are my best friend. The only regret I have is that we couldn't spend more time together. However, you should know in your heart that I will always be with you.

Love,
Lina